FIRST STRIKE: LOUDOUN COUNTY

A.W. Guerra & Kelly Hoggan
First Strike: Loudoun County

Published by BooxAi

ISBN: 978-965-577-939-4

FIRST STRIKE: LOUDOUN COUNTY

A.W. GUERRA

KELLY HOGGAN

CONTENTS

There are so many people to whom I owe gratitude and thanks for a life well-lived, but none more so than my wife Kristie, without whom this novel would not have been possible.

– A.W. Guerra

This book is dedicated to my father, who was an avid reader and introduced me to many books of this genre.

– Kelly Hoggan

PREFACE

This novel is entirely a work of fiction and is not a fantasy of any future that either of us – nor anyone with even just an ounce of sense – would either want or desire. Fiction, though, requires several elements, no matter the genre or style. To us, a decent work of fiction should be complete with heroes, villains, major and minor players, and stories both grand and intimate.

Are some of our novels pulled from today's headlines? Of course they are. To deny that would be to deny reality, which all good fiction must in some way or another rely on at least in small measure.

The question to ask then is this:

"What if?"

PROLOGUE

The Year Before

THE ANALYST WORKED IN A DRAB ROOM IN THE SUB-BASEMENT of an anonymous building, one with an extensive array of innocuous-looking security bollards and barriers disguised as large planters and ornamental bush holders. They were meant to keep car and truck bombs at a safe distance, though their placement had never really been tested for effectiveness. The structure itself sat in an equally anonymous business park in one of the ring suburbs surrounding Washington, D.C.

In the room, which had an impressive bank of exceptionally large OLED monitors mounted on one wall, the man watched a satellite feed nourished by a surveillance drone orbiting in a figure 8 pattern high overhead. It was of the action taking place at Hamid Karzai International Airport in Kabul, Afghanistan.

The chaos and struggle for survival occurring among and between the players on his wall of monitors held him with sick, utter fascination.

No way this isn't going to blow up in our faces, was his frequent thought, usually after seeing one player or another in real life do something that would have gotten said player a long, even permanent, stretch in a federal prison had the action played out back here on the Auld Sod, so to speak.

Just why it was all falling down in so messy a fashion was a bit complicated, the analyst knew, but what wasn't so complicated was the impetus for the chaotic drama now being depicted on his screens.

The US president, newly sworn in just seven months back, had finally had enough of a war-that-wasn't – one that had cost the nation in blood and treasure for far too long, he often remarked. He was pulling what remained of the nation's military forces out of that benighted place after nearly 20 years there. Naturally enough, many Afghans, not eager to once again experience the tender ministrations of the fundamentalist death cult known as the Taliban, wanted out and they were determined to climb into any US or British or other plane leaving the city. The French – a *de facto* part of NATO, though they took great pains to constantly announce to the world that they really weren't – were as always loathe to leave any locale where they were making good money, but even they had seen the truth of things. They were getting their own people out as quickly as they could and tossing onboard their planes any of the local native population that had been aiding them in their endeavors.

As the remaining days of the US withdrawal wound down, many Afghans – along with thousands of American citizens and green card holders also intermixed among them or hiding out from Taliban forces -- were becoming seriously desperate to get out and had proven themselves willing to do anything to escape.

For his part, the analyst had personally seen several clashes among those vying to leave as quickly as possible for fear of permanent sanctioning by a Taliban death squad. Those fights had likely resulted in the deaths of several Afghans each time they occurred, though the bodies were often quickly ground into the dust and dirt and oily grime of the roads and crowded streets encircling the airport. Some of the departed had even been innocent noncombatants, a point that saddened the analyst just a tiny bit, though he also knew it was the way of the world whenever empires tossed their expendables and other trash over the side as they sailed – or flew, as in this case -- off into the sunset.

Certainly, what remained of the Afghan security forces that hadn't already melted away in the face of impending Taliban domination couldn't have cared less what happened to those doomed men, women and children, focused as they themselves were in getting out while they could, fellow Afghans be damned to the deepest depths of *Jahannam*, the Muslim version of Hell. US troops were also under strict orders to not interfere with or aid those outside the now-locked airport gates, under pain of court-martial if they did.

These cold, hard facts on the ground made the fight by the unwashed masses to get into the airport and on a departing flight more like a gladiator-like struggle for survival than something commonplace in the supposedly "civilized" 21st century.

Or like something out of the Hunger Games, the analyst thought to himself as he continued to stare at his monitors, unconsciously shaking his head as he did so.

Blowing out a long, slow puff of air, the man swiveled in his chair to look at his boss, the senior analyst and director of the Afghanistan desk for his nameless, anonymous government intelligence organization. After a pause, he summed up his feelings about the entire debacle.

"We are so screwed on this one, boss."

His voice was low and meant only to be heard by his superior. Within it, though, a casual listener would have easily recognized complete certitude accompanied by a healthy dash of dread.

The junior man's leader accepted the truth of her subordinate's verdict. However, she also knew orders were orders and that all of what was often called "blowback" or "second-order effects" – which were sure to follow in the wake of this disastrous cut-and-run act – would take place after she'd left government service, which would be very soon.

The bloody writing was clearly on the equally bloody wall as far as Afghanistan went.

She'd been around long enough and was tired enough of the whole thing to understand that retirement followed by more lucrative employment with a government contractor, or even a lobbying firm a few years down the road, was preferable to hanging around for what was to come. Many thousands of Afghans were fleeing their country ahead of the Taliban taking over once again, and the United States was going to take all of them in.

In the main, accepting refugees from Afghanistan was the right and proper thing for the US to do. This, the analyst and his boss knew and they were fine with that. Many Afghans had thrown their lot in with America, after all, oftentimes working either directly or indirectly for various American agencies or organizations such as State, Defense or the CIA. In fact, you name the US agency or non-governmental organization working over in Southwest Asia and chances were pretty good that some of the host nation's citizens were earning a paycheck from Uncle Sam, one way or another.

The brutal truth was that if those Afghans stayed in the country, after their benefactors and protectors had left, they would eventually be swept up for execution by the Taliban once that gang of cutthroats, or any other fundamentalist group such as ISIS-K, or the "Islamic State – Khorasan Province," learned of their names. The two American intelligence analysts also knew the Taliban and various other assorted terror organizations were certain to get their hands on those names, too.

No, those Afghans had nowhere to run other than to the United States. The US had to take them in or it would suffer severe damage in the eyes of other people in many other countries that were providing vital intelligence, not only because of lucrative payment but also resettlement in the Land of the Free once they were discovered or their usefulness had otherwise ended.

Unfortunately, both government intelligence analysts also knew the race to supply sanctuary in America to those who legitimately deserved it would also let in a legion of those who most certainly didn't. Long and bloody, this list included Taliban infiltrators, terrorists among several different ISIS groups, and remnants of Al-Qaeda and a multitude of other non-state terror organizations as well state actors such as Iranian Quds Force special operations fighters. All of them wished nothing less than the complete and utter destruction of their mortal enemy, the United States. The analysts were absolutely sure a host of unsavory types and outright terrorist killers and suicide bombers would end up being washed ashore along with the huddled masses of deserving Afghans soon to make landfall.

Upwards of 67,000 refugees -- many of them unvetted or otherwise unverified as having legitimate reason to be let in -- were likely going to be brought to the Washington, D.C. Beltway area alone. Multiply that number by at least ten, scattered all over the country, and a serious security problem for the nation was in the offing due to the Great Pullout, as the two of them called their country's Afghanistan exit.

The senior analyst could do nothing but shrug her shoulders noncommittally and dissimulate slightly, though her subordinate knew it was really just an act.

"It probably won't be as bad as you think, Andy."

It was all she could muster and there was a complete lack of conviction or confidence in her voice. Inwardly, she was honest enough to admit it was probably going to be worse than they could imagine.

"I know you don't believe that Sandy."

More dread in her junior analyst's voice crept out. He knew what was probably going to happen once the assorted bad people among the wave of refugees got to America and then sorted themselves out, complete with access to resources most of the civilian populace would never in a million years be able to possess.

Automatic weapons and all the ammunition a terrorist could ever want? Check. Grenades, ordnance and plastic explosives? Double-check.

Those weapons were bad enough, but there were also worse things, up to and including MANPADS, or "man-portable air-defense systems," and maybe even the Devil-spawns of the terrorist world: radiological devices -- better known as "dirty bombs" – and possibly an array of bioterror weapons such as anthrax and other organisms that would have turned even Adolf Eichmann's stomach. Then there was the unholiest of the unholy: Nuclear weapons.

The intelligence pair knew on an intellectual level that the worst of their fears – dirty bombs, bioweapons and nukes in the wrong hands -- was a stretch, especially given the lack of knowledge and skill among the killers or wannabe killers soon to make their way to America's fair shores, but they also had gained more than enough bitter experience to never put anything beyond the realm of possibility when it came to terrorists and their mindset. They were often doggedly determined and certainly not afraid to die; that much was for sure.

Silence once again reigned briefly between the two. What more could be said that they didn't already know they couldn't say? Doubtless, their conversation was also being immortalized by several listening devices placed in undetectable spots throughout the room in which they worked. Neither wanted such talk either picked apart by those far higher up the intelligence food chain or leaked to some congressional oversight committee or, worst of all, to the news media. In this day and age, they'd likely as not find themselves and their little talk splashed all over some website not entirely friendly to the idea of a Deep State intelligence organization – vital as they may or may not have believed an actual "Deep State intelligence apparatus" to be in the real world, where a nation's ability to gather intelligence could mean the difference between its survival and its extinction.

The man turned to look at his monitors briefly. Another fight had broken out among terrified Afghan civilians massing near one of the airport gates.

Incredibly, it was obvious Taliban "security forces" had been allowed in close to "maintain order." The trouble was, they were far too close to American Marines and Soldiers on the airport side of the gate. The fundamentalists were gleefully breaking up the fight with extreme violence and fatal result, swinging the butt ends of their AK-47s and American-made M4s with wild abandon, in the process trampling children underfoot in the melee. To the analyst, the entire scene was a bit depressing, not least because there was absolutely nothing he could do to alleviate the problem.

The truth was, no one among the throngs of people trying to get into the airfield should have been allowed closer than three hundred meters from the airport fence line until they'd been thoroughly searched and screened by American or other Coalition forces, and certainly not by the Taliban.

Unfortunately, both the State and Defense Departments had at once nixed the recommendation to set up an effective security perimeter and to exclude the kind of Taliban "assistance" being splashed across their monitors. Hamid Karzai International Airport was also situated in some of Kabul's most-crowded neighborhoods, which was another big, flashing red light no one in the federal government wanted to acknowledge.

The tragic fact was that there simply wasn't any way to push a security perimeter out very far, if at all.

End result? Hordes of desperate Afghans -- no doubt with Taliban, ISIS, Al-Qaeda, and Quds Force infiltrators mixed in --were pressing right up against various airfield entrances, including gates that led to the American operational and airplane evacuation areas. US military personnel responsible for keeping an effective security presence were largely at the mercy of Taliban security forces when it came to maintaining an orderly flow of hopeful refugees, and both analysts knew that was simply insane.

Once again, though: What could they do?

The answer? A big, fat nothing.

"Time to wrap this up, Andy," the woman said to her subordinate. She took solace in and was even buoyed by the fact that this time next week it would become someone else's problem. She already had two firm offers of employment, one from a well-resourced D.C. think tank and the other from a government intelligence contractor whose C-suite members she knew well and was very friendly with. Happily, that offer also came with an executive vice-president's perks, including a corner office and a car complete with a driver. The salary on tap from either job offer far exceeded what she was earning as a federal civil servant.

She wouldn't miss this windowless room, in other words, nor its ability to consistently depress her as it revealed the state of the world as well as what was to come. Tomorrow, she planned to let her prospective civilian employers know her decision and then take a well-deserved month off before she jumped back into the fray.

Time to get paid, she secretly thought to herself, though she revealed none of this to her subordinate. No doubt, he had his own opinion on the matter.

"Yeah," he said in a tone showing both that he could read her thoughts at that moment and also that he knew the deal, including what their ability was to affect the eventual outcome of this disaster: Precisely none.

Snapping out of his reverie, the man slowly exhaled once again and then spoke: "Let me log off and shut the system down and we'll walk out together."

"That's fine, Andy."

He moved to his keyboard and began ending the connection to the satellite feed, powering down the ultra-powerful computer system that ran it all. He felt like he'd just ended the lives of countless people in the process, as if his watching the tableau in Afghanistan had somehow been keeping all those people alive.

They're in for it now, he thought.

Another anonymous office in this equally anonymous building would pick up where they were leaving off, with another anonymous pair of analysts, junior and senior, taking up the slack. That new pair would produce the final intelligence report later in the week, after the entire sad tragedy of Afghanistan came to its inevitable and predictable conclusion.

Of course, that document would be stamped Top Secret ("Eyes Only for So-and-So Highly-Placed Government Intelligence Official"). It would also, of course, go absolutely nowhere and affect absolutely nothing in terms of the nation's homeland security policy.

Though he knew he shouldn't let it get to him, the junior analyst still had just barely enough humanity left inside to feel a tiny bit saddened by what it all was going to lead to.

CHAPTER 1
LUKE

Present Day

"Blam! Blam! Blam!"

THE REPORT OF THE SERIOUSLY TRICKED-OUT DANIEL DEFENSE DDM4 V11 5.56mm semi-automatic carbine briefly echoed through the surrounding woods before the verdant green and brown trees deadened the noise completely. The slightly acrid, though not unpleasant, odor of bullet propellant from the ejected cartridges wafted momentarily through the pleasantly warm and clean air before the late-summer breeze carried it away. It greatly pleased the man holding the carbine and brought forth memories of gunfights in faraway places over in "the Sandbox," as he and his fellow service members called Iraq, or over in Afghanistan, which went by various slang names, including "the 'Stan." There were also a few far more profane utterances used to describe the two countries, but they rarely escaped from the shooter's lips these days.

Luke Ellis – a now-retired Special Forces Green Beret and Delta Force operator who'd also served a brief post-military stint as a private military contractor, or "PMC" -- was mostly just a civilian these days.

Right now, he was enjoying the fruits of two decades of hard and often lonely service to his country by concentrating on picking off the collection of targets he'd erected about 100 meters from the rear of his nondescript single-story ranch house. His homestead, all 50 acres of it, was located just north and west of Lucketts, Virginia, a largely rural and semi-rural – as well as tiny, though increasingly trendy – hamlet in Loudoun County, Virginia, which was just a stone's throw from Washington, D.C.

Nourished by a vast array of D.C.-based government agencies, private contractors, and law as well as lobbying firms, "Loudon" – as the locals called it – was officially the richest county in the entire country. The region surrounding Ellis' property, however, was known as the Catoctin District. It probably housed the last remaining large collection of politically conservative people in the four-county Northern Virginia D.C. Beltway region.

"Noh-Vah," as the area was called by supposedly astute political pundits and other assorted know-it-alls, could be counted on as a motherlode of votes for Democrats, or the "Blue team," in other words.

For his part, Luke himself had little interest in such political or ideological goings-on, and he rarely voted anyway. He'd fought for and defended his country, sure enough – and oftentimes with devastating effectiveness -- but that was also through an alternating succession of Republican, or "Red Team," and then Democrat, or "Blue Team," administrations and Congresses. At the levels at which he and his fellow special operations professionals had worked, partisan politics hardly ever reared its ugly head. He and his comrades were given mission sets or developed them among themselves through Army Special Forces Command or Joint Special Operations Command – known as JSOC and pronounced "Jay Sock" -- and then executed them and that was all that mattered. Just which political party would get to claim credit for their work mattered little to men like Luke.

Ellis was proud of the fact he and his peers in SF and over at

Delta almost never "did politics." Such doings were for stiff-necked brass-hat generals and high muckety muck civilian leaders, he believed. He and his kind had lived at the pointy tip of a very lethal spear, where mundane concerns involving national strategy weren't of much import or consideration.

When he'd been a leader at Delta, tactics and the best ways to take out bad guys most efficiently and quickly were what he'd focused on. Even so, Luke had always received glowing write-ups from his superiors about his own high-level strategic thinking abilities, though he'd more often been given the chance to show those skillsets back during his SF days, whenever he'd helped in training native insurgent forces in various hotspots around the world.

The groups he'd once trained had usually been interested in over-throwing the tyrannical regimes oppressing them. To succeed, they'd sometimes ask for and then receive help from Uncle Sam, which would detail one or even several 12-Soldier Green Beret Operational Detachment-Alpha, or "ODA," packages to help out. Those 'A' teams had orders to turn often ragtag rebel forces into at least semi-professional fighting units. Aiding insurgents – or, conversely, training host nation military forces to get rid of them – were the specific roles played by ODAs, which worked in units known as Groups. Those were the classic mission sets for standard-issue Special Forces Green Berets. Ellis had spent plenty of time in ODAs doing just that before he'd been invited to try out for Operational Detachment-Delta, where he was selected on the first try and where his tactical abilities and strategic thinking stood out.

Tactical know-how and strategic thinking had been inculcated in Luke through his years of service in the SF community and only improved by his service with Operational Detachment-Delta and its various squadrons and troops. Collectively, though, they were more commonly known as either "Delta Force" or "The Unit."

Within JSOC and among its planners they'd been called "Task Force Green," a call sign he'd never personally used to describe his organization, whenever he admitted even being associated with it, that is. Generally, Ellis and his fellow operators almost never said anything to anyone about just who and what they were and the Army usually tried not to acknowledge the unit's existence. Besides, he secretly considered the formal JSOC designation for Delta to be just a bit too long and too much of a secret squirrel-type nickname to suit his tastes, so there was that to consider as well.

All in all, though, Luke was satisfied with his life. Sure, maybe one day he'd leverage his skills to again land himself a lucrative gig with any number of State Department-approved "security consulting firms" or PMC companies, but not right now.

Today, he was just happy to be banging away with his favorite weapon system – which consisted of both him and his AR-15 carbine, melded together into one lethal unit. Shooting like this felt really good, to be honest. As good as the intense CrossFit session and five-mile run he also planned to do immediately after wrapping up this shooting session would feel, in fact

Pausing for a moment as he rapidly swapped out magazines, dropping the empty and quickly inserting a fully loaded one into the mag well of his carbine, Luke looked at the dwelling he'd had built to his specifications a few years ago. It sat like a stony silent Roman Praetorian guardsman, utterly intent on protecting his emperor. Ellis could even imagine himself with one hand firmly fixed on the hilt of his Gladius, the short stabbing sword of the Praetorian.

The fifty acres of land surrounding his home made for an ideal training area when it came to his shooting "hobby," he had to admit. Why, it was even close to being a compound though not up to combat outpost or COP standards. Still, the nearest neighbor was a small Baptist community church more than a mile away through the surrounding forest, and they'd never complained about his makeshift outdoor firing range or anything else he did on the land. Knowing those congregants, they'd probably approved of it all, in fact. He'd inherited the land from his father some years ago and had gradually improved it whenever he could carve out some time between deployments as well as during his mandatory instructor tour at SWCS, meaning "the John F. Kennedy Special Warfare Center," which was based at Fort Bragg, North Carolina.

There, he'd taught a wide variety of courses not only to Army special operations personnel but also to operators from every other branch of the armed forces and allied or friendly nations. This included members of the Navy's SEAL teams. Looking back at that second-to-last tour, he audibly chuckled to himself.

During his time at SWCS, he'd sometimes jokingly referred to those SEAL teams as "Squeal Teams," which is what he told their operators they did whenever they ran out of suntan lotion. It was always good for a laugh between them all, Army and Navy alike, and it helped promote a healthy level of competition, he believed. They were all also experienced enough to know both sides had been given unique mission sets and capabilities, and the back-and-forth never got more serious than easygoing ribbing and banter. At JSOC they'd all been playing for the varsity level pipe hitter units and they knew it, so at the end of the day it was a matter of professionalism and pride in one's craft.

Fun and games over, he turned once again to look at his homestead, his critical eye quickly sizing up the tactical layout, including avenues of approach to his dwelling. For a fact, they were cleverly laid out to funnel anyone hostile to Luke into subtle fields of fire that wouldn't be noticeable even if the attackers had a high level of skill in the special operations arts.

Also, the former Delta operator and Green Beret was never complacent, and he always lived his life in what was called "Condition Yellow." Not fully on edge and ready to rock and roll, as "Condition Red" would have called for, "Yellow" was a happy state of being for Ellis. It featured mid-level intensity and good situational awareness, but not the wild-eyed berserker demeanor often needed to succeed whenever a Condition Red situation arose. Besides, "going Red" would have scared all the civilians living around him, and he liked those fine folks.

Okay, okay. He liked *most* -- or at least *some* -- of them.

Fine, then. Maybe he only really liked just a *few*. But he didn't *hate* any of them -- for the most part -- and that was what counted, right?

Somewhat to Luke's surprise, since punching out of the military special operations world he'd greatly managed to dial down the extreme intensity called for to succeed in his old line of work. He'd put his retirement papers in last year, after the Afghanistan screw-up had ended just as messily as everything else there had when it came to policy, rules of engagement, the way latrines in the field were dug... you name it, it had become screwed up over time.

That's what happens when Big Army always gets its way, he'd thought to himself on more than a few occasions. Bureaucracies are bureaucracies wherever they're found, including even in the US military.

Life was better now, though, and Luke felt much more relaxed about most things these days. He sighed contentedly at the way things were turning out.

As a result of his newfound mellowness – relatively speaking, of course -- he'd even declined to sign on to the long-term supervisor contract he'd been offered by the PMC company he'd joined up with not long after hanging up his uniform. Not that that gig had left a sour taste in his mouth – because it hadn't – but during it he'd found himself becoming increasingly attracted to his place in Loudoun County than he'd ever been while he was serving in Special Forces or in Delta. He'd left the PMC world feeling at ease, at peace and eager for whatever came next in his newfound liberation.

So here he was now, out in the fine August summertime of Northern Virginia, happily firing away with his semiautomatic carbine and not having a real care in the world.

Life is good, isn't it? He asked himself.

Yes, indeed. It sure was.

"Enough with the philosophical stuff," Luke said aloud without knowing he'd done so.

He looked down to ensure his weapon was fully locked and

loaded, with safety on, before he laid it down on the wooden bench he used whenever he shot his rifle in what he thought of as his "backyard."

Turning to his target array off in the distance, he picked up a set of field binoculars and looked it over with a critical eye, admiring for just a moment the patterns he'd laid out on individual targets as he'd fired his weapon. All were center mass hits and -- whenever the mood had struck him – a little bit higher than that.

His trigger press was as smooth as ever. Absolutely no jerking or pulling, and he landed his round squarely in the middle of the chest or the head, even if that's where he wanted to put it. Just like every other competent special operator, he'd also silently repeated the well-known mantra "Slow is smooth, smooth is fast" to himself as he prepared to fire. That habit had been so long ingrained within him he was almost never even aware he repeated it constantly when he was target shooting.

Luke's resolve and focus whenever he shot -- or did anything else involving use of his hard-won military skills – was formidable. That single-minded determination sometimes elicited chuckles and knowing shakes of the head from more than a few of the newer denizens in the area was, of course, known by him, but he simply didn't care.

Usually, they thought he was some kind of survival nut or prep-per, from what he could tell.

Generally, those people had moved into the area from nearby Washington, D.C. or similarly wealthy parts of the country to open up antique stores and other businesses designed to attract the well-moneyed and well-connected elite class of the region. Ellis had about as much in common with them as they had with a beggar on the streets of Mexico City.

Luke smiled again. He always looked forward to going out on his five-mile runs -- complete with weighted rucksack, long pants and his old assault boots -- just for the entertainment he knew he was supplying those folks. Almost none of them had any sort of uniformed military service, including Junior ROTC back in high school, he'd learned over time. At best, in their adult years some may have spent a very infrequent day or two running around with a paintball gun or with an Airsoft M4 or AK-47 imitation rifle at some simulated combat ranch, if that counted for something.

In Ellis' eyes, it most definitely did not.

Personally, he believed such games did more harm than good in cultivating what he called a "warrior mindset" because that's what those activities were: Games.

Get hit with a paintball or Airsoft pellet and your most serious injury would most likely be to your self-esteem. That was no way to train a Soldier or a Marine, he thought. Because if you took a live round in the field, meaning in the real world, there was a good chance that would be all she wrote and your new status would be nothing to write home to your folks about.

That is, it would be nothing for the ones assigned to write home to your folks on your behalf because you would be dead and unable to write. Combat was no game, and you didn't train for it as if it were.

Even so, Luke's personal equanimity about such matters was strong enough to allow him to let slide trivialities like Airsoft or paintball "weekend warrior" events. Those folks were civilians, after all. He and many others like him, in all the various service branches of the US military, had been paid and expected to do the hard things needed to ensure that the most serious thing the government drones flitting around D.C. had to worry about in the way of tough times was whether or not the next incoming presidential administration was going to increase government spending by ten percent or only by five. If the latter, said administration would proudly proclaim that it was actually a budget cut and gee, wasn't it great they were so fiscally responsible?

This thought always caused Ellis to chuckle a bit.

Luke paused to look at his watch.

We're burning daylight. Time to get serious again.

Picking his weapon up, he began firing off the fresh magazine he'd just inserted. After that, he'd give himself precisely five minutes – Ellis still referred to the time interval as "Five Mikes" – to gear up with his ruck and a concealed pistol from his extensive collection. He preferred a forty-five caliber 1911-style pistol because of its knock-down power, and it was what he normally had on his person when not out on a ruck run. Tooled up thusly, he intended to hit the rolling hills and roads and run, not jog, at a brisk pace, all just to give plea-sure to those around him and to keep his fitness level up, of course.

Life was indeed good, wasn't it? Ellis smiled broadly with satis-faction at the role he was currently playing within it.

CHAPTER 2
DOMINOES

"KER-BLAM!!!"

THE SUICIDE BOMB BLAST KILLED DOZENS OF MEN, WOMEN AND children, including the bomber's intended target, the President of the United States. He and the others were the unlucky ones. Or perhaps they were actually of the lucky multitude, given a left-handed gift from the gods so that they wouldn't have to deal with the horrible, life-altering injuries the campaign rally's survivors had been dealt by the bomber? That man had, of course, been killed by the blast as well. Such was the way of suicide attacks, after all.

The killed and wounded in the packed crowd had all been within 50 feet of the nondescript man who'd triggered the bomb vest he'd been wearing. That device, which had destroyed wantonly and with an almost devilish abandon, had been underneath the unremarkable man's equally unremarkable and completely Western-looking clothing.

In the aftermath, the air stank of explosive residue and its constituent chemicals as well as the sad detritus that's always left behind when humans violently pass into the afterlife. The ground at the epicenter of the explosion resembled a charnel pit of flesh, bone, blood and gore. All the tragic remnants of an evil act were there, in other words.

The wounded, with eardrums ruptured by the explosion's over-pressure wave, staggered about on legs fractured and torn, with arms equally as destroyed, and in such a state of shock they weren't even aware of how badly they'd been mauled. It was as if a man-eating tiger had rampaged through a village composed entirely of the defenseless, taking its fill of vulnerable human flesh before it melted away into the surrounding jungle. Yet there was no screaming or crying or moaning, though there were plenty of still, broken bodies strewn about as carelessly as a child might scatter her dolls in a fit of anger. Horrible, heart-rending sounds would come soon enough, of course, as they always did after any great human calamity, but for now the newly silent air was almost completely motionless in the aftermath of what the bomber had thought of as Allah's vengeance.

The killer had set himself up perfectly along the rally's barricade. The Secret Service were patrolling it, sure enough, and the bomber could easily pick out just who they were and where they were and thus made sure not to come too close to them or to just as obviously avoid them. His entire demeanor was structured so as to prevent any clear threat whatsoever, in fact, just as his trainers and handlers had intended. He also knew he'd managed to avoid landing on any sort of special-attention list during his time in America, which was a fortu-itous circumstance or the will of Allah or whatever. He'd received no pre-rally visit from the Secret Service or FBI special agent sent to check him out. He was innocuous and completely unremarkable, in other words, and he'd trained long and hard with his Quds Force handlers to look just the part.

It was those men – a pair of Iranians whose intense hatred of the United States easily matched his own – that had supplied his custom-built, plastique-laden and torso-fitted explosive device. It held a new type of extremely potent and highly stable plastic explosive his handlers had assured him was not yet known to the intelligence agen-cies of the US and its allies. It was also vacuum-sealed within its custom-made carrier vest to prevent its discovery by Department of Homeland Security bomb-sniffing dogs and handlers or any sort of infrared, millimeter wave, or other detection device known to be used by DHS.

As a final act of their demonic beneficence, the duo had also thoroughly instructed him in how to get close enough to the US president to use it. In his heart of hearts he knew he would soon deploy it to great effect. That'd he'd also die in the act if it was successful was of little consequence to him. He was a *Taliban*, a Pashto word used in both the singular and plural form. Simply put, he was a "student." Personally, he'd been a *Taliban* been since he was a little boy barely able to speak. The ultra-fundamentalist Muslim religious movement dictated his entire life, in fact.

He'd first been instructed by his father and uncles in the great movement's ways, and once they'd judged him ready, they'd sent him off to a Saudi-financed religious school, or madrassa, in neighboring Pakistan, which served as both a religious training academy and a finishing school in the more obscure, terrorism-related arts. Many young Taliban males had been educated and trained in this fashion, he knew, though he wasn't personally acquainted with any of the others. All the better to keep operational security should he be discovered once he made it to America.

The young man's entire 19 years of life to this point had been dedicated to the Taliban cause. For starters, the movement's leaders had taken great care to ensure his "education" had never been discovered or noted by either US or Afghan as well as broader Pakistani intelligence, including his travel back and forth over the latter country's borders.

He was an almost perfect cypher, in other words, and he took advantage of that fact by quickly aligning himself with US forces once he'd returned from his training. He'd proven himself helpful to American military forces and had never once given even the slightest hint of anything but absolute loyalty to the Afghan government and its US benefactor. He took care, as well, to never rise too highly lest he become the subject of heightened scrutiny driven by a curiosity about his helpfulness and reliability in a country where allegiances might shift on a dime, driven as they often were by a clan warlord's directives.

Indeed, he worked to stay more a low-level asset than anything else, stolidly performing his duties to the best of his ability, to the point where he'd even avidly taken part in the capture of several Taliban fighters, detailing their locations and likely threat to his American masters. Thus, when the opening in the form of the US withdrawal from Afghanistan had presented itself, Taliban leaders quickly seized on the opportunity.

Just last year, for example, they'd ensured he and many of his comrades had successfully made it aboard a multitude of US Air Force C-17 cargo jets, all fleeing Kabul. Those planes had taken them to America, "the land of the free and the home of the brave." For a fact, the man meant to illustrate to them all just how brave they would indeed have to be to defeat him and his compatriots and their blessed movement, for he knew they had the numbers on their side in this idolatrous, wicked nation.

Thousands and thousands of Afghans – some of whom weren't quite so desperate as they made themselves out to be, and more than a few who weren't Afghan but, rather, Iranian, Arab, and even some from Chechnya and Dagestan – managed to pile into those planes. As was always the case with the fat, overfed and overconfident Americans, they either didn't know enough about the ethnic differences among them all or they simply didn't care, focused as they were on helping their supposed "friends" escape the Taliban as their fighters took province after province, city after city, town after town.

At any rate, his paperwork and identity documents had long ago been perfected. They'd previously been surreptitiously entered into the Americans' databases and security systems by skilled hackers working for a section of the Pakistan Inter-Services Intelligence agency, or ISI, which was extremely sympathetic to the Taliban. The entries included his electronic and biometric data, all of which was designed to withstand fairly rigorous scrutiny. Brilliant forgeries, they'd proved his *bona fides* sufficiently enough that the largely apathetic DHS and other US government three-letter-agency background checkers – who'd been looking into his past at the refugee resettlement camp he'd been transported to after landing in America -- had proclaimed themselves satisfied that he was who he said he was.

They'd then welcomed him with open arms and even helped support him while he was "integrated" – their word, not his – into his new country, complete with a small, subsidized apartment, cash payments, English lessons, and a decent and unexciting job that paid him more money than he needed, but which he'd carefully spent so that he could give the impression he'd bought wholeheartedly into what was called the "American dream." He didn't know about anything else, but his own dream had always been of the final, great use to which he'd be put. His entire reason for being was directed at that outcome and today would be the day.

Once he'd planted himself firmly in America the fact he despised everything about his new nation and considered it to be satanic in the extreme was something he had never allowed to appear, either by word or deed, for even just the barest second.

He'd successfully bided his time, playing the part of a grateful refugee and mostly non-religious person. He even stayed away from the mosque in his town, found not far from where the presidential event was being held, on the certainty it was at least under occasional security surveillance. He had even eagerly accepted the nickname his new American friends had given him. They called him "Al," which was supposed to serve as a substitute for "Abdul-Ali," the name on his identity papers. He'd played along, smiling and bowing and scraping and pretending at a gratitude for his American experience that he never in a moment had ever truly felt.

Now, though? Now it was the hour of his and his movement's great triumph. Soon, he'd martyr himself and deal a grievous blow to his adopted country and greatest enemy.

The crowd around him suddenly broke into a loud murmur, with some even cheering a bit. Spying movement at the south end of the barricade, Abdul-Ali knew the American president would soon be near to where he was standing.

And right on time, here the American president was, now standing no more than twenty-five feet from him. Abdul-Ali was careful not to push or shove anyone out of the way or move suddenly toward the man, who appeared a little frail because of his advanced age and the weight of the office he held. The agents of the president's Secret Service detail as well as the security forces no doubt circulating within the crowd, and even the spotters and snipers on the tops of various buildings near the reception area in which he was standing, would be extremely alert to any sort of movement that appeared out of the ordinary in any conceivable way. This, too, had been drilled into his head by his Quds Force trainers.

On the cusp of his great triumph, Abdul-Ali didn't want to risk getting arrested or discovered and then shot, and so he stayed where he was, clapping and cheering just like everyone else was doing. He even held aloft a little American flag he'd brought along with him in case there were video surveillance and facial recognition systems present. As for the latter, his handlers had carefully applied very subtle prosthetics to his cheeks, his ears, his forehead and even his body. These were intended to spoof or throw off any recognition software.

They'd also relentlessly told him never to look up or at any cameras, but to never look like he was trying to avoid them either. Doing one or both of those things risked giving himself away, they'd said, though Abdul-Ali didn't need to be told that. He wasn't about to ruin it all now. He only needed a few seconds to do his job and carry out his sacred mission.

As the moment of his ascension neared, the Afghan refugee silently repeated the *Shahada* to himself. It was the Muslim profession of faith, spoken in Arab by all true believers everywhere: *There is no god but Allah, and Muhammad is his messenger.*

It would be his final message to the infidel president and his supporters.

Now the time was upon them all. There the president was, "pressing the flesh."

Abdul-Ali slowly looked down to glance at his watch, which was visible for all the world to see.

Smiling, he pressed one of the buttons on the side of its face.

The last thing he saw was an almost impossibly bright flash.

That wasn't too bad, was his first thought.

He also found himself mildly surprised, in the milliseconds before he blinked out of this world, at the lack of pain as he and much of the crowd around him, including the US president and his protective detail, ceased to exist.

The US president's assassination was just the beginning. It was the first shot in a war Abdul-Ali's compatriots intended to go on for as long as necessary to subdue the great beast that was America. In one way or another – using one sort of device or technique or another – many members of the government of the United States also exited this mortal coil within five or so minutes of the American president's death.

The Vice-President and several of his staff met their unfortunate end as they were at a separate campaign event for a member of their political party running for reelection to the US Senate. Yet another suicide bomb by an equally dedicated *Taliban.*

The Speaker of the US House of Representatives -- number 2 in the line of presidential succession after the Vice-President – was felled by a remotely detonated vehicle-borne enhanced improvised explosive device as she and her Secret Service detail were traveling to Joint Base Andrews in Maryland, there to fly off to California for a weekend of meetings with various constituent groups. The blast that ended her was so intense windows in homes more than five hundred feet away from Interstate 495 – the route she and the security people driving her in her government-provided and supposedly blast-proof vehicle had taken this day -- were completely and dramatically blown inward from the overpressure wave, something that mentally as well as physically traumatized a good many residents in those homes, unaware as they were of what had taken place.

On and on the wave of righteous *jihad* rolled, complete with blessed martyrdom for the Afghans in the movement as well as those fellow fighters who'd allied with the Taliban for their own purposes. The death count grew greatly over that five-minute span of time.

At its end, others in the line of succession -- the President *Pro Tempore* of the Senate, the Secretary of State, the Secretary of the Treasury, the Secretary of Defense, and the US Attorney General, all of whom were serving in positions suited in one way or another to taking up the burden of presidential leadership should it be necessary -- had also been sent to meet Allah's merciful judgment.

It wasn't over with the deaths of those seven men and women, however.

Off in the distance, in the lands surrounding Washington, D.C., loud booms reverberated, reaching up into the cloudless sky and echoing across the former swampland. It was clear that many bombs had been detonated.

In other parts of the D.C. Beltway region, even louder booms, impossibly bright flashes of light, and a buzzsaw of attacks aimed at many soft targets – including large outlet malls, schools, universities, colleges, churches, and several obvious government agency headquarters buildings, could be discerned. Fellow *Taliban* – and even some women suicide bombers allowed to partake in the great undertaking – struck with deadly efficiency, killing and maiming as many as they could before either dying themselves or making off before police could arrive. The carnage was terrible.

Oddly enough, a few non-evident government buildings were also bombed in the jihadist strike, the first truly massive operation carried out against the United States on its soil since 9/11, and one designed to be far more devastating than Osama bin Laden's had ended up being.

Over in a nondescript suburban D.C. business park, for example, an equally nondescript and utterly forgettable building – distinguished only by the security bollards that had been placed around the building and then disguised as large planters and concrete-encased flowerbeds– suffered a devastating bomb blast. The explosion was so powerful the building was almost vaporized and so were many of the people working within it, making it nearly impossible to identify most of them, including a young male intelligence analyst who just the year before had been working at his agency's Afghanistan desk. How the four attackers in the black SUV -- all of whom were killed during the explosion -- could have first of all learned of the building's actual intelligence-gathering purpose and then gotten in so close as to carry out their strike, was a mystery to DHS and myriad other agents from a large collection of government security organizations, hamstrung as they were in the aftermath of the attack by the loss of national command authority leadership at the moment when such leaders were needed most.

At MacDill Air Force Base in Tampa, Florida, US Army General Pete Dellinger – Chairman of the Joint Chiefs of Staff – was watching the runway rush past the windows of the Air Force C-37A – a modified Gulfstream V executive jet – in which he was traveling. He'd spent the morning meeting with the head of US Central Command and his staff and was now headed back to Washington, D.C. and the Pentagon. The two fighter jets that would escort his plane back to D.C. were already circling high overhead, waiting for the general's C-37A to take off. The local airspace had been cleared of traffic, as was always the case whenever CJCS's jet was coming in for a landing or taking off. Today, such precautions wouldn't be enough, though the general and his people and the crew aboard the airliner would only realize that far too late to do anything about it.

Now 1000 feet in the air, the plane's pilot and co-pilot both noticed a glint, as if some sort of laser targeting device had washed across their bird, and then gray flashes quickly closing in on the nose of the plane as well as the midsection of its fuselage.

Simultaneously, warnings blared on the flight deck.

"ATTACK! ATTACK! ATTACK! TAKING EVASIVE ACTION!" they all screamed.

Both pilots, highly experienced former combat aviators, reacted at once and allowed the aircraft's automated defensive systems to act while they fought to avoid what they already knew they wouldn't be able to avoid.

Back in the passenger compartment, Dellinger's head snapped up at the sudden chaos occurring all around him. A Green Beret and counterterrorism expert, he wasn't ready to give up so easily, though he knew his fate and that of the others on the bird depended more on fate and luck than on any skill his pilots might own. The C-37A suddenly lurched upward and then, almost at once, into a steep dive, momentarily making the plane's occupants weightless as the aviators flying the bird desperately corkscrewed the plane in a final, futile attempt to avoid what they as well as Dellinger knew was now inevitable.

I'm so sorry, was his final regretful thought as he looked at the faces of those who'd depended on him this day to keep them safe. He was profoundly sad that he'd let them all down.

The plane exploded two hundred feet above the ground, victim of two AI-controlled autonomous suicide drones, preprogrammed and let loose from the back of a delivery truck to do their evil work. It had been moving down a lightly traveled road a few miles away from MacDill's perimeter fence.

After rapidly lifting off the drones descended and hugged the nap of the earth. They only popped up once they'd found their target moving down the runway prior to takeoff.

There it was.

The drones raced with single-minded purpose for the twin-engine jet, which suffused the surrounding air with a heat signature impossible to miss, though the devices didn't rely solely on infrared to track down their prey.

The two infernal devices – inhuman in their determination to close with their prey -- completed their mission well before any ground-based defenses or the two F-15s orbiting a few thousand feet above could react and do anything to prevent their strike.

Members of the Joint Chiefs of Staff and other civilian and military leaders – including the secretaries and assistant secretaries of the several branches of the nation's armed forces as well as the Reserves and the National Guard -- met similar fates. Some were sent on to the next life while being driven to their offices at the Pentagon or in the course of business at some military base or another while others and their protective details – usually two agents from the government's various executive protection organizations -- were caught unawares at home, on leave, or in various other locations.

One met an explosive, fiery end sitting in her government vehicle at a Rockville, Maryland, traffic light, the engine of her destruction seeming to race from among the forested areas of nearby Rock Creek Regional Park. She'd just finished an annual physical at Walter Reed National Military Medical Center in adjacent Bethesda and was pleased at the "healthy as a horse" pronouncement issued by the physician looking at her exam results.

At least one AI-controlled suicide drone had been detailed to each designated target, though some merited two or even three of them. The latter was the case for one service secretary, who traveled with a larger protective unit, as well as the Commandant of the Marine Corps, a former Force Reconnaissance officer who prided himself on being the hardest of hard targets.

During the First Gulf War, he and his small team of Force Recon Marines had been victorious after 72 hours of house-to-house fighting against seriously determined Iraqi Republican Guard forces after running into them in a small Saudi border town that had apparently been of some value to Saddam Hussein. He'd been awarded the Navy Cross, second only to the Medal of Honor in terms of valor awards, for his actions. Though he'd never admitted it to anyone, the four-star general felt himself bulletproof to this day, sincerely believing he'd die an old, retired Marine far off in the future, going to wherever it was Marines such as Dan Daly or John Basilone or Chesty Puller or a legion of other heroic Devil Dogs went to when they finally stacked their rifles for good.

In the end, of course, he found that he wasn't so bulletproof after all.

Finally – and for obscure reasons US authorities managed to avoid discussing in the aftermath -- cities large and small, as well as many towns around the country and especially in various areas of the several Virginia counties facing Washington, D.C. across the Potomac River, also came under attack. These included by car bomb in addition to well-armed hit teams of four to six terrorists. Special targets, though, saw squads of twenty shooters dispatched to take care of business. The attackers were men -- and even a few women -- who'd patiently bided their time, awaiting their orders before they struck with deadly, wanton disregard for life. Almost all succeeded greatly, though with one very glaring exception.

More on that very glaring exception later.

Bridges linking the American capitol to Virginia were also destroyed by vehicle-borne explosive devices using synergistic liquids so powerful they approached that of a US Air Force MOAB, or "Massive Ordnance Air Blast," which was also called the "Mother of All Bombs." In cases where such structures weren't destroyed by chemical-based munitions, they were at least temporarily made unusable by small explosives-based radiological devices, better known as "dirty bombs." Theoretically, none of these attacks on infrastructure such as bridges, roads and God-only-knew-what-else should have been possible given the level of security scrutiny and layered defenses focused on what was called the "National Capitol Region," but it had indeed all clearly been pulled off.

That was the nature of surprise, wasn't it?

Again, though, the how and why of it all would have to wait. The human disaster now confronting federal and state authorities was threatening to tear the nation apart and it had to be stopped at once before everything collapsed. There was a method to all the madness but those coming under fire in that moment didn't have time to think on the "why." All they had time to dwell on was the "how" of immediate and very personal survival.

At the end of it all, the official Designated Survivor -- the Secretary of the Interior – who was a former Member of Congress and a prodigious campaign fundraiser nominated for his cabinet-level position as a reward for his formidable ability to shake the trees and make it rain money on behalf of his political party – had now become the new President of the United States of America.

To say he was unprepared to become Commander in Chief of the nation's armed forces, as well as the most powerful man in the world, would have been an understatement.

CHAPTER 3
LUKE

Ruck run and CrossFit session over, Luke Ellis was freshly showered and shaved and otherwise looking and feeling good as he piloted his crew cab, four-by-four pickup truck southeast toward Lucketts, the Virginia town nearest to his home. The truck -- bought with some of the hazardous duty and combat pay he'd earned over the years while serving as a Green Beret and Delta operator -- was about the most-common vehicle driven by US special operations personnel next to the lifted and highly modified Jeeps that seemed to multiply like weeds whenever any US military SPECOPS unit was back on base after an overseas deployment or mission. Ellis had once owned one of those Jeeps but preferred the versatility and capabilities of his pickup truck these days, especially given the size of his homestead and its maintenance needs.

That he could also carry an ungodly amount of guns, ammunition, and other "special items" if he needed to only added to the truck's appeal. In fact, Luke had had the rear passenger area and bed of the truck outfitted with all kinds of special compartments and useful bins for just that sort of emergency if the need ever did arise. Until that day, though, those same compartments and bins worked just fine to haul groceries, tools and other supplies.

Glancing over to his right to assure himself his daypack – which in his military days he'd called an assault pack -- was where it should be, Ellis subconsciously checked to ensure his concealed carry handgun was where he could quickly get to it if needed, and then mentally pronounced himself satisfied at the current state of things. The daypack itself was filled with useful items Luke might need if he ever found himself in a situation where he was cut off from outside aid, including police and fire services. These included a nice Suunto MC-2 compass and waterproof topographic maps of the county and the surrounding region, small flashlights, matches and a few butane lighters along with a ferrous rod and striker, a quality Gerber field knife, some bottled water along with several energy bars, a small first aid kit with bandages, a couple of Special Operations Forces tourniquets, and aspirin and ibuprofen along with antibiotic cream for medicinal needs, a waterproof poncho and small one-man tarp, and even an extra change of clothing with a couple of pairs of clean socks.

In the rear passenger compartment, Ellis also openly transported a long gun – in this case, his AR-type Daniel Defense carbine along with several loaded magazines. *No one ever died from being too prepared,* he reminded himself whenever he stopped to consider whether he might be taking things a bit too far these days. He *was* retired from his former line of work and no longer in the game, after all.

The "Old Dominion" – as Virginia called itself -- had a long history of support for gun rights that went back to the colonial era. As long as you had a valid concealed handgun permit, which Luke, of course, did, you could generally openly carry your rifle on your person and in your vehicle, even when it was classified as a so-called "assault weapon," a term many politicians tossed about as if it really meant anything.

Personally, Ellis thought it was too glaring – and made you far too visible a target -- to walk around with a rifle slung over your back, but to each his own, he supposed. Add in that the state allowed for long gun transport in cases where someone reasonably believed that a loaded rifle or shotgun was necessary for their personal safety in the course of their employment or business, and the former Delta Force operator felt he was rolling along pretty clean and well-equipped to deal with any trouble that might arise. He knew he could get to his setup, meaning his rifle, ammo, body armor-equipped chest rig and other gear very quickly if he needed to, though he couldn't imagine why he might need to do so. These days, Ellis mostly dealt with supermarket and store clerks and waiters and waitresses whenever he went into Lucketts or even Leesburg, which was about 15 miles farther south of his little hamlet, and unless he'd missed something about those fine people, they weren't likely to be active threats to his life or limbs. In fact, since he'd settled down and become part of the local scenery, they'd all been unfailingly polite and not too nosy, which was just the way he liked it.

While a casual observer might have thought Ellis' focus on his personal security to be a bit extreme, he wasn't taking any chances. Over the years, both he and the Army had gone to great lengths to keep his true identity as obscure as possible on the valid assumption that more than a few of the non-state terror groups he'd fought against might seek some payback down the road if they discovered his real name and whereabouts. Knowing that that was just the price of poker in the SPECOPS world, Luke made sure he was always ready just in case.

Nearing the outskirts of Lucketts, Ellis shut off the truck's air conditioning and powered its windows down. He was pleased not only with life but with himself. The late-August air was warm and the very-late-afternoon day – some might even call it early evening -- was still sunny, with the lengthening shadows cast by the lowering sun off to the west being the only evidence of impending nightfall.

Luke mindlessly hummed along to a song playing on his truck's stereo while he drove. It was from one of his favorite rock bands of the 1980s, a music era he'd been introduced to by an older cousin when he was just a boy and which he'd at once taken to. According to the band's singer, Dee Something, they weren't gonna take it anymore. He completely sympathized with them.

Looking to his left, Luke returned a friendly wave by one of the locals, an elderly man lazing the day away out on his small home's front porch. Though Virginia was seemingly growing increasingly populous, especially around the D.C. Beltway areas of Loudoun and the other counties bordering the national seat of government, up here around Lucketts it was still a given that most people knew each other on at least a casual basis. So, waves and nods of the head were the order of the day and Ellis was fine with that, as it also helped him blend in and become part of the background.

True enough, the retired Green Beret was six feet, two inches and solidly muscled, but so were plenty of other men around the area – as obsessed as many seemed to be with CrossFit these days. He couldn't do anything about his personal physical attributes, he knew, but to compensate he always took care to wear everyday clothing. Nothing too "tactical" or noticeable, in other words. Jeans and an untucked, comfortably lived-in t-shirt or polo shirt, for the most part, and a smooth-shaven face, though his one concession to his past life was a quality pair of military assault boots, usually Danner, which he took care never to be without.

Rounding out the ensemble, the ballcap he wore -- which concealed a still dark head of hair -- wasn't anything special and it didn't sport any memorable sayings or American flags or other attention-grabbing graphics. Even the sunglasses that helped conceal his blue eyes looked run-of-the-mill, though they were actually of very high quality and durability. His wristwatch – all rubberized black surrounding its face and with a thick, sturdy rubberized wristband -- was also relatively inexpensive when compared to some of the truly pricey ones he'd once worn, including a Rolex for a time, but this one was water resistant and shock-proof and did everything he needed it to do. *Never try to draw additional attention to yourself by sporting the latest high-speed, low-drag wrist ornament,* was his rationale for wearing it.

Overall, Luke neither stood out nor was completely invisible, but that was only at the surface. Behind his sunglasses, his eyes never stopped scanning, his head never stopped subtly swiveling, his ears never stopped listening and his mind never stopped evaluating. It was what he did and who he was and he suspected he'd be that way for the rest of his life. All things being said, it was yet another side of his personal demeanor that was just fine with him.

Ellis was now driving his truck through Lucketts, the objects of his affection looming just up ahead and to his right. There, a small farmer's market and a supermarket stood off to the side, small and welcoming in appearance. They were both run by locals like himself and had been passed down over the years from generation to generation. Those homespun businesses were followed in turn by similar establishments, all still family-owned as well.

"Not too many cars for this time of the day," Luke murmured aloud as he pulled up into the dirt-and-gravel lot fronting the farmer's market. One of them stood out, though, at least to his trained eye. Black in color and with dark-tinted windows, it practically screamed "government vehicle." The license plate also gave it away as probably belonging to the General Services Administration's motor pool. Ellis noted the plate number, thinking he'd maybe conduct a little research later, if only to satisfy his professional instincts.

He also made a snap decision to carry his daypack -- complete with body armor, chest rig, and extra ammunition – into the store. He quickly broke down his AR-15 and put it in the pack as well. "Just in case," he again murmured. Cars like the one in the lot, in an out-of-the-way place like this farmer's market, often carried important people, and important people sometimes attracted others who might not like them very much.

By and large, Ellis was pleased he wouldn't have to elbow his way through any sort of crowd, not with so few cars and trucks in the lot. If he'd come during the weekend – something he almost never did except in an emergency -- he would have had to maneuver his way through a fairly decent-sized crowd. That was when the big-spending visitors came up from Leesburg and points south or west, including from Arlington and Fairfax, two counties whose residents seemed avid to explore the various antique stores now popping up with abandon in and around town, as well as the larger farmers markets dotting the area.

Like many in his former line of work Luke had a natural aversion to large crowds and what he thought of as "soft targets," which this market and the other stores surrounding it definitely were. His well-honed caution when it came to such places also jibed nicely with the attitude of most men when out shopping for non-interesting goods.

His aim was to go in, get what he needed and then leave, taking as little time as possible before moving on to the supermarket next door, there to repeat the same shopping process. Unless he was in his home, he preferred to stay mobile and able to respond to whatever was thrown his way. Such was his way of life.

Exiting his truck, after making sure his windows – tinted to the maximum extent allowed by Virginia law – were closed tightly, with doors also locked and alarm enabled, Ellis made his way into the farmer's market, daypack slung casually over his shoulder and hanging by a single strap. He kept his right hand free and able to quickly access his carry piece if he needed to. Doing so was yet another habit he'd cultivated over many years and was nearly subconscious at this point in his life. Fruits and vegetables for the rest of the week were his focus at the moment and Luke didn't expect he'd be inside for very long.

CHAPTER 4
THE MARKET

"Hey, Mister Ellis! Only 17 years old, the checkout clerk was one of the owner's kids, Luke knew. Her name was Annie. "How are you doing today?" she asked.

Annie was in her last week working at the market before her mom and dad drove her to Charlottesville to begin her freshman year at the University of Virginia. Ellis recalled her parents remarking to him about how proud they were of her earning an academic scholarship from the school, which made it vastly easier for them to send her to the prestigious, nationally renowned state university.

"Just fine, Annie. How are you? You all packed and ready for your first year of college?"

Luke wasn't normally so talkative, but the girl had always been unfailingly polite and courteous to him and was obviously the product of a good upbringing, so he made sure his voice was friendly and welcoming.

"I sure am, Mister Ellis!" Annie had trouble keeping the pleasure out of her voice. She was excited to head into the next part of her life. "Mom and Dad are driving me down there this weekend to move me into my dorm."

"That's awesome, Annie!"

The gruff, old Delta operator couldn't keep the pleasure out of his own voice. He was genuinely glad for the teenager's good fortune. Looking over his left shoulder at his pack, he took it off and held it in his hand. "By the way, do you mind storing my backpack behind the counter until I'm done with my shopping?" Ellis didn't want to appear out of the ordinary in any way and walking around with his somewhat bulky pack would make him stand out a bit.

Annie was only too pleased to accommodate the former soldier's request. "Sure thing, Mister Ellis," she said, hefting its impressive weight before putting it behind her counter. She was used to this particular request from Luke, whom she thought of as "that really nice ex-Army man."

"Thanks, Annie, I really appreciate it. Me and that pack's been through a few things together and I like to keep her close by." Luke rolled his eyes and then winked at the girl, letting her know that he was joking more than anything. It was an act he used to keep her at ease.

"Hah-hah, Mister Ellis!" Annie laughed at the big man's self-deprecation. The backpack felt pretty heavy to her, but she'd seen him hold it in one hand like it weighed hardly anything at all.

Ellis understood Annie's excitement at leaving the nest so that she could spread her wings, though his own nest-leaving experience had involved a military entrance processing station, induction into the Army and a flight to Columbus, Georgia, before reporting to Fort Benning for boot camp followed by infantry advanced individual training and then Airborne school. The Special Forces Q Course, his Green Beret and, finally, Delta Force had all come after his first baptism in the Army, of course.

"We're going to miss you around here, Annie," the former Delta Force operative remarked. "You're not nearly as grumpy as your younger brother, Darren." He again winked broadly and grinned.

Annie laughed once again, clear and lighthearted. She could tell Luke was joking. Her brother was about the least grumpy boy she knew. Small in stature at 12 years old, she knew his physical size would eventually grow to match his already impressive courage and good nature. Plus, he was a whiz at all things electronic and had even built his own ham radio after reading a few online articles and studying briefly the general theory of such communications.

That boy knows his stuff when it comes to comms, Ellis thought to himself, and he secretly hoped Darren would consider putting those talents to good use once he grew up and filled out, such as in Special Forces, which could always use talented soldiers skilled in various communications technologies. "Special Forces Communications Sergeants" worked all manner of comms gear while also recruiting, organizing and training "indigenous forces" to help the US and its allies fight what Luke called "the bad guys" – whoever they happened to be at the moment.

Darren's got potential, Luke had thought to himself on a few occasions. For one, he certainly never quit anything once he put his mind to it.

He turned his attention back to the teenage girl as she spoke to him once again.

"Thank you, Mister Ellis." Annie looked at Luke, brown eyes sparkling merrily. "I'll sure miss selling you so much fruit and vegetables. I think you practically paid for my dad's new truck over this last year."

Luke appreciated the remark. He wasn't a tightwad by any means, and he didn't mind paying for quality merchandise and service – with cash whenever he could get away with it -- and that's what he'd gotten from Annie and her parents.

"Glad to hear it, Annie. I like to do my part for the local economy, that's for sure." Rubbing his hands briskly together, Ellis motioned toward all the fully stocked bins. "Well, I guess I better get to it, then."

Annie nodded, glancing down to make sure the Army man's backpack was securely placed under her counter, out of the way of prying eyes. From its weight, she also suspected there was more in the pack than just some candy bars and a water bottle, though she wasn't curious in the least about finding out. Her dad thought very highly of Mister Ellis and his military service and that was good enough for her.

"Sure, Mister Ellis. Strawberries and apples just came in about an hour ago and so did the tomatoes and carrots." Annie waved over to her right, where the bins holding those items sat.

Luke noted the three other people in the market who were strolling around at the moment, as the evening crowd hadn't yet begun showing up. There were two men and a woman. The men were each about six feet in height with the kind of haircut that said "cop" or "bodyguard."

To Ellis' practiced eye, the pair looked to be in decent physical shape and they certainly paid attention to their principal, or protectee, and were careful to not let her wander too far afield without at least one covering her while the other eyeballed the area around her, though they were more or less trying to be subtle about how they worked. The untrained eye might not have picked them out at all, in fact.

Luke was anything but untrained, though.

The woman herself was kindly looking and middle-aged in appearance. She had dark hair, though slightly graying at the temples, with wisps she probably had trouble keeping under control, as if she'd spent a lifetime picking at them and then trying to put them back into place. Her eyes, however, were bright hazel and piercing and they radiated intense intelligence.

She was the one squeezing and thumping melons and checking out the fresh strawberries and Ellis got the impression – just from his very quick scan – that she applied her undoubtedly formidable intellect to almost any task set before her, including boiling a two-minute egg. She also didn't appear bothered or put out by the two men hovering near her and it was clear to Luke she'd long ago accepted the necessity of having them around, and so did her best to accommodate herself to their likely continuous presence.

Ellis could detect slight lumps showing possible firearms being carried beneath the bodyguard duo's light jackets. This confirmed his suspicions about the vehicle out in the parking lot and the fact it was likely transporting someone the government thought of as important enough to warrant protection.

Almost without knowing it, he unobtrusively sized up the men and classified them as feds. Probably diplomatic protection service or similar, meaning they would have some military service in their backgrounds, perhaps as airborne infantry or even Rangers. He could tell they were decent at what they did. Good, though not great, but likely able enough in most circumstances. And what sort of circumstance, here in a local farmer's market, would need any higher level of skill and competency? Even Luke, as experienced as he was, didn't think the odds of anything serious happening at the market were all that high. Still, the former Delta operator filed it all away for later consideration and then returned to the here and now.

Ellis looked over his shoulder as he started toward the strawberries. "Thanks, Annie. See you at checkout." Pushing a small shopping cart -- which he'd picked up at the market's entrance -- Ellis figured he'd be in and out in about 10 minutes.

"No problem, Mister Ellis. I'll be –"

Annie stopped mid-speech. The building rumbled and the ground shook slightly. Outside, a loud boom shattered the summer's somnolent ease. Echoing in the distance, it sounded like it was off toward the east.

Suddenly, another boom reverberated in the warm air, this time off to the west.

Worse, there was also gunfire just up the road, right in town.

To Annie -- whose own parents had never owned a firearm but who also had watched her fair share of action movies with her little brother whenever she babysat him -- it sure sounded to her like that's what it was.

The teenager nervously looked about, her eyes landing on Luke Ellis. Her parents were down in Leesburg attending to some business and they trusted her completely to mind the store while they were away.

Without them around, though, Annie looked to Luke, who was the nearest adult she knew and trusted, for answers. His change in demeanor shocked her, as did the pistol in his hands, which he was carrying at the low ready position. And what were the two men and that woman doing? The men also had pistols in their own hands and they were hustling the woman toward the exit. They seemed intent on getting her outside, probably to the car they had parked in the lot.

Upon the merest inkling of the first rumble and boom – which he'd noted well before the teenager – Ellis had tensed up like a jungle cat. The gunfire echoing from farther up the road only served to confirm his suspicions. Seeing the trio hurrying to the exit also did nothing to put him at ease. Just like Annie, he figured they were putting Plan A – "get the protectee out of the danger zone" – into action, though he personally thought they were moving a little too quickly without considering what was going on outside. Yet another thing to file away and process as he began sizing up the tactical situation.

The woman was their problem right now. He believed Annie and her safety was his.

Luke sprang into action, all senses acutely attuned to the environment, and he went into an operational state of alert, a kind of human-centric DEFCON 3, or even DEFCON 2. At this point, he was only a half-step away from going into full-on DEFCON 1, or complete combat action mode.

Moving with a purpose over to the counter, Ellis silently motioned the teenage girl out of the way and reached behind it to pull his daypack out and to his side. Satisfying himself as to his and Annie's personal safety at that moment, Luke scanned his immediate surroundings for any potential threat and then extended his senses outward, eyes and ears acutely attuned to any sign of danger while he watched the woman and her two bodyguards continue hurrying toward the exit.

The retired soldier looked down briefly to ensure his concealed carry pistol was now in his hands, round in the firing chamber and ready to go. He'd done all these things in only a scant couple of seconds and with no conscious volition on his part. He intended to service enemy targets with all of his weaponry if he had to. He looked once again at Annie – who was wandering toward the exit as well -- and spoke using what he called his "Command Voice."

"Annie! On me! NOW!"

The girl abruptly pulled up and stopped moving. Turning around, she obeyed Luke's command at once and rushed over to take up a position directly behind him.

Luke's eyes were constantly moving now, searching for any threat within his environment. Pausing, he motioned with his left hand toward a cinder-block, windowless office in the back of the market. He was surprisingly calm, considering all the chaos going on outside.

"Annie. I need you to get into your dad's office and then lock the door and stay out of sight. There's gunfire down the road and it sounds like it's headed this way."

Annie nodded silently. She visibly fought to keep from panicking and running away as fast as she could to escape the fury that was booming and thundering over in town. Her eyes were as wide as a deer's and she trembled slightly.

"Ye-Ye-Yessir," she said. "What about those three people?" She meant the two men and the woman. They were at the market's joint entrance and exit. The men were scanning the outside for any visible threats.

The retired soldier took a breath and essayed a slight smile, looking to keep the scared 17-year-old from becoming too frightened. He'd seen this sort of attack play out before over in the Sandbox and he knew a panicked rush out the doors wouldn't be good, so he was slightly pleased that the woman and two men were now taking their time somewhat, though he also knew death could just as easily claim all of them as well no matter how slowly or quickly they moved.

Taking a breath, he decided to warn them.

"Hey! Hold up!"

One of the men turned toward him, pistol at the high ready. Ellis kept both hands down and in a nonthreatening position. He didn't want to risk getting shot at for his trouble. The man with the pistol considered Luke while never moving his gun off the former Delta operator's torso. He only spoke a single word:

"What?"

The man was clearly a little tensed up, and rightfully so.

Luke kept his voice even and reasonable.

"Are you folks going outside? Not sure that's the best play right now, given we don't know what's going on out there." He continued to keep his arms low and hands lower still.

The man, whoever or whatever he was, didn't say anything. It was obvious he was waiting for the all-clear from his partner and he kept his weapon aimed at Ellis. Now, the other man spoke in a terse, clipped voice:

"We're good to go. Let's move!"

At that, the man with his gun on Luke turned and the trio went through the glass doors and to their car at the double-time. The woman was nervously hovering at the back of the bodyguard to her front. The one to her rear closed the gap and took up position slightly off to her left. Outside, they would probably maintain position, the one to the front leading the woman to the back of their vehicle while the one in the rear dove for the driver's side and the means to exit the parking lot as quickly as possible.

Ellis didn't interfere. He had enough on his plate and time would tell if he was right or not about the woman and what the attack taking place outside and down the road was really all about. He strongly suspected she had something to do with it, though not as an enemy combatant. Rather, if his suspicions proved true, she was probably the reason for why his little hamlet was now being taken under fire.

Luke bent down and rummaged around in his daypack. He pulled out and then quickly assembled his AR-15, making sure a 30-round magazine of 5.56 mm ammunition was securely in place and that the rifle was charged and ready to rock, with red dot on and set properly. He didn't want any "red wash" from an overly bright reticle to obscure targets he might have to fire at. Satisfied as to his progress so far, he paused to listen to the goings-on outside. The trio's car hadn't yet started up.

"POW! POW!"

Two shots rang out.

They had the distinct sound only a sniper rifle could make. Twin barks from a fair distance, followed by dual thuds as two bodies toppled to the ground, shot either in the chest or just a bit above, in the throat. Two more shots echoed off the market's front face, each likely meant for a head in case anyone already shot was wearing body armor. *Shoot 'em 'til they're down, and then shoot 'em some more* was a mantra of the infantry fighter everywhere.

The woman who'd left with the men screamed and ran back inside the market, eyes frantically casting about for help. She quickly fixated on Luke and Annie and ran over to them. She wasn't crying, but she was clearly scared witless at the moment.

Ellis kept his voice as calm as possible, right hand holding his AR-15 now that he'd holstered his pistol. He held his left hand up and began speaking:

"It's okay, it's okay, ma'am. You're safe."

Luke wasn't sure if the woman would run away from him and try to hide someplace not quite as safe, but he didn't want to take any chances.

"Puh-please. Puh-puh-please! Help me!"

The woman said all this in a low, almost-whispered voice. Her eyes and her head were on a swivel and she was shaking and trembling as well. The former Delta operator had seen the same reaction in many people who'd come under fire for the first time in their lives and he wasn't surprised by it.

At the moment Luke cared only about the situation at hand, though he was even more convinced now that the woman was the reason for all the shooting going on outside, and that he and Annie and her brother Darren – wherever he happened to be right now, and Luke knew he was going to have to figure that out sooner or later – were standing in the way of the bad guys fulfilling their mission. He also knew the attackers likely wouldn't spare even a second's consideration before they killed whoever else was in the market or around town.

Nonetheless, he felt he still had a responsibility to do whatever he could for the woman.

Pointing at the office, Luke spoke to both females: "Go on, now. Get in the office and stay there."

Annie and the woman nodded vigorously and took off for the designated sanctuary. Once they were inside, Luke could hear the girl lock the door and the muffled sound of discussion within, though that also quickly faded away.

Silence now ruled the building.

Outside, down the road, it was an entirely different matter.

Ellis' mind had already moved on to the next tactical problem, which was to figure out when an attack might occur and how to get out of having to fight it. No doubt, the bad guys had the front covered, but did the enemy – and that's how he now thought of the shooters outside – have any rear exits under observation? He couldn't hear anyone crawling around on the market's corrugated tin roof, so if there were any other attackers nearby, they were likely out back somewhere.

Time to see what's going on out back and in those woods, he thought to himself.

Luke sized up the situation.

One: Of the three people to rush out of the market, two had been shot and killed, with only the woman making it back into the building. There was still shooting going on just down the road and around the slight bend leading into Lucketts itself. It sounded like a mix of handgun, semiautomatic and automatic rifle fire, as if some people with pistols and an AR or two were duking it out with several better-equipped terrorists. The latter always seemed to favor AK-47s or

M4s whenever they could get them, and it sounded like M4s were the weapons responsible for the chatter of automatic and three-round burst fire he was hearing.

Two: The snipers covering the market's front had probably been assigned to provide overwatch fire support for their comrades -- the ones who'd somehow ended up in a firefight with several townspeople – once they arrived at the market.

Three: Or maybe the local police had been joined by some good old boys who were carrying their own firearms and both sides were now involved in a major league slugfest?

Luke didn't know just yet. The latter scenario seemed as good a reason as any for why the aggressors hadn't yet stormed the place to take what they'd come for, which seemed to him to be the woman now hiding with Annie in the windowless office to the market's rear. It helped give him a tactical insight into how they'd behave if they were successful in finally making their way to this building, and he knew what he should do if it at all possible, which was run away and hide somewhere else until he could find the police or some other armed, friendly force that could protect him and what he now thought of as "his people."

As the firefight down the road continued to rage, Luke considered what might be outside at the rear of the market. For starters, a wooded area – lush green and thickly forested – stood only about fifty yards away. Ellis expected that the enemy would have set up some sort of fire position or hide back in those woods on the chance that the target and her guards would try to make a run for it in that direction.

It's what I would do, he thought.

Making a snap decision, he reached into his daypack again, pulled out an expensive handheld imaging device and then leaned his carbine against the market's rear wall.

Looking around, he found what he was looking for: A small rectangular window about eight feet off the ground. It was one of about a half-dozen spread out along the rear wall to allow sunlight in.

The window he chose supplied a direct view of the wooded area behind the market. It and the other windows were also covered in reflective silver film on their outside faces so that no one could see in, but which also allowed an observer on the inside to see out. Luke knew this was so, as he'd made sure in the past to case the building before he'd entered it, noting ingress and egress points as well as any helpful features, such as those windows.

The former soldier grabbed a step-stool and climbed it, careful not to let his head pop up into the window's face until he was ready. He turned his ballcap around, with its bill covering his neck, and moved the imager's viewer to his eye, and slowly raised his head just in case someone in the woods happened to be scanning the window and looking for any hint of a reflection or movement in it.

Nothing happened. He hadn't really expected a shot at the glass, but better safe than sorry, he knew.

Adjusting the device and switching through different filters, Luke landed on the one best suited to his purposes at the moment. Now, the woods were bathed in shapes discriminated only by the heat signatures they gave off.

Almost the entire wooded area was cool, with not even a small, furry rodent or another mammal around to heat things up, so to speak.

It was possible, Ellis knew, for any security element placed in the forest to be hiding under a thermal blanket or two to obscure their heat signatures, but his imager – one of several gifts given to him by upon his retirement by his friends at JSOC – was precise enough to pick out even the smallest thermal leakage from under such blankets. It could also detect even a very small patch of ground warmed up merely from an enemy standing or sitting on it. Plus, any sudden movement, or even just twitching or jerking on the part of anyone hiding out in the woods, would alert the imager to the fact someone or something was trying to avoid its all-seeing eye.

Luke continued scanning the area slowly and methodically, all while listening to his 'six,' or behind him, for both the sound of the firefight still going on down the road as well as anyone trying to creep up closer to the building or even enter it.

He'd have liked to have had someone guarding his back, but the two dead men out in the parking lot had ruined that chance after ignoring his advice to stay put and wait things out a bit longer. There was no change, as yet, to that situation. Good guys and bad guys alike were apparently still going at it hot and heavy, the "KERR-RACK!" of rifle fire interspersed with the slower and more deliberate popping sounds of 9 millimeter handguns joining in on the devilish symphony now playing out in Lucketts.

Ellis didn't know how long the good guys – likely some towns-people with a couple of cops mixed in, from the sound of things – could hold out.

Probably not for much longer, he thought, given the pace of true assault rifle fire – meaning long guns with select fire capability – that seemed to be aimed in their direction.

Sooner or later, Luke knew, superior firepower would win out. It almost always did in these kinds of slugfests.

Spotting a flare of orange light out in the woods, Ellis fixed his optic on that particular spot, waiting.

Success at last.

There you are. Two men were hiding in the brush.

They were camouflaged well enough, the retired Delta operator thought – plus, they'd also taken care to ensure neither they nor their gear were overtly visible and that they'd made no perfectly straight lines because there are no such things in nature -- but they very fool-ishly were far too close to each other at barely a small tree trunk's worth of distance apart.

Even stupider still, one was smoking a cigarette. It looked like he was trying to cup his hand over the glowing end, thinking that that would be enough to hide it from anyone wandering around outside on the rear lawn facing the woods in which he and his partner were hiding.

Only a moron – *Or a very poorly trained terrorist*, Luke thought –

would smoke while on a surveillance and fire or ambush operation. The odor of burning tobacco could often be detected a hundred meters or more away, depending on the wind direction.

Satisfied with what he'd seen, Ellis climbed back down the step stool and reached once more into his daypack, pulling out a high-quality suppressor, another of the gifts his friends at JSOC had given him at his retirement. Bringing his weapon around, he quickly attached it to the muzzle of his AR and checked to make sure he was locked and loaded.

Luke went motionless, listening intently to the world outside his little piece of real estate, and cocked his head to the left, almost like a Rottweiler listening to his master's voice.

Was the gunfire down the road slackening a bit?

It sounded like it, and it gave new urgency to the mission at hand, which was to end the opposition in the woods and then get his charges out of the building and on the move, hopefully toward safety. In the back of his mind, he knew he'd also have to find Annie's brother, Darren.

Ellis moved up to the edge of the wall opening out onto the ground-level cement slab at the rear of the building. He knew he'd be able to gain an unobstructed view of the wooded area where at least two of the bad guys or terrorists or kidnappers, or whatever they happened to be, were hiding.

Luke had already fixed their position in his mind, but he wanted to check one more time just to be sure.

He switched his carbine to his left hand for a moment and brought the imager up to his right eye, slowly moving the smallest possible part of both it and his head out from behind the wall for the merest possible second.

In that interval, his trained eye managed to pick out both shooters. They were still in the same position as before.

Snap shots it is.

He returned the imager to his daypack and otherwise made ready to go to war.

Breathing slowly and steadily, forcing his heart rate to slow way down, Ellis mentally counted off the seconds until he'd make his move.

"Three, two, one..." Luke's movements were slow and smooth, which meant that in the apex predator's world he'd once dominated, they were also fast.

Carbine up, the retired Delta warrior rapidly found both men and placed his red dot over the chest of the one on the left. He was the one who'd been smoking. Ellis pressed his ultra-fine trigger's mechanism until he was slightly surprised by the nearly nonexistent recoil of the weapon as it sent its deadly cargo downrange.

What was left of the rifle's report as his bullet exited the suppressor was little more than a "POP!" It would be hard for those two men in the woods to hear.

"THUD!" Even though the sound was very low, the man hiding in the woods no more than 50 yards away instantly fell to the ground as if he'd been poleaxed and moved no more.

Luke took all this in in a flash. He and his rifle were a single living, breathing entity, and everything he did was aimed at servicing the targets in front of him.

Immediately after feeling his AR's recoil, Ellis moved his red dot slightly to the right, sighting it in on the second bad guy's chest. He pressed the trigger once again and saw the same result: A very slight recoil, no muzzle flash, a low "POP!" and another dead terrorist.

Looking through his optic, Luke satisfied himself that both men were down, but he still put another round into each to make sure they stayed down. No movement came from either after he shot them a second time.

Slinging his rifle on his back once more, he reached down and brought his imager up, quickly sweeping the woods from left to right and back again, looking for any telltale sign of more enemy troops.

Nothing.

Time to move.

Turning around, he headed toward the office, grabbing a couple of 2-liter bottles of water along the way and stuffing them into his daypack. He had high-calorie protein bars and enough water for himself stowed in it already, but Luke knew stress could make people thirstier than normal and that both of his charges would no doubt need a drink or three of water once he had them in the woods and on the move.

The retired soldier was a realist, especially when it came to the kind of combat situation he found himself living once again. If the people doing all the shooting in town – as well as the shooter or shooters out front -- suspected their quarry had escaped or had gotten to some kind of help and was now fleeing through the woods he and his protectees would soon find themselves outmaneuvered and gradually caught in an ever-tightening noose.

Real, honest-to-God combat wasn't a Rambo movie, where a lone man with a really big, ugly knife always prevailed against all odds. No, it was chaos and blood and terror and the side with more people and more guns almost always won. In the cold, cruel calculus of war, Luke knew that one man – no matter how skilled he was – stood little chance of defeating a well-armed and determined enemy and he was now weighted down with two other people, neither of which were armed.

Ellis had no problem with this reality. He'd lived on the razor's edge for more years than he could easily recount. It was what it was. So, he intended on taking the cards stacked against him and throwing them back into the enemy's face.

Luke quickly calculated the odds of making it to his truck and using it to bug out. They were nil and none.

No way I can get us to any vehicle out front, he thought as he neared the market's office. Not with shooters out front and him having no idea where they were positioned.

Long story short, they'd shoot him down like a dog. Also, if they were armed with sniper rifles, they would probably be hundreds of yards away. No matter how good his AR-15 was, no matter how fine a shooter he could boast being, his carbine simply didn't have the capa-

66

bility to take them under fire in a long-range shoot-em-up, even supposing he had all kinds of time to find them and then take them under counterfire.

The voice in his head was rueful when it came to him and Annie and the woman being unable to use one of the two available rides out front.

That dog just ain't gonna hunt.

To make a play for his truck – really, any motor vehicle at the moment – would be the height of foolishness. Ellis hadn't gotten to the age he was, which also included not having been awarded a Purple Heart among his many rows of medals, ribbons, badges, and uniform tabs, by being foolish.

In truth, he and others in his world had often joked that the Purple Heart was nothing but an enemy marksmanship badge and he had no desire to receive one of those, especially now that he was officially an Army retiree.

No, it was time to egress the area, which at this point meant getting himself and his people outside and into the woods and then running away and hiding until the cavalry arrived.

"Great," Ellis said aloud. "I have no idea just what the cavalry might consist of, or when it might arrive, but I do know how to run and hide."

Now at the office door, he knocked firmly on it and spoke in a calm voice.

"Annie? Ma'am? This is Luke Ellis. We're safe. Come on out."

The 17-year-old girl threw the door open. The older woman was standing behind her. Both looked scared, but it was to their credit neither appeared anywhere near hysterical or unable to obey commands. Both moved up to face the former soldier. The woman spoke first, voice plaintive:

"Am I able to leave now?" she asked Ellis. "Can I get to my car? Are the ones who shot my friends gone?"

Luke knew this was no time for fooling around. He spoke to both Annie and the woman in a matter-of-fact voice.

"I have no idea, ma'am, and I wouldn't want to chance it. I managed to spot two men hiding out in the woods to our rear. It was clear they were there to cover the building in case anyone ran out and tried to make it into that brush."

The woman's face fell slightly at Luke's situation report. Annie spoke up:

"I don't understand, Mister Ellis." The girl was indeed scared, but she wasn't paralyzed by fear, a fact the retired Delta soldier admired a little. "I thought you said it was safe now. How are we supposed to get away from here?"

The older woman stayed silent, waiting for Luke to respond. His voice was clear and still matter-of fact and he smiled slightly to put the two females at ease.

"We are, Annie. I ended the threat to our rear, and that's the way we're going to leave this place: Through the woods until we can get out of this area. But we have to leave now, so let's get going."

While he spoke, Luke accompanied his directives with slight hand and arm movements to show his desired direction of travel as well as the urgency of the situation.

The older woman still seemed somewhat hesitant, though, and broke the momentary silence that had dropped over the trio after Ellis had summed up the plan to escape the building.

"Uh, Mister Ellis is it? Yes. Good. Look, I need to make a phone call. If I can do that, I promise you help will come quickly."

Luke nodded in the affirmative. "That's fine, ma'am, but we need to be moving while you're calling, because I don't know how long we have until the fellows doing all that shooting in town get tired of playing war and start heading this way."

Finishing, Ellis looked directly at her while Annie watched and listened to their interaction, head moving from one to the other as the duo conversed.

Ellis spoke to the mystery woman once more, this time with a bit more assuredness.

"Obviously, all this shooting and gunfire has something to do with you, ma'am."

Falling silent, he looked directly at her, waiting for her response.

The woman pulled up short and looked back at the former soldier. She sketched an innocent, befuddled look and planted it firmly on her face.

"I don't know what you mean, Mister Ellis." Her voice was calm. "I'm just as confused about what's going on as you are. Really, what kind of town is this where drug gangs or criminals can just come in and shoot everything up? My two friends are dead out there in the parking lot, caught in some sort of crossfire between warring gangs, no doubt."

She capped off her denial with a vigorous nod of the head, as if her pronouncement about drug gangs was now irrefutable.

To this, Ellis said nothing. Annie had no idea what to say, either. The situation was completely beyond her lived experience.

Rather than say anything else, the woman looked back down at her phone and continued tapping numbers into its touchscreen, her fright causing her to misremember the 11-digit string she was intent on entering.

Luke wasn't fooled. Shaking his head, he counted down the seconds until he could move everyone outside and into the safety of the forest. He'd give them 10 seconds, in fact, before he physically propelled the girl and the woman outside.

Glancing over at Annie, he nodded at her and received one in return. Ellis could tell she'd put two-and-two together as well when it came to the older woman and her presence in the store.

The two dead bodyguards in the market's parking lot, combined with how protective of the woman they'd been before they'd all gone outside, told the teenager everything. After the men had displayed their firearms, she'd quickly determined the older woman was someone important. Soon after both men were shot, but not the woman, she'd also known her assessment had been correct.

Now, she looked to Luke to help get them out of the mess they were in. He was "the Army guy," after all. If anyone around town knew what to do in a situation like this, it had to be him.

Ellis moved. They were nearly out of time.

It was obvious all cellular service was down. A glance at his own phone's touchscreen showed zero bars and an "Out of Coverage Area" message blinking in red and yellow. He'd never seen his phone do that before. He also suspected if he picked up a hard-wired land-line, he'd hear only an endless, repetitive beeping similar to a busy signal, though much faster.

The woman was standing stock still, looking down at her cell-phone in disbelief.

The sound coming from her phone's speaker – to Ellis' trained eye, it looked to be one of those fully encrypted models given to the privileged few within the federal government's Senior Executive Service – also told him what he needed to know:

Whatever had happened, there was no phone service, at least on every available cellular network in the region, including the "special" ones reserved for people having the kind of phone she had. Luke would also bet good money the lady and her two protectors had a pretty good satellite phone in the glove box of that car of hers, though fat lot of good it would do him with at least one sniper covering the front of the building. He'd never be able to get to the car, open it, search the glovebox or the center console, find the phone, and then retrace his steps back into the market without taking a .308 round or something similar right in the chest or back, there to bleed out while Annie and the woman awaited their fates.

Ellis quickly summed everything up in his head while he took the teenager and the mystery woman by the arm, rushing them toward the rear of the market until they could begin moving of their own accord.

What was happening looked increasingly to the experienced former special operator like some sort of direct action operation, one aimed at capturing the woman. He could also feel in his bones that if they went out the front in an attempt to get to his truck or the lady's car, at least he and Annie would find themselves shot. Halting them all for a second, he spoke to the woman once again, clapping his hands together and then pointing at the phone she held limply in her left hand:

"Ma'am," he told her firmly, "whatever's going on with your phone, with my phone, with all our phones, it doesn't really matter for now." He made ready to begin moving her toward the rear of the building once more. Annie was bringing up the rear and he could see she'd go where they both went.

"Buh-buh-but..."

The faith the older woman had put in the ability of the two men with her to keep her safe, along with the loss of her electronic lifeline, had finally disoriented her. She was struggling to regain her equilibrium.

"But nothing," Ellis replied to her. "We've got to get moving, NOW."

Annie spoke, her voice a little reedy and querulous but certain, nonetheless. She looked at the woman in front of her:

"Mister Ellis is right, ma'am." She pointed at the rear of the building. "We have to get out of here because this building sticks out like a sore thumb, someone shot your two friends but not you, and the people doing all the shooting in town will probably be heading this way soon enough."

The teenager was no fool and she knew all the firing just down the road likely presaged something worse once it stopped. Inwardly, she prayed they'd have the time to avoid whatever was coming.

Taking a breath, Annie looked at Luke before pointing at him. When she spoke, her voice was firmer and surer, as if she'd made the ultimate, fateful decision to entrust her fate to Ellis' skills and experience.

"I trust Mister Ellis completely, ma'am. You should, too."

The girl inclined her head toward the man she'd mostly thought of in the past as "that really nice ex-Army guy." In her eyes, he was one of those Serious Men her father spoke about every once in a while, much as her dad and mom had said her paternal uncle, who'd been a Marine officer for several years, had been. Personally, she'd never known her uncle because he'd died of cancer when she was just two years old, but her parents had told her the same uncanny awareness and quick reaction to perceived danger Uncle Jared had owned also lived within the man standing in front of her.

Now, fully attuned to what he was or maybe what he'd been in a past life unknowable to her until today, she could see Mister Ellis was a very dangerous man. She could also tell, though, that the danger he radiated was only directed at those who threatened him and anyone he was trying to protect. At present, this meant both her and the older lady standing with them. That the woman was likely the source of all their problems didn't really matter right now. Mister Ellis was certainly right about that.

Thinking back to her past encounters with him, she remembered he'd been friendly and unfailingly polite to her at all times. In retrospect, she'd always suspected there was something much deeper residing within him. It was at once both scary and yet comforting and reassuring, as if Mister Ellis were a giant sheepdog sent into a pasture to protect the flock against the predators moving around just out of sight in the deep, inky black night.

And now here he was, his might and courage on full display for all to see if they cared to look. All of this had run through the girl's head in a flash, and she looked gratefully at the man and the weapons he carried.

Luke nodded at her in return and began moving them once again toward the rear, daypack now firmly on his back and suppressed AR-15 pointed outward at his front quarter.

At some point, though Annie hadn't even seen him do it –because he was that fast and that smooth and subtle -- he'd put on some sort of camouflaged vest. It was a little bulky and there were rifle and pistol magazines and a few other things on it that she couldn't describe. No doubt it was the "body armor" her little brother pointed out to her whenever she sat with him to watch what she called his "war movies."

She wasn't personally a fan of most of those flicks – though the one starring Tom Hanks that was about World War Two and D-Day always managed to hold her interest. Still, she watched them with her sibling out of a sense of loyalty to him as well as to make sure he didn't see anything too scary.

Thinking back once again, she was grateful she'd done so because she understood, if only just a little, what Mister Ellis was about. Annie thought he wore that camouflaged body armor with the natural grace of someone who'd worn one practically forever. The black rifle he held in his arms also seemed like it was naturally attached to his hands and he maneuvered it around them without even seeming to think about it. She could see that he never deliberately or even carelessly pointed it at either her or the woman with them.

Right now, she felt safer with him than she would with anyone else.

Annie decided Mister Ellis must have done all of this stuff a million times during his Army career and her estimation wouldn't have been all that far off the mark. The man and his gear were now a single organism. He was mated to his weapon and his support gear, all part of a single system focused solely on the mission at hand.

Luke held up his left hand, right one on his carbine. He halted them at the edge of the same wall he'd earlier peered around in search of the pair of shooters he'd spotted in the woods. Annie and the mystery woman pulled up short behind him.

Turning, he looked at both and spoke once again in the same calm-yet-firm voice he'd used before:

"Okay, this is it." Ellis paused a moment to make sure he had Annie's and the woman's full attention. "We're going to go outside and then move off the patio and cross the 50 yards and head into the woods. Do you both understand?" He waited for a response.

"Yes, Mister Ellis." Annie was the first to speak.

"I do."

The older woman's voice was terse and it was obvious she was still on the edge of breaking and running away. Ellis wanted to prevent that from happening and looked at her with eyes fixed firmly on her own.

"Ma'am? You good to go? You're not going to ghost me and go running off on your own, are you?"

The woman's voice sounded a bit miffed. "I'm not going anywhere but with you two," she replied. "Where would I go anyway?"

Ellis looked down at his watch and then at the two females.

"Fine. Let's go.

With that, the trio left the market and headed towards the woods, unsure of what awaited them.

CHAPTER 5
THE WOMAN

THE WOMAN'S SHOULDERS SLUMPED SLIGHTLY AS SHE ADMITTED the futility of trying to strike out on her own. Her bodyguards were both lying dead out front in the parking lot. At least one sniper was out there, too, and there were no doubt other people intent on grabbing her – not that she was in any way eager to admit she knew more about the situation than she'd so far let on to the man Ellis and the girl Annie. What they didn't know couldn't hurt her, she'd already decided.

She needed to get to a secure phone. Tragically, the one in her vehicle was very much out of reach. The tracking bracelet she normally wore was also sitting on her dresser drawer today, left behind in her haste to get into Lucketts to do some light shopping. It had been one of the few pleasures she allowed herself these days.

In truth, she was rarely given to such quaint diversions. Some years back, she'd finally accepted that she really was as important as the government had long ago decreed her to be.

Unfortunately, familiarity – combined with a complete lack of threat over the years – had slowly bred carelessness and a casual underappreciation for security procedure within her. Her thoughts on the matter were succinct:

Well, I'm paying for that disregard now, aren't I?

The woman wasn't trained in the ways of espionage, nor of anything remotely related to military operations. Rather, she'd once been among the most highly educated and trained scientists in the world and probably would have been recognized as one of its greatest had she ever been allowed to publish her research. That had been completely out of the question back then and was even more impossible these days, she admitted to herself.

Though many wouldn't believe it, the world was an even more dangerous place today than it had been back when the Soviet Union and the United States had fought a long, mostly cold, war in the nooks and crannies and shadows that made up what the typical naïve and foolish political scientist called "international relations."

She knew for a fact there were organizations and even nations out there eager to bring about a global Armageddon if they could. As well, relations between what she called "the Great Powers" – the US, Russia, and Communist China – were on shaky ground at best. All it would take to fatally upset the delicate balance existing between the three biggest, meanest tigers in the jungle would be a little push.

She knew something much more powerful than a little push was on tap if she was ever captured or died anything less than a completely natural death.

The world could end in nuclear fire, and she might even welcome the sterilizing blast of alpha, beta, and gamma radiation that would result. Because believe it or not, there was something much worse than even nuclear war. She shuddered inwardly at the thought of what might escape if she couldn't make a phone call or get to a radio soon.

To add insult to injury, the woman now knew she'd stupidly grown far too used to the good offices and the protection and resources of the people and officials and government agencies hovering menacingly over her, yet also simultaneously cocooning and protecting her.

All of this is totally my fault, she admitted. To be fair to her protective detail, the pair of men with her today, as well as the others who'd worked to keep her safe, had never really understood who it was they'd been guarding.

For one, they knew almost nothing about her – which was by design, both for the government's as well as her and her detail's protection.

Her identity – who she was and what she'd been – had been completely scrubbed from every database known to the federal government and all its intelligence agencies. No fingerprint card nor any sort of DNA sample existed anywhere. There was not even a simple photo to be found, including from her kindergarten days, she'd learned. The government had been thorough in this regard, she grudgingly admitted. It really could make someone disappear if it wanted to.

Shortly after her great discovery (she'd thought it great at the time, though not so much these days), her death in an auto accident had been faked and a cremation urn dutifully presented to her parents, along with a government life insurance check large enough to ensure they'd never have a financial worry in their lives ever again.

To the woman's utter sadness, both her mother and father were now gone and she'd never been able to reach out to them or simply comfort them once she'd been disappeared. On an intellectual level, she accepted that she and her government couldn't afford to let even a hint of her existence leak.

That was small comfort on an emotional level, though.

Her mother had been irreparably broken by her brilliant only child's death and she'd been the first to go to her grave. To paraphrase Ernest Hemingway she'd wasted away, gradually at first and then suddenly.

That left her father, who'd been an orphan, bereft and alone in the world. He was felled in his early seventies by a massive stroke. He, too, had passed the years until his death bitterly angry and saddened by both the loss of his daughter and then, several years later, his wife.

Thinking back on everything that had taken place before the last 10 or 15 minutes of her life, the woman was forlorn. Inside, she sighed deeply at the cosmic unfairness of what she'd had to put her parents through. As was her habit when she looked to find some small, threadbare measure of comfort, though, she would weigh their loss – and the loss of all she'd loved and cared for – against the potential loss of nearly all human life on Earth.

Ninety-six, maybe even ninety-seven, percent of all humans.

That was how dangerous what she'd created really was and why she'd practically become a woman without a country, or at least a country that couldn't afford to let news of her continued existence become known.

She supposed she should be grateful – and she really was, she told herself – that she hadn't simply been killed in a tragic "accident" after the powers that be realized the full import of her discovery. Certainly, she'd known of a few people above her in the food chain who'd advocated for just such an outcome.

It was to her government's credit, she thought, that she was allowed the life she now found herself living.

"Well," she'd said to the mirror in her bathroom on more than a few occasions, "it might also have a little to do with the fact the government knows I set up a failsafe in the weekend between my discovery and when they brought me in from the cold."

She liked the phrase "in from the cold." It implied leaving a threat behind and moving into security and warmth and safety.

The reality was an altogether different thing, she'd learned. She probably lived only because her government feared what would happen if it made her die.

At any rate, she hadn't spared her superiors from the knowledge that leakage of her creation to certain other governments – some of them far less scrupulous than her own, including the aforementioned few motivated by a religious fervor downright scary in its intensity – would occur if she should somehow suffer an unfortunate "accident," like falling up the stairs and breaking her neck or committing suicide by somehow shooting herself three times in the head with a really big shotgun.

The number of people who now knew she was alive and kicking could be listed on a ten-line sticky note, with several of those lines left over. To be in on that secret was to forever have a target painted on your back, after all, and she'd never wished, even in her darkest moments, to have anyone else share the burden of what she'd created.

And so, she knew her life had to be what she'd made it into. The men and women helping keep her safe had also never known anything about the work she'd carried out and the deadly secrets she kept locked in her head, and that was the way she'd wanted it because it kept them alive, too.

Such is the perverse nature of fate on occasion, though, that the need to protect her had also brought with it the potential seeds of her destruction. Over time, repetition, routine, and even boredom had infected not only her but those within her orbit. Even the few people in the rarified strata of government allowed to know of her work had grown far too used to quiet and a lack of threat.

To all of them -- immensely powerful officials and bodyguards alike -- she'd over the years somehow become just another high-level government VIP. The woman had never been able to divulge anything to disabuse them of that notion, either. She'd once created something in a stroke of genius not replicated in all the world since no matter how hard the vast research apparatus of the government had tried, but if she breathed a word of it, nations might end up fighting wars with each other just to capture her and her secrets. To make matters worse, she wasn't even completely sure these days just how she'd done it, though she couldn't afford to admit that to anyone. She'd been somewhat sloppy with her notes and had thought the path down which she'd gone was nothing more than another dry hole.

Why keep extensive notes in that case? she'd once reasoned.

Such an idiot she'd been.

Eventually, the woman began to realize she was taking some things for granted, but she also didn't care, secure as she was in the belief that nothing could penetrate the world she'd created for herself.

And so, she began to hector and even plead and soon enough demand and threaten. With the implied threat of a failsafe hanging in the air like the Sword of Damocles the woman got what she wanted (somewhat to her surprise, to be honest). Now, she received an occasional day trip here or there and even a drive into Lucketts and the immediate vicinity so she could pick up a little farm-to-table fresh fruit, something she prized for her breakfast.

And now look where she was at.

She was with a young girl hardly aware of the danger into which she'd been thrust as well as with a man who posed another type of danger, though not to her, she could tell. She had to admit that, just like the teenager with her, she found herself comforted by his presence. He practically radiated deadly skill, and at a much, much higher level than Chris or Tom, her two guards, had had. That much was clear to her.

She didn't know what the man the girl called "Mister Ellis" was, or maybe what he'd once been, but she could tell he was serious, very experienced in the way of war, and that he currently had the only weapons around. Ergo, she needed to stay by his side and she also needed to stiffen her spine a little.

She had to play for time.

More importantly, while she played for time, she needed a phone. Unfortunately, no commercial landline or cellular network was working. She kept looking at her watch, hoping the man wouldn't catch her doing it.

Time wasn't on her side.

Size up your situation, girl!

She couldn't allow herself to be captured. It would be very bad for all three of them as well as the rest of the world if a determined enemy managed to get their hands on her and then pry her secrets out. Even if they had no idea how to at once use what she knew, she also accepted it would only be a matter of time until they would.

She also couldn't die during all this, though if she'd hadn't become lax with her personal protective measures, she'd have gladly killed herself now to stop what she knew from leaking out into the wild. Stupidly, she'd hadn't disarmed her failsafe before heading out. It was what others might call her "dead man's switch." There was also no way to deactivate it without a working phone or, at minimum, a radio. And forget about the internet. No doubt, it was even more messed up at present than even simple forms of electronic communication.

Fortunately, her failsafe would accept a radio transmission as long as she used the proper code words, so until she could make that happen, she accepted that she had to stay among the living. It was a bitter pill to swallow, though, and she almost sighed out loud.

I'm damned if I do, and damned if I don't.

Being brutally honest, she knew she should be damned for all eternity anyway for what she'd done. Hitler, Stalin, Genghis Khan, Mao – all of them, combined with every other genocidal maniac throughout the length and breadth of human existence – would pale beside her if the thing she'd created ever escaped its restraints.

She once again stole a glance at the man and the teenage girl. He was telling her they were going to move into the woods in just a few seconds. She could see him silently counting down until he would make them both come with him and so she nodded at him, seeing and reacting but not really hearing. She'd mentally disconnected for a second to consider things.

One of her favorite movies – it had come out during her doctoral studies -- had been the original "Jurassic Park." In it, the scientist asked to assess the reborn dinosaurs at the park -- after seeing the havoc resulting from their creation -- had made a keen observation:

Your scientists were so preoccupied with whether they could, they didn't stop to think if they should.

The woman knew she'd been a peerless intellect in the ways of science but also a naïf when it came to such piddling things like the ethics attached to her work. Looking back, she now knew better. In her arrogance she'd never stopped trying to create, but she'd also never stopped to take even the barest, briefest second to consider whether she should.

How was I to know what would happen?

What a giant, steaming load of horse flop! her more honest side exclaimed. *You knew and you didn't care. You wanted fame, riches, glory, an appearance on "The View," you name it, you wanted it.*

The woman imagined her other side. That woman was shaking her head in disgust at her and she hated to admit it, but that one was right.

She'd always known this day might come, that what she'd helped create in the past might return to finish its destruction of her, and that its continued existence made both her and anyone else near her a prime target if word ever got out about what she'd created.

Stop whining!

That was her honest side again. *Get moving with these people and take advantage of the opportunity to make right what you once made very, very wrong. And if you can't, I hope the world will forgive you one day, though I doubt it's possible.*

For some reason, her honest side always sounded like her mother.

My honest side is a real pain, isn't she?

The woman sighed inwardly once again, resolved to do what she could. That began with making sure the man and the girl didn't find out what she knew. To know would be a death sentence for them both, and they did seem like good people. After all, she wasn't yet so far gone in her personal circle of hell that she wanted others to join her there.

The man caught her attention, breaking her reverie by snapping his fingers at her. She'd blanked out for longer than she'd intended. She also saw the girl roll her eyes slightly, though the teenager quickly managed to hide her frustration.

"Yes, what is it?"

"Ma'am, it's time to move, and Annie and I need you in the here-and-now if we're going to do this." Despite what had to be his pique at her, the man's voice was evenly modulated and he was honestly trying to be patient.

"So, you ready to do this?" he asked her.

"I'm fine, I really am." Inside, she really wasn't, but he didn't need to know that.

The man and the girl couldn't find out what she knew, if only for their own sakes, though the fate of the world might also hinge on the knowledge they might glean if she wasn't careful. She spoke once more and motioned her hand toward them both.

"I'm ready when you are."

She cocked her head slightly. The gunfire in town had tapered off. It sounded like only a single pistol and one of the rifles -- like the one the man Ellis was carrying -- against four or five other rifles.

In her estimation, there was now only a minute or so left before the people she knew with absolute certainty were looking for her would, indeed, be able to pursue her. As if to confirm her fears, the glass in the market's front doors exploded as rifle rounds -- from the same sniper who'd killed her two bodyguards – started hitting the front of the building.

Ellis nodded. He knew better than she did what was happening outside.

"Looks like whoever the bad guys are, they're ready to wrap up their little brunch and they've told their shooters to try to keep us pinned down and helpless until their main body of attackers can move to this location."

The man paused and spoke to her again.

"Of course, by "us," I mean *you*. They don't know I'm in here and armed and Annie wouldn't be of any concern to them. Just saying. On the plus side, I'm also sure they don't know I took their guys in the woods out of the equation."

The woman felt she should issue at least a *pro forma* protest and insist on her innocence once again, but she could tell the man would ignore it at this point. Instead, she remained silent.

Ellis motioned for quiet.

Annie and the woman at once looked at him. Out in the woods, near the two dead attackers, they could hear the sound of a tactical radio.

Luke recognized the language. It was Pashto, common in Afghanistan, though he could also make out Dari, which Iranians spoke, though Afghans living near that country's border also often spoke it as well.

It was yet another piece of the puzzle he was assembling in his head. Afghan, and possibly Iranian, terrorists here in Lucketts, and they were after the woman he was now trying to protect. His thought was immediate.

This is crazy!

Instead of saying anything, he just shook his head and concentrated on matters at hand.

Annie was a bit miffed that Mister Ellis thought she posed absolutely no threat to the attackers, but she was mature enough to also accept it as true. She wouldn't matter in any firefight even if she had a gun, which she really had no idea how to use anyway.

"Mister Ellis?" She was eager to escape this deathtrap and get into the woods and then to her brother.

"Yeah, Annie. Time for us to leave." Ellis began counting down once again.

"Three, two, one... GO!" He stepped out onto the patio, with the two females trailing him slightly. He moved smoothly and evenly, not too fast but also not too slow. His carbine was up and ready for action if need be.

Out in town, the last scattered shots from the good guys echoed in the still air. At the front of the market, sniper fire picked up even more. The man, the teenager and the woman could make out the sound of motor vehicles starting up, with engines racing as men no doubt piled back into them. Their evil work was done for the moment, and now it was time to head for the market.

Luke knew what time it was, too.

"Ladies, it's time to get moving."

Ellis, Annie and the mystery woman with them all moved toward their new destinies.

CHAPTER 6
BARADAR

"GOD CURSE THIS HATEFUL COUNTRY AND ALL ITS PEOPLE," Hasan Baradar swore under his breath. He looked around momentarily as his fighters – the ones left after they'd stumbled into a gunfight with a pair of American police officers and several townspeople – began piling back into their two SUVs, which now looked much the worse for wear after their impromptu gun battle.

This town – called "Lucketts," a name the commander was sure blasphemed Allah in some way and which he now despised even more than he despised America, a godless land of idolators and infidels – was nothing more than a waypoint along the path to something much more important, which was still out there and no doubt alerted to their presence by now.

The thought of potential failure in this regard threatened to send him into paroxysms of rage, and so he stood still and breathed deeply while he calmed down. He took a second to check his gear and reload his M4 and then jumped into the front passenger side of their two-SUV caravan.

The mission goal wasn't all that far away. Merely up and around the slight bend that lay directly in front of them. He needed to make haste to scoop up their prey, especially now that she was alone and defenseless after his men had taken out her protective detail. Earlier, by secure encrypted satellite phone, he'd double-checked to ensure he had two experienced shooters positioned to cover the front of the building the woman would enter and two in the woods near its rear in case her bodyguards decided to get her out that way. He'd also stationed himself and his group, the main element of this attack and kidnapping, in a copse of trees just north of the town. At his command they headed for the target location, expecting to be there in no time at all.

There'd been one problem, though.

They hadn't counted on police pulling them over in a routine traffic stop just inside this town for "excessive tinting on motor vehicle windows" according to the American police officer just before he died in a hail of gunfire from one of his men, a fool named Amir Khan.

At that point, and from out of nowhere, it seemed – including from the beat-up pickup truck of a man old enough to be committed to a nursing home – Americans with guns started appearing! Baradar, who as a boy had heard stories about the Wild West and the cowboy culture of the United States -- but who also believed Americans were weak -- couldn't believe it.

At one point during the gunfight, he and his men had found themselves facing a dozen civilians armed with a mix of handguns and that most common of rifles in America, the AR-15. It was similar in nature to the US military M4s he and the rest of his cell carried and in the right hands, it could be just as deadly.

The commander didn't know precisely from where his own cell's weapons had originated, but he strongly suspected they'd come from the vast quantity of armaments left behind by the US when its military had left Afghanistan in such haste.

The other policeman -- the one who'd survived their first volley of rifle fire -- had been armed only with a service pistol, a semiautomatic Glock 19 or similar. Regardless, he'd assiduously used it to shoot at and even wound a couple of his men. Insult of insults, the lawman had even managed to kill one of their number!

This deeply offended Hasan Baradar's sensibilities and he vowed to take his revenge on everyone in this town as soon as he completed his mission.

The civilians who'd quickly come to the police officer's aid had pulled guns and rifles seemingly from out of thin air. This included that elderly man with an AR who'd stopped his equally elderly pickup truck in the middle of the road and then began blasting away at Baradar and his men.

Before the old man had finally had the good sense to die – shot through the head by one of his men – the terror leader noted his maniacal grin and shouts of "COME GET SOME!" whenever he fired his weapon, which was quite often and with obvious glee.

For his part, Hasan Baradar had no idea what "COME GET SOME!" meant, but it was doubtlessly employed by the shooter to appear more fearsome than he really was.

Whatever.

The old man and the rest of those civilians – who for a brief few moments had given as good as they'd gotten -- now lay dead in the street.

Once his impromptu defense force had gone down – all victims of superior firepower and the will to indiscriminately use it -- the surviving police officer fell back into the woods, his pistol now silent. He was still running away, Baradar thought, though he didn't have the time to send his fighters after the man to track him down.

No, he was still on mission and he and his men needed to complete it as soon as possible.

"God curse that Amir Khan," the cell's leader swore under his breath at the thought of the fool. He was always too eager to go to the guns! He never thought logically! The fact his wife and two sons had died in a US airstrike a decade ago had no doubt colored his emotions. Understandable, but still...

At any rate, there was nothing to do for it now but to keep

pressing forward, and so he and his men did. They threw their two dead fighters – who'd both been shot cleanly through the neck just above their body armor, one by the American policeman and one by that obscene old man -- into the back of the trailing SUV. For this operation they knew they couldn't leave any of their number, either wounded or dead, behind. That much was clear to both him and the rest of his cell. They were to grab their high value target, who was shopping at a farmer's market just up the road and then disappear, leaving no trace of their presence in this blasted town behind.

He paused for a second to reflect on how he'd come to be here, leading this particular attack.

His original identity documents had proclaimed him to be one Hasan Baradar of Kunduz Province in Afghanistan. They were so good and yet so unremarkable they easily passed the Americans' scrutiny once he'd been transported here to Virginia last year, so eager were the fools to welcome him to his new "home," not that he meant to stay in it any longer than necessary now.

Baradar really had no idea how his masters had known when the woman -- who was no doubt as unclean and impure as every other woman in this benighted land -- would be in this town at this time, and he didn't care.

He only knew the day of reckoning for this country, which he'd hated his entire life, had come at last.

Once the word was passed to him and his small cell, using an extremely high level of tradecraft and caution and mostly through electronic means as well as cutouts they'd never actually met, he and his men had gone into action.

All of them were fellow "refugees" like himself, vetted by his masters and their organization and evaluated in the past for absolute loyalty to the Taliban and the movement's cause.

In Afghanistan he and the others had all managed to insinuate themselves over time into either the Afghan government or the US mission there. Once the inevitable American pullout occurred, they rushed to feverishly proclaim themselves in need of exfiltration and then refugee status in the United States for fear of Taliban reprisals should they be left behind.

The plan had worked magnificently.

Now there was a veritable army of men -- and even some women -- like Hasan Baradar, with most ready to martyr themselves for Allah and the Taliban cause. He was one of the estimated 82,000 non-vetted Afghans who'd gotten to America during the military withdrawal the year before. Since then, he'd taken great care to live a life of scrupulous blandness and visible dedication to the United States.

But no plan ever plays out perfectly in every single respect, as this idiotic gunfight had proven. He knew the Americans called what had happened, an example Murphy's Law in action.

If those policemen hadn't pulled them over, they'd have already secured the woman and been on the road by now. From there, he was supposed to bring her to a certain set of map coordinates.

After that, his masters had told him, he and his men could shoot as many Americans as they wanted and bomb without hesitation so as to make life very miserable for the people of Virginia. Once they were nearly out of ammunition and other ordnance – and he did have an AT4 antitank weapon with him – they could then allow blessed martyrdom to claim them, preferably while shooting down police or other first responders.

Baradar and the other members of his cell understood their effort to be part of a grander attack, though they had no idea of its size. In truth, it would make 9/11 pale in comparison. Today, the Taliban would announce to the world that they'd taken their vengeance on the United States for what the Great Satan had done to them and the country they'd ruled all those years ago.

Vengeance on behalf of God is as good a reason as any for my men to die, the commander reasoned.

He looked at his watch. They were still within the time parameters he'd laid out previously.

At worst, the woman might stumble into the woods out behind the market in a futile attempt at escape. Ajmal and Hamid – the men he'd positioned there – were in position and would scoop her up if she did.

Entirely unnecessary firefight now over, the terror leader keyed his tactical radio and checked in with the two shooters covering the front of the building he knew she'd entered earlier.

"Tayyab, Mohammad. Do you copy? Over."

The response from the pair of shooters was almost instantaneous.

"We copy, Commander." The radio was silent for a second, as if the two shooters were discussing what to say next. "There may be a problem. Over."

Baradar rolled his eyes, beseeching Allah for patience, and spoke once more, this time a bit more heatedly:

"Problem? What do you mean? Over."

"We can't raise Hamid and Ajmal on the radio. They've gone silent, and no one has come out of the front of that market since we took out the woman's bodyguards. Over."

"Shoot at the front of the building! We're headed to the location now! And don't leave your posts until we arrive! Now fire! Over and out!"

He could make out the sound of gunshots through his radio's speaker before all sound cut out as the man he was speaking with unkeyed his own radio to begin shooting his weapon. In the distance, he could make out the shots fired by his two-man team.

"Let's go!, Let's go!" He slammed his left hand on the dashboard of his SUV.

Baradar uttered a series of profane oaths under his breath, cursing not only America but also the woman who was the focus of his mission. He even cursed the two dead members of his cell lying lifeless in the back cargo area of their second SUV.

Once he had the God-cursed woman in hand – which he knew he would soon have, and Ajmal and Hamid had no doubt failed him by either falling asleep or wandering off to relieve themselves, he thought – he intended to make this country burn.

Now moving, his black SUV rounded the short bend of the road and he saw the market just up ahead and to the right.

His men had shot out the building's front windows as well as the windows of the car in which the woman had ridden. Disregarding the two men lying dead in the parking lot, Baradar saw there was also a pickup truck parked nearby. It was one of those four-by-four trucks many Americans considered their most prized possession.

Maybe it's the market owner's or maybe it belongs to a customer hiding inside, behind some watermelons or something?

It didn't really matter, though.

Other than the woman, they were going to kill everyone else in that building. Doing so was not only necessary as a security measure but also as part of the attacks he and many others like him were now pulling off across the country.

Baradar personally didn't know what else his masters had directed his compatriots to hit, but he could guess that they'd strike cellular towers and their data and routing centers in addition to as much of the internet backbone of the United States as it was possible to reach. Not that the terrorist leader knew it – or would even care if he did -- but it was fortuitous for his cause that around 80 percent of all global internet traffic was routed through this particular part of the American state of Virginia.

He shook his head.

"Focus!" he said to everyone in his SUV. The men with him all nodded their heads in agreement.

For Hasan Baradar, it was enough to successfully carry out his part of the attack. He trusted in God to give the rest of the people, no doubt taking part in the many other attacks this day, the help they needed as well.

He keyed his radio again.

"Cease fire! Cease fire! We're coming in!"

The rifle fire from off in the distance halted just before his two-SUV caravan came to a screeching halt in the lot.

The Afghan jumped out, turning and facing the direction where he'd placed his shooters.

He waved both arms overhead in the universal "Stop firing" sign.

Two of his men raced around toward the back of the building.

"The rest of you, let's get inside and find the woman, NOW!" he barked.

Once there, it was clear she'd already left.

"GOD CURSE THIS PLACE!" Baradar swore loudly. He and two of his men quickly moved toward the building's rear. They recalled from their memorization of the structure just where it was and what lay behind the place. It was the forest.

"Fayaz, Tawab. What do you know?" The commander spoke to the two fighters he'd sent around to the back from the outside of the building. His tone of voice made it clear he wanted no hemming or hawing.

"The woman is nowhere to be found, Commander," said the younger of the duo, the one called Tawab.

"I know that you fool! Where did she go?" Baradar thought he already knew the answer but asked more out of frustration than anything else.

The younger terrorist cringed inwardly at the threat implied in his leader's voice.

Both men silently pointed at the woods. It was the only place the woman could have gone.

Why haven't Ajmal and Hamid radioed in?

He spoke into his radio:

"Ajmal, Hamid? Do you copy? Over."

Nothing. Not even return static. Just dead silence.

By now, the rest of his men had joined him outside. He turned to them, fire in his eyes.

"The woman is no doubt in those woods." He pointed to the forested area.

"Spread out in a line and begin searching it. She couldn't have gotten far! And find Ajmal and Hamid!"

For Hasan Baradar, the mission was now officially in trouble.

He and his men quickly moved up to the edge of the forest. It was thick with brush and undergrowth in spots and was also lushly vegetated.

Ajmal and Hamid had to have wandered off, as bored and stupid as they are.

Cousins to each other, they were unpopular within their tribe precisely because they sometimes screwed up the simplest jobs. This latest piece of ill-disciplined behavior was just such an example of their laxity.

This is the first and last time they fail me. I'll see to their punishment myself!

Returning to the here-and-now, Baradar knew they were going to have to move with some haste to capture the woman. Moving so quickly was something the terror leader normally abhorred, but how dangerous could a lone, middle-aged woman be, after all?

"Alright, brothers. Time to move. Find the woman and find Ajmal and Hamid. And burn this market to the ground. NOW!"

Baradar's last word made it very clear that no failure would be tolerated going forward. Two of his men raced about the building setting as many small fires as they could. Soon enough, the market was a flaming inferno.

Now sufficiently agitated, the Afghan terror chief and his men set off into the forest. The heat of the flames from the farmer's market that Annie, her brother Darren and their parents had worked so hard to make a success rolled over the terrorists in waves, so intense was it.

Their leader couldn't have cared less.

Where are those two fools?

Baradar looked left and then right for the two men he'd chosen to guard the market's rear area.

Nothing I can do about that right now.

He saw that his men were properly spread out and able to run the woman down. She couldn't have gotten very far.

Just then, he felt his boot hit something. Maybe a tree root or a fallen limb.

Looking down, he saw two lumps concealed under camouflaged thermal blankets. A very faint odor of tobacco lingered in the air around the pathetic pile.

"Stop!"

His men froze.

He motioned one of them over to his side. Together, they pulled back the blankets to reveal his wayward rear security men in all their nonliving glory.

Both had been shot cleanly through the chest and the head. Two shots, and only two shots, for each. Stupidly, they hadn't worn the body armor he'd ordered them to don. Too hot or too constricting or whatever.

"Fools!" Baradar exclaimed, enraged yet again at their stupidity. He examined them more closely for a moment and then straightened back up.

"Their M4s and their ammunition, as well as their radio, are missing."

His men began to cast nervous eyes in every direction.

"Such equipment is of no use to dead men, is it?" he asked rhetorically, expecting no answer and receiving none from the fighters he had with him. Just more nervous glances.

What Ajmal and Hamid had been turned into – and it couldn't have been by that woman – was the end result of their natural stupidity.

Suddenly, Hasan Baradar knew that this operation had become something more serious and possibly more deadly for him and his men.

GOD CURSE THIS PLACE!

His men, all of whom had gathered round to gaze at their former comrades, were looking increasingly uneasy and nervous. Their bodies were still warm and they looked almost lifelike. Except for the two bullet holes that each of them sported, that is.

"Someone is a very good shot and it's not that woman!" The terror chief's voice raged.

Baradar knew he had to rally his men and get them moving again or, in the way of many poorly trained Afghan fighters from certain tribes – and he had plenty of sons of idiots in his cadre -- they might start running away from danger and never stop.

"We've seen enough here. I'll personally avenge Ajmal and Hamid when the time is right. Until then, you men know what you're supposed to do, correct?"

The terror chief waited for his men to acknowledge his question.

Silent nods of the head from all concerned. That was good enough for him.

"Okay," he breathed, his voice surer of itself now. Looking at his men, he pointed at each in turn, clearly letting them know that if they weren't careful, their own fates might match those of the dead men lying before them.

"The woman may have had another security person we didn't know about. Or one of those rifle-carrying cowboy Americans happened to be in the market and helped her escape after killing our poor men."

Personally, Baradar thought the latter proposition more likely than the former. His masters had made clear she only traveled with a two-guard security detail these days. He spoke to his men once more.

"Whatever the case may be," we must find her and bring her in. Are we all clear on that?"

Nods from all concerned.

"Good. The plan stays the same. Spread out and track her down and anyone else with her. Those people we'll do with as we please." Baradar smiled grimly at his men. They knew what he meant.

His need to please his masters and deliver on the promise of this nationwide attack was urgent. Now time had priority in his mission.

The woman simply couldn't be allowed to escape.

I'll kill her myself!

He was sure his superiors would accept her death in lieu of his cell bringing her in. Who knew what she might do if she were allowed to remain free and alive? Her survival would be a testament against the movement, after all, and that simply couldn't be tolerated. For sure, whatever it was, the people above him wanted her, for they also wouldn't want her to fall into the hands of the Americans again, there to do whatever devil-trickery it was she'd done for them in the past.

She has to die.

Baradar looked down at his watch, considering things. He made the "move out" sign, raising his right hand over his head, index and middle finger raised, twirling his hand several times in a circular motion.

It was time to hunt.

CHAPTER 7
ALLIES

"WHERE ARE YOU TAKING US?"

The woman's voice was a worried whisper. She could hear people moving around in the forest to their rear, off in the distance, though they weren't as yet visible.

They're looking for me.

Ellis, hearing the mystery woman ask him yet again where they were going, merely turned his head and, holding his index finger to his pursed lips – a sign universally recognized as "be quiet" -- pointed in a northerly direction, motioning for the woman and Annie to follow him.

For her part, Annie had no problem obeying Luke Ellis' directives. The sooner and the farther away they could get from whoever it was chasing them, she thought, the better. She had no desire to either shoot at someone or be shot at, and that's what would likely happen if the men chasing them managed to catch up. She thought back to just a few minutes ago.

When they'd come upon the two men Mister Ellis had obviously shot and killed – and she was still processing the reality of that situation -- she'd watched as he stripped them of their weapons and spare ammunition as well as their radio in addition to various other items he found on them.

Annie was no fool. She saw that before Luke approached the dead men, he checked the area around them for signs of any booby traps or tripwires and such. He also quickly but thoroughly checked their bodies for any live grenades or other devices meant to explode if they were moved. Fortunately, there hadn't been anything.

Looking back at the event, Annie was amazed at how quickly her guardian – and that's what she now thought of Luke as -- had moved since all the chaos had started.

In what felt like the blink of an eye, he'd finished with those men and then silently handed her one of their black rifles – he whispered to her that it was a "US M4" and told her to use its sling to carry it on her back, which she was now doing.

She was also being careful to keep it from rattling around, just as Mister Ellis had instructed. That was easy, as the sling on it was some sort of elastic or bungee cord that snugged the rifle securely up to her body.

She noticed that Mister Ellis also had a similar setup for his own rifle, though his was much more professional looking. He'd also kept all the spare ammunition he found on the men, which was several magazines worth. Those he put into various pockets on the side of his backpack. He had enough magazines for his own black rifle on that camouflaged vest of his. Annie didn't know how he could make carrying so much weight look so easy. Just the rifle on her back felt like a hundred pounds and she knew without a doubt that if she'd had to carry anything more, she'd quickly tire out and be caught and probably killed by the people chasing them.

The teen noticed as well that her protector hadn't given it to the mystery woman with them. Instead, he'd positioned her near to him and just slightly to his left front.

The better to keep an eye on her, Annie surmised.

She was trying to stay as close as she could to the man who was protecting her without making any unnecessary noise in the underbrush around them, especially because they were moving at a fairly quick pace. Annie knew she was no soldier, but she also knew these woods and how to use the shortcuts lying within them to quickly get to other places around town. It was obvious that Mister Ellis certainly did as well. She was comforted by that fact.

Right now, I'm running on adrenaline, she admitted to herself. It was also helping her make good use of her flight instinct. No doubt, the mystery woman was doing the same.

Annie saw that Luke Ellis didn't need any adrenaline to do what he'd been doing. The change in his demeanor, once all the shooting and the explosions they'd heard off in the distance started up, had been something to see. It was like something out of one of her brother Darren's war movies, in fact, though much more serious.

This is no game. We could all die soon!

Mister Ellis had already impressed upon her and the mystery woman the importance of being as quiet as they could. The woman, who hadn't yet told them her name and didn't seem inclined to do so anytime soon, nodded silently at his directive, just as she'd nodded silently at everything Mister Ellis had told her once he took them into the woods and the cover it promised.

To Annie – and surely to Mister Ellis, the girl hoped – it seemed like the woman was also waiting for a chance to either slip away or to run to some other form of help or protection she probably believed was headed her way.

The teenager didn't think she'd be successful. There was no phone or internet service, and no sounds of sirens approaching her town, even after the really big gun battle that had occurred there.

The only sounds she could make out were those being made by the people who'd attacked them all.

"I hope we're not cut off, Mister Ellis" she whispered to the big ex-Army man guarding them.

"Don't know yet, Annie. Time will tell."

His voice was also a low whisper. Then he placed his index finger to his lips yet again.

Luke listened to the words coming from the tactical radio he'd taken off the two men he'd killed. Conveniently, it also had an attached earpiece, which ensured it couldn't be heard by the bad guys trying to track him and his people.

He kept his little group moving forward, working around the outskirts of Lucketts. He wasn't about to go into the town. There wasn't anything or anyone there, he felt, that could help them at this time.

We're better off getting into a concealed observation position once we shake the bad guys chasing us.

Ellis' many years of experience were telling him to go to the ground and hide once he and the two people he was trying to protect could safely do so. There, they'd await nightfall and either try to slink away or barring that, sit tight and wait for help.

Inside, Luke seethed at the thought of having to move during the day, like they were now. There was just too much that could give them away, but it couldn't be helped. They had to escape or at least find a really good hiding place to avoid the men looking for them.

Looking for the woman, you mean. Ellis knew it wasn't about him or Annie.

Once night fell, he had more options available. For instance, they could even very slowly and very carefully make their way over to his place – provided he could get his charges through the woods without being detected, that is.

While his homestead wasn't all that far away, at least in terms of a forced march – barely five kilometers now, according to his compass and topographic map – there were people chasing them and at least one of the females he was protecting probably wasn't up to a 5K run through the woods with men chasing her and bullets whizzing overhead.

For the moment, though, he was glad he didn't have to make a final decision as to just where to go. Once he shook off their pursuers, he and his people could double back and approach Lucketts from the rear or simply head to his place. Luke definitely preferred the latter – because he had even more in the way of "good-ies" stowed away on his property than this current bunch of bad guys could ever suspect.

The most important thing, though, was to keep his charges safe. Luke planned to get the truth, the whole truth, and nothing but the truth out of her once it was safe enough to do so. She was hiding something and to him it felt like it was a really serious secret.

Ellis looked at the horizon. Towers of smoke rose from several directions. There was much more going on than just this simple snatch-and-grab by some bad guys. Cellular and internet service was completely down and the only traffic he could find on the radio he'd taken from those two dead shooters had come from the same men pursuing them.

One thing was for sure: Whoever the fellow was that was commanding them, he was seriously ticked off at the effort Luke, the woman and the teenager had put forth so far. The fact he didn't yet have the woman in his grasp had clearly enraged him. They'd seen evidence of his anger in the column of black smoke that suddenly appeared in the sky over Annie's store. The girl couldn't help but let out a low moan of sorrow when she realized where the fire was raging.

"It'll be okay," Annie" Ellis whispered to her, though he didn't have a clue at the moment just how it would, indeed, end up being okay.

Luke couldn't tell much more beyond that from listening to the captured radio, though. The same man – who'd spoken in both Pashto and Dari, depending on the person responding to his commands -- had ordered his men to switch to a secondary secure channel. Static came from the radio at that point. No doubt, you had to enter at least a four-digit code to access the new channel and the ex-soldier had no way of knowing it and no time to experiment with discovering it. From past experience, he knew it might also fry its circuits at any minute as well.

Sizing up their current situation, and the urgency with which the man on the radio spoke (his troops referred to him as "Commander"), Ellis knew they badly wanted the woman.

As evidence of this, their pursuers were now making much more noise than he'd have ever tolerated from either himself or his fellow operators.

"They're trying to spook us into bolting and running," he whispered to the two females. They both looked at Luke and then slightly nodded, taking care to not make any serious sudden movements.

"They don't know what they're up against either," he continued, "and whether it's just our lady friend here or whether she still has a bodyguard or two helping her get away."

Annie looked over at the woman as if expecting her to say something. All she received for her effort was silence. In fact, she was trying not to look at either of them.

"Look," the retired Delta Force operator went on after fixing his gaze on the two females, "if they're trying to scare us into running, it means they've got people to our front and sides – meaning our flanks -- somewhere out ahead of us, just waiting for us to stumble into them. The men to our rear will close the trap door on us, so we're going to have to be careful moving around, but we also can't avoid dawdling, understand?"

Annie's eyes were as big as saucers once more. "Yessir, Mister Ellis."

"I can assure you that I understand the fix we're in, Mister Ellis." The woman was working hard to hide the increasing anxiety she felt about what would happen if she didn't contact her failsafe in time.

Luke had a plan for dealing with their current situation once he needed to. What the men chasing them – including their commander, no doubt -- didn't know was that the prey they were chasing was being accompanied by a creature much more dangerous than a cougar or a grizzly bear.

Probably, they're assuming some local good old boy with an AR in his truck had decided to help out, was his first thought.

Ellis also guessed he could figure out what they were thinking right about now, too: The good old boy had managed to get the drop on their two comrades, sure enough, but he was no real threat now that they knew about him, correct?

Luke knew this sort of operational and tactical ignorance and disregard on their part gave him an advantage in his fight against them. Plus, he had his daypack and all it contained, including his high-tech imager and a pair of night-vision optical devices or NODs along with enough ammunition to deal with any close encounters of the non-alien kind.

Ellis raised his left hand. It was balled into a fist, telling them all to halt. Both Annie and the woman did so. He slowly turned around and looked backwards, checking for any signs of movement in the woods to their rear.

There was nothing, though he could still hear sounds coming from a distance. It was now a little farther back than it had been just a few minutes ago, when he'd performed the same check.

Good.

Time to move again.

The ex-soldier turned slowly, looking closely in all directions. Satisfied nothing dangerous was approaching, he signaled to Annie and the woman, and they all started moving once more. The county road was still about a mile away. At their current pace, they would come near it after nightfall. That suited Luke just fine. American soldiers liked to fight at night, after all, and they were the best in the world at it.

"SNAP!"

The sound of a twig breaking froze them dead in their tracks.

"Down!" Luke's whisper was urgent. The women went into a crouch.

"Quiet!"

Neither Annie nor the woman even tried to breathe, though each was sure the sound of their racing heart could be heard all the way down in Leesburg.

Luke slowly moved his eyes and took in their present position.

Good cover and concealment.

He slowly, ever so slowly, moved his head towards where he heard the sound of that twig as if someone had mistakenly stepped on it while trying to move silently through the woods in front of them.

Ellis froze.

There he is.

It was a lone man dressed in a police officer's or sheriff's uniform. He was about 50 feet to Luke's right front and moving from that direction to his left.

The man had a pistol in his hands and up in the high ready position, moving it slightly from right to left in an effort to sweep his front for any sign of trouble. It looked like a standard-issue 9 millimeter Glock 19 to Ellis, who was of course intimately familiar with both the brand and the handgun model.

Most surprisingly, there was also a young boy, who appeared to be about 12 years old -- though slightly undersized for his age – trailing closely behind him. The ex-soldier saw that the boy was also carrying, on his left shoulder, the kind of messenger bag or satchel popular with teens and younger adults. There were a few bulges in it as well.

Ellis of course knew who he was.

Blonde-haired, the youth wore a dark t-shirt and khaki shorts along with athletic shoes of some sort. He had a determined look on his face and, though it was clear he was scared it was also clear he wasn't about to run away. To the retired soldier that was a good sign. It might just be that he and the cop could be of use.

The sight of the boy had the most startling impact on Annie, however.

Upon seeing him, she exhaled slightly, almost in relief, and would have stood up and raced over to the young man had Luke not stopped her with a gentle squeeze on her forearm. Annie looked at the former Delta operator with startled eyes and tensed up but then relaxed and slowly nodded her head and leaned in closer to the man so that she could whisper in his ear.

"It's Darren." The teenager was clearly relieved to find him safe for the time being.

"I know Annie. Who's he with?"

"That's Deputy Holman... Alec Holman."

The mystery woman also relaxed a bit upon hearing the girl's revelation, though her urgent need to get to a secure phone was hammering away at her brain, not that she could reveal any of that to the man trying to keep her safe, of course. Doing so would lead to far too many questions that shouldn't be asked and couldn't be answered. So, she remained silent and watched her comrades while they dealt with the question of the man and the boy with him.

The girl spoke in a low whisper once again.

"Alec Holman is one of the good guys. He comes in the market sometimes and buys fresh fruit for lunch while he patrols the area." She looked once again at the man and the boy cautiously making their way through the trees. It seemed to her like those things were looming menacingly over them all right now.

"What's he a deputy of?"

The tone of Luke's voice told Annie that he was measuring and weighing the man. The teen already knew the ex-soldier could easily take her brother Darren from the other man at any time and probably without the latter even being aware he'd been right next to them both.

Annie's whispered voice was reassuring.

"It's fine. Alec's a Loudoun County deputy sheriff. I don't know how Darren hooked up with him, but you can see my brother trusts him, and Alec is obviously protecting him, so please don't shoot him, okay?"

Luke was slightly bemused, and he briefly wondered what sort of powers the girl must think he owned. He was no Superman or a cold-blooded killer. He was just a man with many years of extensive and very difficult military training.

"Don't worry, Annie. I'm not going to hurt or shoot anyone. I just want to make sure we can safely link up with them both without starting a gunfight out here in the woods, is all."

The ex-Delta man leaned in even closer to the girl before whispering once more. "We can't afford the noise, remember?"

He looked into the woods behind them before speaking once more.

"Right now, we're being hunted. I suspect your brother and that man Holman are as well, so let's get together with them and then get moving again, okay?"

Finishing, he cast a glance at the woman with them, who nodded at him in agreement.

"Okay, Mister Ellis." Annie was relieved at finding her brother. Not only that, but he was also with a law enforcement officer. Plus, Deputy Holman was armed, which was also reassuring. There weren't any other adults around to help them out, to be honest. At the moment, the woman with them was more of a hindrance. It was clear that the mystery lady clearly wanted to be anywhere else she could and would likely desert them the first chance she got.

She might even surrender to the people chasing us and give us away, too!

Annie was instantly ashamed of herself. To take her mind off things, she looked back over at Mister Ellis.

His attention was on the man and the boy. He noted, approvingly, that the man was very carefully moving through the forest to get away from town and then deeper into the woods. He'd likely been involved in that big firefight in Lucketts and had somehow managed to survive it.

Good on him. He might even make it out of this alive.

As the three of them watched, the lawman halted and keyed his radio mike. It was attached to a loop sewn a few inches above the badge pinned to the left breast of his uniform shirt.

Naturally, nothing intelligible came from the mic. Just static. Luke wasn't surprised in the least.

Whoever the bad guys were, they were being helped. There was a widespread cellphone and radio communications outage, something that was way beyond the capabilities of most criminals and terrorist groups.

The former Delta operator listened carefully as the deputy sheriff, Holman, spoke into his radio microphone. His tone of voice was slightly worried, though not overly so, considering he'd just walked away alive from one heck of a gunfight, from the sound of things.

"Dispatch, dispatch. You copy? Over." The man called his dispatch office three times, pausing between each one for several seconds. He also kept busy checking not only his rear but the rest of his personal perimeter as well.

Luke was again mildly impressed. The man's movement through the forest had also been a bit stealthier than most people's efforts

He still gave away his position, though, so don't give him a medal just yet.

Still...

That noise could hardly have been avoided at this point. Also, we need more guns in this fight and the man's a law enforcement officer. Probably knows his way around a rifle in addition to that pistol of his. If he survived that firefight in town, he's also lucky.

Personally, Luke felt he'd rather be lucky than good any day of the week.

The retired soldier made his decision. It was time to make contact.

In a low crouch, Luke silently moved away from Annie and the woman. He could still keep them under observation and covered by his rifle if he needed to and he didn't want to risk them being struck by a bullet if the cop panicked and shot at him once he was hailed.

Luke checked to make sure he had good cover behind a small boulder just in case the man shot first and then asked questions later. He cupped his hands and sent a low, whispered call his way.

"Alec Holman!"

The police officer froze and quickly fixed his pistol in the direction he thought the voice had come from, seeking out the person who'd hailed him.

Ellis saw all this and mentally counted off a few seconds before he called to the policeman once more.

"I'm a friendly, so don't shoot me! You're liable to give us all away to the men that attacked the town."

Luke saw the policeman was clearly torn. The man wanted to both engage the enemy yet also run away even deeper into the forest. That he now crouched slightly and was prepared to engage raised his stature, just slightly, in the retired Delta operator's eyes.

Good. I can use this guy.

"Who are you?"

The police officer's voice sounded a bit strained but didn't seem excessively nervous. Rather, it was more cautious than anything, as if the man behind it was making a series of quick decisions and knew that he was cut off and alone as well. War makes for all sorts of allies, both soldier and police officer knew.

"My name's Luke Ellis. I'm a retired soldier and I live outside Lucketts. I was in the farmer's market on the other side of town when some sort of gunfight started up not far away." Ellis paused to let the policeman speak.

The man's voice was still cautious and his handgun never wavered.

"Go on."

Off in the distance, the sound of men moving through the underbrush became louder. Luke knew they didn't have much time.

"I've got two other people with me. A teenage girl named Annie and a woman whose name I don't know. Annie's parents own the market and the woman was shopping in it. Her two companions were shot in the parking lot when the three of them tried to leave the place."

At the mention of Annie's name, her brother Darren perked up, looking for and then spotting his older sister. He sent a wave her way, which she quickly returned. Her brother also couldn't keep a grin off his face. Proving that he was smart, though, he remained in a very low crouch just in case either of the two men talking to each other started firing their guns.

The police officer nodded at Ellis' mention of Annie's name.

"Annie? I know her. Where's she at?"

The girl answered him, also in a low whisper. She recognized the lawman.

"I'm over here, Deputy Holman."

At this, the deputy – who looked to be in his mid-20s at most -- turned and looked toward the sound of the girl's voice. Annie slowly moved her head out from behind the tree she'd been using as cover. He now visibly relaxed and whispered back to both her and Luke.

"Annie! Good to see you and thank God you got away safe!" He looked down at Darren, who gave him a thumbs-up, and then once more in Luke's direction.

The soldier hadn't yet moved from behind the boulder's cover. Holman motioned toward Ellis and spoke:

"You folks come over to where I'm at. I'll cover you as you move."

The lawman made a "come here" gesture with his left hand before he placed it back on his pistol's grip. Next, he shifted his weapon slightly so that he could fire on anyone approaching from behind Luke and his people.

Luke was now even more confident he could work with the man. Looking to his left, he could see that Annie and the woman were waiting for his command to start moving.

Ellis gave them the "move out" signal and the three of them quickly covered the fifty feet between them and then converged on the officer and the boy. The latter was instantly swept up into a fierce hug by his big sister.

CHAPTER 8
REUNION

"OOF! Easy, Annie!"

Darren struggled a bit to catch his breath after having it knocked out of him and wriggled in a bid to escape from his sister's tenacious grip. He was glad to see her, of course, yet also embarrassed at being hugged so tightly and so publicly. He might catch girl bacteria or viruses or amoebas or something else equally nasty.

Gradually freeing himself from his sister's Anaconda-like embrace, the 12-year-old boy moved to free himself from her embrace. She almost looked on the verge of tearing up over him, he noted with satisfaction. Usually, she just ordered him around like she was the boss of him or something.

"I'm okay, Annie! It's all right. You're squeezing me to death!"

Finally breaking free of her grasp, he stood back and looked quickly around the woods. His body language told her he was anxious to get moving again. She hadn't seen what he'd seen just a few minutes ago, and he didn't want her to ever see it.

He'd been there to witness the big gunfight Deputy Holman and his poor partner had found themselves in. That man had gotten himself killed in the first wave of shooting by the guys in the two SUVs the lawmen had pulled over to the side of the road. They'd each been in their own sheriff's cars. Quicker than you could say "BOO-YAH!" the shooting had started. That other deputy got hit first. After that, it was nothing but pure chaos.

Darren knew exactly what kind of danger they were all in.

For one, the men were now chasing his sister and the big ex-Army man with her, whom he'd always addressed as "Mister Ellis," and probably the woman with them as well. Just why they were doing so the boy didn't yet know, though he was eager to find out.

Possessed of a quick wit and a very sharp mind, the 12-year-old also noted that the woman certainly wasn't talking, just looking nervously at her watch and mumbling something under her breath.

Something's up with that lady. She definitely has a world-class case of nerves going on.

It didn't matter right at this moment, though. Only their survival did. The boy briefly reflected on what had brought him to this spot.

Before he'd run off into the woods, he'd seen Deputy Holman almost overwhelmed by the amount of gunfire coming from the men in those SUVs. Another few seconds of such furious fighting, with only him and his pistol against many more men, and the deputy would have been done for. The boy also knew there'd been absolutely nothing he could have done to help, either.

"Run and hide," all his teachers had told him, over and over, in response to a school shooting.

And so, he had. As quickly as he could.

Looking back, Darren felt mildly ashamed for fleeing like he did. But he also knew his parents and Annie, and certainly, Deputy Holman would have wanted him to. He'd watched more than his fair share of online Afghanistan and Iraq war documentaries to know that the kind of fighting he'd witnessed wasn't like in the movies. In the real world more people with more guns than you had usually meant you were going to lose.

Fortunately for Deputy Holman – and Darren was utterly amazed at what had happened -- several townspeople, all armed with a variety of handguns and rifles, had suddenly stopped whatever it was they'd been doing and began firing at those bad men, too.

The townspeople included an older man who'd come to a screaming stop near the deputies' cars and then jumped out of his old mid-90s pickup truck with his own rifle. He began firing at the bad men as well. Frequently cranky and irascible, the man was a Vietnam War veteran and local fixture around town. Aptly, his name was Jeremiah Battle and boy, did he ever give battle. Right up until he got filled full of holes that is.

Darren had seen it all too clearly to ever forget it.

Before that sad happenstance, though, he'd also seen Mister Battle take great pleasure in shooting at the men who'd piled out of the SUVs, even hitting and killing one of them. All the while, the old man had been shouting a string of choice swear words at those men intermingled with the demand that they should "COME GET SOME!"

Get some of what? It was a mystery to him, though he suspected it meant "Come get some more of my bullets!" -- which Mister Battle had proven himself more than ready to give them.

Darren mentally paused for a second to reflect on his part in the whole mess.

Before the shooting began, he'd been casually strolling back to his parents' market from the community center where he and a couple of other boys had spent part of the day exploring the woods bordering it. They'd also spent the afternoon testing the small communications radios they'd each built as part of a group summer project assigned to them for extra credit by their science teacher, Miss Jenkins.

The radio he'd constructed, after much painstaking research and testing over the summer, helped explain the bulge in his satchel that Luke Ellis had quickly noted. In the heat of battle, though, he'd now forgotten he was even carrying it.

Darren was a smart young man. He also recognized the danger in speaking loudly, so he kept his voice low as he spoke to his sister, who did so in return. Currently, she was the one doing pretty much all the talking.

"You dork!" the 17-year-old girl whispered to him with some feeling. "How did you end up in the woods with Deputy Holman?"

Annie released her brother from the death grip she'd had him in and stepped back slightly to check him for any sign of injury. Her parents expected her to make sure he was safe whenever he was with her, to tell the truth.

Earlier in the day, she'd wanted him to stay with her and help out at the market while her parents were down in Leesburg, but her mom and dad overruled her.

"Boys need to get together with other boys and do boy stuff every once in a while," they'd said.

She knew that the center and the wooded area Darren loved exploring were also very close by and then, after looking at her brother, ordered him to be at the market before sunset and the evening after-work customer rush. Annie felt her parents mostly treated her brother with such consideration whenever they felt she was becoming too motherly – or, better yet, too bossy – towards him.

Bet they won't be thinking that now, was her only thought at the moment, though she was ecstatic her brother was okay even though she was now doing her best to hide it from him.

Luke interrupted the group confab.

"Everyone, we have to get moving again. NOW."

Ellis' whispered tone of voice was clear: There would be no argument on that point. In his old world, movement was life and, right now, they weren't moving, meaning the chances of them all dying were growing by the second.

The woman helped his cause by adding her own two cents.

"Mister Ellis is correct. We need to go. I can't tell you how important it is we're not caught." She stopped speaking for a second after realizing she might have inadvertently given away more than she meant to about just who was in the woods and why they were stalking her.

Both Ellis and Holman stopped and looked directly at her. Their eyes told her she'd tripped herself up.

To recover from her misstep, she spoke once again.

"I mean... I mean, it's obvious these people are crazy, right? There's no telling what they're up to and why they shot up this town."

Now she was stammering.

Bang-up job there, girl, the honest side of her pronounced.

"It, it... well, it was probably a criminal gang or a terrorist attack. I don't know!" The mystery woman looked down at her watch to buy some time to collect her thoughts before she spoke again.

"Anyway, we need to get going!"

She looked around the woods dramatically and lowered her voice even more, speaking in an almost-conspiratorial whisper. "I don't know about you, but I don't feel like being shot."

Upon her final pronouncement on the matter, she clammed up and motioned for everyone to move.

Luke didn't say anything. He just eyed her for a second before giving the "move out" sign once more. He didn't believe a word of her little spiel, but he also knew he didn't have time to interrogate her more thoroughly right now.

Soon as we're safe, the two of us are going to have a little talk.

She was lying to him. Her verbal slip-up only cemented what he'd already come to believe: She was cause of the day's events.

CHAPTER 9
HOLMAN

THE GROUP, NOW GROWN TO FIVE PEOPLE, MOVED OUT. THIS time, Alec Holman brought up the rear and Luke Ellis went up front to take the point. He'd placed the women and the two young people between them both.

The deputy had already holstered his Glock 19 and was now carrying one of Ellis' two M4s. The retired Army soldier – who he now recognized as someone seriously skilled in military operations – had given it to him after directing the teenage girl Annie to hand it over, which she'd done at once and with no questions asked. That she trusted Ellis so completely spoke volumes about him and put the lawman somewhat at ease.

While they all made their way through the forest as quickly and as quietly as they could, Alec reflected on the weapon – a true assault rifle – he now held in his hands. It was far from the first time he'd used such a firearm, of course, though it had mostly been the civilian-version AR-15. The tactical training Loudoun County sheriff's deputies regularly received had made sure of that.

After taking it from the girl, he made sure it was locked and loaded and that he was also carrying a couple of extra magazines for it, which he'd stowed in his front pockets. They were a little bulky, but he didn't care. They didn't rattle around and that was good enough for him.

Holman also didn't know what distance his M4 had been zeroed to or sighted in at, but figured it was probably 100 meters, which was standard. At any rate, he didn't think he'd need to worry about distance shooting. If they mixed it up with the terrorists, or whatever they were, while moving through these woods, it would be from a lot closer than a hundred yards, that much he knew.

The sheriff's deputy was smart. He'd graduated from the University of Virginia with a degree in cognitive science a few years ago and was serving a stint in local law enforcement to add to his record while he waited for his application to the FBI to be considered. So far, his "short stint" as a deputy sheriff was now at three years, with no end in sight. To be sure, though, he was indeed grateful for not only the employment but also the law enforcement experience he'd gained.

Though only 25 years old, Alec Holman could also read most people like they were an open book. In this case, the book he was interested in – meaning, the mystery woman – was about 10 paces ahead of him. He closed the gap until he was nearly behind her and then leaned forward to whisper to her.

"Who are you, ma'am? Are you from around these parts?"

Though he'd kept his voice as evenly modulated and friendly as he could, Alec could see the woman's back stiffen and tense up upon his inquiry.

"I live in Loudoun County. My friends and I were just in the wrong place at the wrong time, I guess."

Alec's senses told him the woman wasn't lying about being from the county, but that she was leaving out a lot more and also wasn't in any hurry to clear things up.

He decided to press his case a bit.

"Where in the county do you live, ma'am? I've never seen you in Lucketts and north of it or near the river." The deputy meant the

Potomac River, the waterway separating Virginia from Maryland and the District of Columbia.

"Oh, I'm farther south, down in Leesburg." The woman figured the town of approximately 50,000 people was sufficiently large enough to ensure the annoying lawman questioning her wouldn't be able to easily detect her lie.

In truth, she had for years been living in a complex nearly 200 feet underground and with a footprint the size of a big time university or NFL stadium. It was also a Level 4 facility rated to handle all manner of nightmare-level viruses. Billions of dollars had once gone into its construction, all completely off the books and deep black as far as what Congress knew and didn't know. It had been built completely under the nose of county residents in a masterpiece of misdirection and covert construction and was a lot closer to Lucketts than anyone knew, including almost everyone inside the government. The woman was also acutely aware no one with her had even the remotest need to know when it came to such matters.

The lawman wasn't fooled, however. Alec looked at her back as they moved through the forest.

She's lying through her teeth.

To be fair, though, training and experience also told him she wasn't doing so out of nefarious or malign purposes. More likely, he thought, she was doing it to keep all of them safe.

She knows what's going on but doesn't want to tell us for our own good.

That was sufficient for the moment, though he knew he'd have to explore the matter more once they reached some sort of safety. Like the retired soldier up at the front of their group, he was certain she was the reason for all this shooting. The fact that her companions – probably bodyguards – had been shot dead but that not a hair on her head had been harmed told him much.

Nothing I can do about it right now, though.

Putting it all aside, the lawman looked down at his watch for a brief second and shook his head. Their need to move a bit quicker than they should have made him a little uneasy, but there was no avoiding it. The people behind them were obviously intent on closing the gap, and with just himself and the man Ellis skilled enough to do something about it, they couldn't sit in ambush to wait for them to get closer. They'd end up quickly outflanked and probably dead if they did. He also had no idea if any of the bad guys' comrades were trying to find his little group.

They probably were. No doubt, they had more people than just the ones pursuing them from behind, and it was a dead certainty those men were also on the hunt.

Alec Holman prided himself in knowing a little about a lot. This included the people who lived in and around Lucketts, which fell within his patrol area. Luke Ellis was now definitely of interest to him. He'd heard the man had been some kind of Army special operations soldier before he'd retired last year. Personally, he thought he'd probably been a Ranger, maybe.

Like most law enforcement officers, Alec had a keen eye for detail. Right now, the man Ellis certainly looked the part of a special operator. His body armor and chest rig looked as natural on him as could be and he radiated deadly competence. He also had not one, but two, true assault rifles: One slung on his back and one he had Annie give to him. They were both select-fire M4s just like the ones the men he'd recently fought against had used.

Real M4s couldn't normally be owned by civilians, Alec knew. He badly wanted to ask the man Ellis where he'd gotten those rifles, but the pursuit behind them sounded closer than ever before and the retired soldier was now quickening their pace through the woods even more.

Holman could tell they were headed toward the county road which lay less than a mile away. Most likely, they'd cross it once night fell and then double back around the outskirts of Lucketts so they could enter it from the rear during the night.

It's what I'd do, he thought to himself.

For now, though, they had to increase the separation between themselves and the people looking for them because gaining some defensive space was vital.

After speaking into her brother's ear – who'd turned his head to look toward the woman and the deputy sheriff with them -- Annie dropped back a little until she pulled even with him.

The girl was anxious. "What happened in town, Deputy Holman? My God, it sounded like World War Three."

Alec hesitated before speaking, mentally reassembling what had gone down and looked up ahead to the back of the man Ellis. He was still moving with some urgency.

"I don't rightly know, Annie," he replied.

Holman was clearly frustrated at the unfairness of it all. He and another deputy who'd been in the area in his own patrol car – Eric Simmons, a good man with a wife and kids -- had together pulled over a couple of shady looking SUVs with excessively tinted windows. It had mostly been out of curiosity, though, and neither had even planned on writing the people driving those vehicles a citation if they checked out.

Annie spoke once more: "Well—"

She stopped whispering and froze.

Mister Ellis was up ahead, clenched fist in the air and still as a statue.

She looked sideways at Deputy Holman, who'd also halted and made sure both the woman and the boy had done so as well.

They looked at the deputy and the teenage girl with questioning, fearful eyes. He shook his head very slightly, his own eyes telling them not to move a muscle.

Off in the woods, a distinct "CLICK!" echoed, as if someone had mistakenly flicked off the safety on their rifle.

"DOWN! DOWN! DOWN!" Ellis suddenly shouted before he began firing his carbine.

The woman, the girl, and the boy hit the deck hard, hugging the forest floor for all they were worth. There was a slight depression in the ground only a few feet away, and the three dove for it.

Alec went down on one knee, M4 up and ready to go.

The forest around them suddenly filled with the sound and fury of rifle fire.

CHAPTER 10
EYES ON

Luke looked down at his watch, noting the time.

Not long until sundown.

He and his little group had been making their way through the woods abutting the rear of the now-destroyed farmer's market.

A little faster than I really like, he thought ruefully.

It was from there that he, the teenage girl Annie and the mystery woman had managed to escape, and just in the nick of time from what he could determine. Luke had to get everyone through this part of the forest and positioned near the county road so they could cross it once full darkness arrived. Every single one of his tactical senses told him they were being vigorously hunted by persons unknown and that they were definitely out for blood. Once it was dark, they'd have more options available to them, including being able to double back into town and then take refuge in several potential hiding places or they could continue on to his homestead, which he'd carefully fortified over the last year.

One thing was for sure: The woman with them was extremely anxious to keep moving, a fact she gave away with every tilt of her head, look at her watch and frustrated exhalation as they stopped to check their 'six,' or the area behind them.

She'd become especially antsy once he told her he had a vehicle large enough for all of them – an older 4x4 SUV he'd bought at a municipal auction and then fixed up. The retired soldier even had radio-based communications gear. It didn't rely on cellular or satellite coverage to get the job done.

"I really think we should make for your place," she'd said to him several times since then, her tone of voice slightly desperate now.

Or maybe she'd said that more than several times?

Actually, it was more like every 2 minutes or so. At this point, even Annie was rolling her eyes each time the woman voted for heading to his place. It might even have been funny if the situation wasn't so deadly serious.

Luke came to a sudden halt.

Something's wrong.

He raised his right hand, now in a fist. It told everyone to freeze.

What's that up ahead?

Over the years, the ex-Delta Force operator had grown figurative eyes in the back of his head and had developed near Spiderman-level ultra-senses, a necessity in his former line of work. Without turning around to check, Luke could tell the other four members of his band had obeyed his hand signals and come to a complete stop.

They were waiting for his command. Even the woman had managed to stop her fidgeting and silence her impatient exhalations.

Ellis' eyes and ears probed the forest in front as well as on their flanks, seeking anything that didn't belong. His nostrils flared as he subconsciously brought his sense of smell into the effort. He'd have to trust that deputy sheriff, Holman, to guard their rear and he hoped they'd all live to regret it if something went wrong in the seconds ahead.

Everyone behind him waited. Would it be fight or flight?

Slowly and carefully, Luke's eyes took in the woods and under-brush around him, looking for anything out of the ordinary. He gradually raised his carbine up to the high ready position.

Scanning from his center front to his right, his eyes suddenly stopped. Something looked out of place in a forest full of unevenness and natural disorder.

There were no perfectly straight lines in nature.

The barrel of a long gun such as an M4 or AK-47 presented a perfectly straight line unless the person holding it took steps to camouflage it.

There were at least two such perfectly straight lines ahead, one slightly to his left and the other just to his right. Luke's ears, attuned to what should be making noise in a forest and what shouldn't, suddenly picked up the sound of a "CLICK!" just to his right front, as if a safety on a rifle had been flicked off.

"DOWN! DOWN! DOWN!" he shouted.

Luke started into the forest in front of him.

His rounds were quickly met by return fire. Almost right away, rifle fire erupted to his right, telling him they'd walked into an L-shaped ambush, though one he'd managed to detect before it could be fully brought to bear against him and his group. He also suspected the bad guys hadn't fired for fear of hitting the woman.

If his theory was correct – and he was certain it was – they wanted her alive and unhurt.

All these thoughts went through Luke's mind in just milliseconds.

Bullets snapped and cracked in the air around him as he shot and moved, never staying in one spot for even close to a second. He now brought every reflex and learned behavior – developed and honed through countless near-ambush immediate action drills and actual firefights – to bear against the enemy confronting them. Toward the rear of his little column, Luke detected M4 rifle fire coming from the lawman Holman, who'd also quickly gotten into the fight. It wasn't scattered or disorderly, either.

Good, was all Ellis could think as he continued to shoot while looking for muzzle flashes from enemy firearms.

When he detected one, he shot at it, all while continuing to move to better cover and concealment.

"BLAM! BLAM! BLAM!"

For the moment, Ellis had his hands full dealing with the people in front of him and he could only hope the sheriff's deputy supplying rear and flank security for their group could stay in the fight long enough for Luke to do something about helping him and the others. He had to take out as many enemy fighters as he could, he knew, or they were done for, especially with even more terrorists no doubt moving up through the forest behind them.

"THUD!"

What?

Suddenly, he felt as if someone with a Louisville Slugger baseball bat had swung it right at the center of his chest. It knocked the breath out of him and he stumbled backwards and then fell.

"WOOF!" The air rushed from his lungs as the Level 4 multi-hit ceramic body armor he was wearing took the blow from an M4 5.56 millimeter round.

I'll be all right, Luke told himself. This wasn't the first time he'd taken a round to his body armor, after all.

I have to get back in the fight!

He struggled to sit up and return fire.

A black curtain slipped over his eyes, though, and he fell into unconsciousness.

At the rear, Alec Holman was doing everything he could to help, which meant firing at anyone he could see out toward his right flank while avoiding fire from his front.

Right after the ex-Army man leading them had shouted and began firing, Alec and his charges also came under fire. Fortunately, he and the others had gotten just enough of a warning to drop down and out of the way of the swarm of bullets – all sounding like angry murder hornets – sent their way.

Whoever was out in the woods shooting at them, they were taking no chances and were filling the air with lead. Holman looked briefly to his left. Annie and her brother were trying to get even lower to the ground than they already were. Admirably, though, neither one of them were shouting or screaming.

The woman was also on the ground, curled up and with hands and arms knitted over the top of her head, as if doing so would protect it from 5.56 mm or 7.62 mm rounds. He thought he could hear a low moaning coming from her as well.

No time to worry about that.

Alec kept firing his M4 in hopes of suppressing the bad guys' own fire. To his horror, he saw Ellis take one to the chest and go down.

The lawman didn't know if he was dead or if he was just unconscious, but it didn't matter. The situation was now dire. He had the only rifle on their side currently in the fight and once the bad guys figured that out, they'd likely bum rush him and they'd all be either captured or killed.

Only one thing left to do. Darren and Annie and the woman are counting on me to protect them.

"Annie!"

Her head snapped around, eyes wide as she tried to shield her brother with her body. She said nothing, though. Just listened. The sound of gunfire and the chaos they'd stumbled into had shocked her, Holman could tell, but she didn't look as if she was on the verge of losing it. The deputy's admiration for the teenage girl climbed even higher.

Alec took his Glock 19 out of his holster as well as the last spare magazine for it that he had and slid them both over to the girl. She took them without saying a word, her eyes even wider than before. She'd never fired a gun in her life, but she and her brother had seen plenty of action movies.

"It's a Glock, Annie!" the lawman shouted to her, the cacophony of rifle fire splitting the air around them. "Just point it at those guys and shoot it!"

That was about all the time he had for handgun instruction.

The 17-year-old gulped and nodded, fingering the magazine release as she did so. She knew if it came down to her and the pistol Deputy Holman had just given her, they were pretty much dead, but she would do what she could. She looked down at her brother Darren. He was practically glued to her side and hugging her tightly. He nodded slightly upon seeing his sister take the pistol from Deputy Holman. Things were really, really bad and the gunfire in the air had shifted from murder hornets to out-of-control freight trains barreling down on them all.

Darren looked at everything going on around him, wide eyes wincing every time the deputy sheriff fired his black rifle at whoever was shooting at them. By now, the fire coming from both sides was nearly continuous.

As if it really mattered.

The boy idly wondered just how much ammunition Deputy Holman had left. He'd also seen Mister Ellis get hit and fall backwards into the underbrush. He didn't know if the man was dead or alive. He only knew that the ex-soldier couldn't help them right now.

In other words, things were really, really, REALLY bad.

Darren was scared, sure enough, but like his sister he wasn't inclined to try a mad dash deeper into the forest to escape this place. He'd already figured out what would happen to them all if they did.

They all three could see, however, that the woman was another matter. She was sobbing silently to herself and her ribcage and chest heaved from the exertion. She appeared to be on the verge of hysteria and maybe even a scramble away from the temporary sanctuary they had.

To do so would mean death for them all, they knew.

Annie reached over to the woman and placed a hand on her shoulder, squeezing it slightly in reassurance.

The mystery woman looked at her, eyes reddened from sobbing, and quieted down slightly. She knew she was no gunfighter and there was nothing she could do to help at the moment.

Looking around at the other three on the ground with her, the older woman knew they'd mistakenly assumed it was fear of being shot and killed that had her so worked up.

In truth, she had little fear of death these days, only of what would happen to the world if she couldn't reach out soon and prevent a potential global cataclysm from erupting. That she and the rest of humanity now found themselves with the Sword of Damocles poised to fall on them all, guilty and innocent alike, was because she'd self-ishly taken steps in the past to ensure her continued presence among the living when she should have eagerly sought to become one of the dead for what she'd done -- though only after destroying the demon she'd created, of course.

Now it's too late!

She hid her head and face between her knees once more and resumed sobbing.

Looking at her, the three of them knew she'd be useless in the deadly fix they were in.

Annie looked at her younger brother, frightened nearly to death of what might happen but also determined to fight to the last. Beads of sweat popped out on her forehead and she felt as if her racing heart would fly out of her chest.

"Oh, God!" She silently prayed for help. Seeing Mister Ellis go down like he had, though, she had little expectation of aid or of the cavalry arriving in time to save any of them.

Now resigned, she let out a sigh and gripped the pistol. She waited for the moment when she'd have to use it.

Alec angrily shook his head at the tragic absurdity of it all – where a teenage girl and her little brother might have to fight for their lives against men trying their best to kill anyone not on their own side – and returned his attention to their front.

Peering intently ahead, he thought he could detect movement. Perhaps two or three people, all trying to inch their way closer to where he and Annie and Darren had gone to ground. To drive them back, he fired off two more bursts from his M4. He hoped he could keep those men from charging the little depression they were all huddled within. It supplied scant cover, but even just a little of it was better than none at all.

Not much longer, now!

Sensing the situation growing increasingly desperate, he knew it was time to do the only thing he knew he could do, if only to take as many of them out as he could before he went down.

If he'd had an M9 bayonet for his rifle, he'd have already fixed it to the barrel. He owed Annie and Darren nothing less, after all. Holman was a good man caught in a life or death situation. Like good men everywhere, he knew there were women and children that needed his protection.

Preparing himself, the young deputy dropped his half-empty magazine from his rifle's mag well and slammed a full one into it, checking to make sure he was locked and loaded. He stuffed the half-empty one in his front pocket and took a deep breath and then began mentally counting down.

The bullets whizzing in the air all around the forest told him that the men shooting at them hadn't yet figured out he was the only gun in the fight left on his side.

Almost time to move.

Alec took a deep breath and steeled himself. It would be a last, desperate charge.

His muscles tensed up.

"Three, two, one," he whispered.

Zero!

With a yell, he fired his M4 and then leaped to his feet and began running to where he thought the enemy would be.

Well, it was a nice life!

He felt a momentary sadness that he'd never see friends and family again.

"BLAM!BLAM!BLAM!BLAM!"

That's rifle fire coming from my left!

It was definitely single-fire, not three-round burst or fully automatic.

Probably from an AR-15.

As far as he knew, the only man in the fight with an AR was the ex-Army man Ellis.

Could it be?

The crack and bang of M4 fire right in front of him brought him back to the here-and-now. That none had yet hit him was a major miracle.

Maybe my suicide charge confused the bad guys and now they're just panic firing?

Alec concentrated on rapidly firing to his front while charging forward. He still had at least two, if not three, people shooting at him and he knew from his tactical training and all the times he'd spoken with the several Iraq and Afghanistan veterans in his department that you had to assault your way through an ambush. His tactical instructors and his fellow deputies who'd also served in the military had all told him it was one of the things you could do if you found yourself in an ambush and the odds weren't looking too good. He and his fellow deputies had also practiced the technique, too.

Holman moved quickly, constantly firing his weapon and trying to suppress the return fire coming from his front. He also prayed mightily that the people shooting at him wouldn't get their act together before he made it through their line. He would then wheel on them and shoot them from behind.

Like every lawman, Alec knew there was no such thing as a fair gunfight. He had to kill those men before they killed him and his people, simple as that.

"BLAM!BLAM!BLAM!BLAM!BLAM!"

For a brief second, he heard even more rifle fire off to his left. If it was indeed Ellis, he was doing a heck of a job over at his position. And even though he knew he was shouting Holman couldn't hear the sound of his primal screams of rage. They were directed at the bad guys firing at him, of course, but also at the cosmic unfairness of it all.

"BAM!" "POP!"

A round from one of the people in front of him suddenly passed so close to his right ear the noise from its 900 meters per second muzzle velocity assaulted his eardrum. Worse, it passed by so closely that the heat from it briefly scalded his ear lobe. It might have even grazed it, for all he knew. It certainly felt like it.

The shock of coming so close to death suddenly started slowing things down. Alec felt as if he were moving in super slow motion but also nearly instantaneously, as if he could teleport himself from one part of the woods to another through mind power alone.

Wouldn't that be quite the lifesaving trick right about now?

His thoughts on the matter were interrupted yet again.

"BLAM!BLAM!BLAM!BLAM!BLAM!BLAM!"

Alec stopped and crouched, though he continued to fire his M4. Well before his consciousness detected it, his senses told him there was a change in the direction of the rifle fire that had been making such a racket off to his left. Now it was passing in front of him, directly into the spot where men were shooting at him.

He saw a blur of motion. A man in body armor was racing to near where he now crouched. He was firing his AR-15 to devastating effect. The first bad guy went down, shot twice in the side and once in the head, and then a second one, also shot several times.

Neither moved from the ground onto which they'd fallen like carelessly discarded trash. Confirming his suspicions, a third fighter also jumped up – no doubt to bugout -- and ran headlong toward the perceived safety of the woods behind him. There, the man's comrades would be able to help him.

A thought occurred to Alex at that point: Perhaps the ambush had been meant to slow them all down or fix them in place until even more enemy fighters could arrive on scene?

Right now, Holman didn't know and didn't care. The one running away couldn't be allowed to link up with his buddies. The lawman took careful aim with his M4 and shot the man through his side, dropping him instantly.

Still moving in slow motion, he waited and watched.

More movement to his left.

"CEASE FIRE! CEASE FIRE!"

US English and a clear, crisp command to stop shooting?

Lo and behold, it was Ellis! He'd been the one off to the left who'd gotten the drop on the three men trying to ambush him.

Space and time suddenly returned to normal.

Holman stopped firing. He watched as the ex-soldier ran past him. The man glanced at him for just a second before he caught up to the third fighter, the one Alec had shot through the side.

"BLAM!"

He saw Ellis shoot the fallen man one more time to make sure he was dead and then kneel down beside the permanently inert figure, AR-15 slung to his side and out of the way. That last, violent act by the man offended Alec's law officer sensibilities but not so much that he felt compelled to do anything about it.

Sucks to be that dead guy, right?

Breathing heavily from adrenaline and exertion – after surviving his part in the firefight -- Luke checked the man he'd seen the deputy sheriff, Holman, shoot. The lawman had certainly just proven himself a cool customer with that insane suicide charge of his!

No signs of life. The enemy fighter was dead.

Good.

The former Delta Force operator searched the terrorist for anything of value, such as spare magazines and ammunition as well as a radio and any documents or written materials. Time was of the essence, though. There were still men in these woods hunting them all. He could hear the racket they were now making as they tried to quickly close the distance between themselves and Ellis' group. Soon enough, he knew, they would also begin firing into the air over Luke's and the others' heads to harass them all and keep them pinned down long enough to finally catch them.

Luke wasn't about to let them do that, and he intended to get his people away in the next 15 or so seconds. They had to keep moving, or they would be caught and killed.

For the last minute or so, the retired soldier had been almost like an automaton. He'd been knocked down, HARD, by the 5.56 mm round he'd taken to the chest. His body armor had saved him but at the price of a precious few seconds of unconsciousness. Fortunately, almost as soon as he'd blacked out, he'd regained his senses.

To Ellis it had been easy to sit up, once he popped his eyes open, and then shoot the two men to his front who'd been firing at him. They'd stupidly approached him after landing their blow -- assuming he was dead -- instead of shooting him some more until they were sure of it.

They paid for their idiocy, didn't they?

It made no difference to Luke. He was alive and they were dead, as was right and proper.

He paused to take two full magazines and another tactical radio off the dead terrorist, and then pounded the man's carbine into the ground to render it useless. He had no time to take the bolt carrier group assembly. He looked once more at his watch. It was nearly time to go.

Nearby, the deputy sheriff had already rejoined the three other people in their party. The ex-soldier could see them gathering themselves, this time around the lawman.

Good man in a fight, isn't he?

The young man had come through for them and fulfilled his responsibilities just fine. Better than fine, in fact. Magnificently, even.

It might even be on par with Army Distinguished Service Cross-type performance. In the former Green Beret and Delta Force operator's experience that was a rare thing among even trained soldiers.

Ellis stood up and looked around at the chaotic scene. There were now five dead enemy fighters in these woods, seven if you counted the two he'd killed before getting Annie and the mystery woman out of the market and into the forest.

The people chasing them weren't going to like that at all.

Luke cast his eyes about one more time. It was clear the ambush had been meant to take all of them out except for the woman. He could tell they'd avoided shooting at her, even after she'd stayed frozen in place for several seconds before diving for cover. During that time one of the attackers could have easily shot her, but they didn't.

Why is that?

Ellis didn't know, but he was going to find out.

He checked his carbine and made sure he had a fresh magazine and then eyed the weapon to make sure it was locked and loaded and ready to go.

Satisfied so far, Luke trotted over to the spot where Holman had assembled everyone. There was now a gun in Annie's hand. No doubt it belonged to the deputy sheriff.

War makes everyone grow up much too soon, the retired soldier thought sadly, shaking his head. He looked all of them over one more time.

"We have to get moving, folks. Right now."

They all eagerly nodded, especially the woman. Her eyes and nose were red from crying, but she appeared more motivated than all of them to press on through the woods.

Time to make my move.

"Deputy Holman, can you take the point? I'll bring up the rear." The retired Delta soldier looked at the woman in their group before he spoke once more.

"Ma'am? You can hang back with me. You'll be safer next to me than up front or in the center." Luke kept his voice calm and nonthreatening. He didn't want to spook the woman any more than necessary, especially as he made ready to closely question her while they all hurried through the forest.

The woman was definitely no fool and she suspected what was going to happen. But she had nowhere to hide or run off to or she already would have. The man – who was now checking her out closely, she could sense -- didn't seem like he was easily fooled, either. Plus, she'd just seen him shoot another four men as casually as you might pick up something you'd dropped onto the floor.

What would he do to me if I refused to cooperate?

She suspected that, at minimum, he would probably tie her up and fireman carry her over his broad shoulders until he had them all away from danger, whereupon he'd then question her more vigorously.

And he would get the truth out of her.

She looked at the man Ellis and shrugged her shoulders. Nodding her head, she took up station near him and then examined herself and what she'd done to this point.

I'm tired, she thought.

She just didn't have the strength or the resources to keep the demon bottled up on her own any longer.

Another thought forced its way into her consciousness: *I'm tired of running, tired of living, tired of everything.*

She felt terribly sad at the realization she'd been the cause of all this violence, but she knew she had to see this one through to its end no matter what.

I can't lay down and die until I've made this right!

She badly needed help, though. Humanity might not survive because of her stupidity and she couldn't bear the thought of her responsibility should that come to pass.

What was going on here, though? Why was she suddenly so concerned about the fate of others?

She honestly couldn't say.

The woman only knew that she had to do something, confess something, ask for something, and only the people with her – especially the man Ellis, who had to be some sort of ex-super soldier, given what he'd just done to those men shooting at them all – might be able to help her set things right.

Time was rapidly running out and she was no closer to reaching out to her failsafe than she was back in the market after the shooting started. Looking at the last hour, the woman knew the flight into the forest and then the ambush and firefight had made her far more percipient in regard to her situation than she'd ever been in the past.

Up until this point, she'd always believed – foolishly, as it turned out – that she'd be able to successfully hold a tiger by its tail for pretty much forever.

How utterly stupid I was.

Starting just a little at the sound of his voice, the woman paused to listen to the man speak.

"We ready to go, everyone?" Ellis tapped the face of his wristwatch.

The woman looked from him to the rest of their group. The teenage girl Annie and the boy nodded their heads. They wanted to get out of these woods as soon as they could, she could see.

"Let's get out of here, Mister Ellis." The girl was vehement on that point.

"I'm with Annie, Mister Ellis," her brother said, voice slightly shaky but not overly so considering what he'd just survived. He looked first at the ex-soldier and then at his older sister.

To the woman, the girl was clearly the leader of the two, though after seeing how well her sibling had held up during the ambush, there was no doubt about his courage or his tenacity. She found herself comforted by this revelation. For a very brief second, the woman thought that maybe the world wasn't in as much trouble as she'd believed, but then she quickly snapped out of that delusion.

We're in big, big trouble.

Alec Holman fell silent for a second, carefully eyeing Ellis and then the mystery woman with them, the one who'd been constantly looking at her watch and unsuccessfully trying to urge them all on after he and the boy Darren had linked up with her and the others.

Saying nothing, he nodded slowly, understanding what was going on. He'd quickly developed his own suspicions about the mystery woman and he wanted them answered as well.

There's more than just a kidnap job going on here.

Alec didn't need a degree in cognitive science to see that something was horribly wrong. It was written in big, bright neon letters all over the woman's face.

"Yeah," was all he said in reply to Luke. "Let's move out."

Holman began walking. Annie and Darren bunched up behind him.

Luke turned slightly to the woman, a grim smile on his face.

"Well, ma'am. Looks like it's just you and me."

CHAPTER 11
FUTILITY

THE UNITED STATES WAS A NATION UNDER ASSAULT.

Unfortunately for the country all the blood spilled appeared to be due to terrorism. This fact made it extremely difficult for the powers that be – or those powers that remained after the first bloody spasm of attacks, that is – to put it all together sufficiently enough to react with anything resembling speed.

Government rice bowls were still rice bowls, after all, and they had to be jealously guarded. The various three-letter national security agencies that still had a functioning command and control structure were busy fighting each other for primacy in responding to the attacks. The end result was a scattered and largely uncoordinated immediate response by both the federal government and the states. Governors activated what militias and Guard units they could, of course, but none had been constituted to respond within the amount of time needed to confront this existential crisis.

For its part, federal response had been kneecapped by the attack and no plan developed after the terror events of 9/11 had conceived of what had so far taken place. Certainly, no sand table, computer, or real-world exercise had ever been undertaken to train to the scope and scale of what was going on.

For one, the President and his national security advisor and chief of staff were all dead in the first strike. Likewise, the Vice-President – along with the emergency powers that went with his position – was gone. The Speaker of the House was also dead, and the list of who'd been killed was longer at this point than the roll call of those who'd been spared.

The dead included the Chairman of the Joint Chiefs of Staff and the civilian and uniformed leaders of each of the several branches of the Armed Forces – Army, Navy, Air Force, Marine Corps, Space Force, Coast Guard and Guard and Reserve forces alike, not to mention more than a few of the many combatant commanders. These were the four-star and three-star generals and admirals who could lead their staffs in a coordinated military response. With a few exceptions – such as for combat air patrols to protect the nation's borders and the like -- it was an open question whether the US military could even respond with anything close to its full might.

The military's own command authority had also been decapitated. There were still plenty of lower-ranking leaders left, sure enough, but contingency and continuity of government planning hadn't envisioned this sort of grievous, near-mortal injury to its command structure.

Simply put, the US military was a rudderless aircraft carrier for the moment. It couldn't steer itself in the right direction and it was likely to remain so afflicted for at least the next several hours.

Many of those in government leadership who'd survived the first bloody wave of terror attacks were also being spirited away to various secure and supposedly unknown locations.

This included the new President of the United States, the former Secretary of the Interior and the official "Designated Survivor." He had to go to ground in one of several highly fortified locations set up for the purpose of ensuring continuity of government because the White House was under serious threat, given all the attacks on other federal government buildings. For the moment, it was a shaky sanctuary at best and Secret Service and other federal agents weren't entirely sure who they could trust. Obviously, no single terror organization or cell could have pulled this strike off. It had to have been the work of years, though some factor in the recent past must have served as its impetus.

There was no time at the moment, however, to get to work on running down the malefactors. The carnage had thrown everyone in the federal government who'd survived to this point – as well as their agencies – badly off balance. Being human beings, many could hardly think of what to do without first envisioning what had become of their own leaders, friends, and compatriots, or how narrowly they themselves had managed to avoid being killed.

All the men and women of government killed so far had also been delivered into the hands of Death through a variety of means.

Suicide bombers, suicide drones, enhanced improvised explosive devices, car bombs, truck bombs, suitcase bombs, individual assassinations using rifles and pistols, even a few stabbings. All those and more had been used to effectively eliminate US national command authority.

The new President of the United States, Thomas C. Masterson, now confronted the carnage before him. In this, he was currently supported only by a small cadre of aides and his chief of staff, a woman who was a recognized veteran of Washington power politics. She'd never envisioned managing the power – through her boss – he was now expected to wield.

She and her boss weren't quite ready for it. That much was plain to everyone around them. But who could they turn to for help and advice? Several members of the National Security Council had been killed in the attacks and there also wasn't a secretary of state or other old Washington hand around to guide them. As well, those of any importance to the government that had managed to survive were even now being moved to a myriad of secure locations or they were in hiding with whatever federal, state, or local law enforcement help that could get to them.

The trouble with protecting everyone in government needing

security was that communications throughout much of the country had also taken a serious hit. This was turning out to be a huge problem and it wasn't easily solvable. To start, it was now nearly impossible to make use of cellular and internet-based communications. Satellites were fine, so far, but the physical and electronic infrastructure needed to route communications beamed down to the ground was under serious stress.

The internet was also under a massive DDOS, or Distributed Denial of Service, attack and buildings housing routers and servers in many locations had either been blown up, or the people working at them had been attacked as they arrived or left, with more than a few killed as they worked from home or their vehicles and wireless laptops and handheld devices as they were trying to piece together their own emergency protocols.

Imagine the terror felt by the people charged with managing the flow of all that data.

Soon enough, they too began to go to ground, hiding or seeking sanctuary wherever they could. Naturally, the internet and many other forms of communication started experiencing service drops that quickly turned into massive outages. It was one of only a dozen ways in which the attackers were killing off US and even global internet activity.

Plus, terrestrial radio and television capabilities were also being degraded.

Blow up a few television and radio stations and all the people in them and soon enough a mass exodus of people from the remaining stations begins to take place.

Assassinate a few network heads and their lieutenants and watch how the others run to find a safe hiding place. There weren't enough executive protection firms in the country to keep safe everyone of importance who suddenly felt the need for such protection. Police and other law enforcement agencies also have their own problems at this point, so they aren't a possibility, either.

End result?

"Run away and hide" becomes the key phrase of the day.

Security experts – both in and out of government – had been warning ever since 9/11 that the nation's critical infrastructure, or CI, was highly vulnerable to terror attack. Water treatment plants, interstate and other highways, air transportation systems, bridges and tunnels, utilities, important buildings housing a vast array of functions needed to run the country... all of them faced either the threat of attack or they'd already been struck and were struggling to survive intact.

Maddeningly, not a lot of the CI even had to be destroyed. Just enough to cause widespread panic.

Water treatment plants supplying fresh water for Detroit are attacked. A metropolitan area of more than 3.5 million people is suddenly afraid to use the water coming from faucets and taps. There is also no TV, no radio or internet, and electrical power is shaky at best.

Highways and roads in many major cities are clogged as people try to flee to perceived safety elsewhere. Enormous, unfixable gridlock results and it traps people wherever they've stopped their vehicles.

A series of electricity substations out in the Mountain Pacific and in the Northeast are taken out. Tens of millions of people -- maybe even a hundred million or more -- are without electricity for at least a day, though probably longer. Emergency power crews assigned to get electricity restored are shot at and a few are even killed. There aren't enough police to protect them all and state Guard units also several hours away from being deployment ready.

Slowly, the lights go out and don't come back on.

Hospitals and other first responder agencies such as police and fire and emergency medical services go to backup power generators, but even some of those aren't protected well enough and several are destroyed by car bombs or suicide bombers.

The number of such attackers seems endless. A few of them are even genuinely spontaneously motivated "lone wolves" who take up whatever weapons they can find to strike out at the nation that once gave them sanctuary.

It's a fine madness or a mass psychosis, even. Many people hide, but some are drawn to violence like a moth is drawn to a flame. Anarchists, for example. Name the radical affiliation, and chances are good at least a few adherents have seen the opportunity and are now trying to take advantage of it.

Already stretched thin, police now have to keep officers off the street and near power generators, safeguarding them until state National Guard and US military units can be sent to relieve them. How long that will take, nobody knows.

Soon enough, looting and other violent crimes start increasing until they become a tsunami washing over some cities and larger towns and their police forces, especially in areas where gun laws have prevented citizens from adequately protecting themselves.

The attack rolls on.

A few commercial jet airliners taking off or landing – both periods when they're at their most vulnerable – are shot down by terrorists using MANPADS weapons. Those men have the will to die if they're confronted by airport police or federal and municipal law enforcement officers that might happen to catch them in the act. In the aftermath, both the Federal Aviation Administration and the Transportation Security Administration act to ground all flights nationwide until everything can be sorted out.

To speed the shutdown along, groups of very committed men and women assassinate as many air traffic controllers and their managers possible, along with a number of government regional and national air transportation leaders, oftentimes catching them as they're leaving their homes to head to their jobs.

Somehow, their identities and positions had been found out by the terrorists.

Perhaps it was just the fruits of the 2015 data breach at the federal Office of Personnel Management – which maintained millions upon millions of records with personally identifying information, or perhaps it was something even worse. Whatever it was, someone had access to an incredible amount of data about those working within the federal government.

It doesn't matter right now, though.

It only matters that people in many key positions who were managing parts of the nation's critical infrastructure were being killed, and authorities didn't have a coherent strategy for stopping it other than to advise everyone to harbor in place, preferably in their homes, and to not show themselves until help could be sent to them.

How long would that take? A few hours? An afternoon? A day? A week? Maybe forever?

In many cases, the terror attackers either melt away in the chaos or, if they're confronted by police, kill themselves and the unfortunate law enforcement officers trying to apprehend them, usually by detonating a suicide vest of varying design. Some of those vests are quite crude, but others are masterpieces of demonic engineering.

After all, that who in their right mind would want to fly anywhere or drive anywhere, or take a train anywhere – or even walk anywhere -- until they were sure it was safe?

International air travel also quickly grinds to a halt, at least until other governments can be sure it's safe to fly again.

When will that be?

Once again, no one can come close to a reliable prediction.

Attackers also go to shopping malls, supermarkets, sporting events or most any large gathering of people and once there, they do their worst.

No one, no matter how old or how young and no matter their race or religious identity is spared. Largely gun-free zones, these places are essentially hunting preserves set up for evil people.

Even in areas where citizens are allowed to carry concealed personal defense weapons the ferocity of the attacks often overwhelm any defenders that can bring their guns to bear. Combine extreme ferocity with suicide bombs and even more panic ensues. It happens every time.

Maddeningly, Congress and the Supreme Court – the other two branches of the federal government -- now face their own chaotic situations.

Several senators and representatives have been killed. Some of the attackers even manage to fire off a mix of AT4 antitank weapons and man-portable air-defense systems – those infamous and devilish MANPADS – as well as classic rocket-propelled grenades or RPGs at the Capitol Building and the Supreme Court. In the past, less than eight months ago, Afghanistan's ruling Taliban had even threatened to inundate Washington, D.C. with 2,000 suicide bombers.

Perhaps those lunatics had finally made good on their threats?

God only knew where all the attackers had obtained their weapons and bombs and other engines of destruction. There was simply no time to find out, either.

After they fire off their infernal devices and destroy as many people as possible, the attackers then detonate suicide vests or are killed in exchanges of gunfire with federal agents, Capitol and District of Columbia police, and even DC National Guardsmen ordered into the fray with whatever small arms they can grab from their armories or even from their private collections.

Unfortunately, it wasn't much -- especially in the face of a determined enemy intent on achieving martyrdom.

Naturally, Congressional leaders as well as the Justices of the Supreme Court have been scattered to the four winds. As many legislators and Justices as possible have been placed under whatever protective measures that can be thrown together in a moment's notice.

It isn't close to being enough.

The Chief Justice of the Supreme Court was on a fishing trip up in New Hampshire. Funnily enough, he was driving his rental vehicle near the town of Loudon – no second 'U' -- just outside Concord. The Supreme Court he led wasn't due to meet in formal session until the famous "First Monday in October," and his vacation plans had long been known in DC and elsewhere.

At the moment -- after being pulled over by three Marshals dispatched from their headquarters at the US courthouse in Concord – he's in their government SUV and being rushed to a C-37A executive jet at a nearby general aviation airport. The two Marshals not driving have Colt 9 mm submachine guns fitted with Knight's Armaments Company suppressors and they look deadly serious.

The Chief Justice feels comforted by their competency.

Not today, he thinks to himself upon imagining some terrorist force trying to get to him.

The Justice, a man with decades of government judiciary service, doesn't believe there's any way for the people attacking his country to do to him what they'd already done to so many others.

Just to be sure, he looks first at the state police vehicle ahead of his SUV and then turns around to look behind him at still another state police car.

Four uniformed police officers in total – two in each New Hampshire State Police vehicle – are escorting his SUV. All the state police officers know is that their country is under a godawful terror attack and the man the Marshals are guarding is a VIP of the highest order who they have to get to the airport and in the air.

That's good enough for them.

They also know to stay off the radio as much as possible. No one knows just how the enemy is finding targets of opportunity but listening to radio communications is a distinct possibility.

The C-37A is warmed up and ready and waiting for immediate departure at the airfield. The Marshals guarding the Chief Justice are anxious to get him airborne. After takeoff, his plane will rendezvous with two fighter jet escorts out of Pease Air National Guard base in Portsmouth. As the Chief Justice is flown to a designated secure location, the escorts will hand his plane off to other Air Force or Air National Guard fighter jets. It's true enough that Justices of the Supreme Court don't normally move about with a federal protective detail when they're away from the District of Columbia and the Court isn't in session. However, their whereabouts are also well-known to the US Marshals Service and any law enforcement agency the federal law enforcement agency decides has a need to know.

Today, every law enforcement agency has a need to know.

Seven law enforcement officers – three federal and four state – now have one of the most important persons in the United States under their protection.

The Marshals take comfort in knowing that their protectee will soon be in the air and guarded by warbirds piloted by people ready and willing to kill to protect him, just as the seven men and women guarding him now are ready to kill if needed. They take comfort in knowing that the man is as safe as can be.

The two suicide drones come from seemingly out of nowhere.

They blow the Marshals' SUV and the state police vehicles sky high. The blast overpressure wave from the high explosive each drone carries is so powerful it flattens the white pine trees lining both sides of the two-lane road on which the little motorcade is traveling.

The Chief Justice, his three US Marshals and the four state police officers helping to guard him are all killed instantly.

The United States continues to descend into complete chaos.

No one is really paying all that much attention to the seemingly low-level terror attacks going on in Loudon County's Catoctin District.

Figuring out what was taking place in that region, so near to Washington, D.C. -- yet also so far away, now that every bridge across the Potomac River and even a local ferry on the Virginia side has been severely damaged or destroyed -- would just have to wait until a coherent federal and state response could be developed and then coordinated.

The Catoctin District and Loudon County are on their own.

After all, they're just one of a multitude of locations needing help and there just isn't enough of it to go around. Not nearly enough Virginia National Guard or state militia units and little in the way of readily available sheriff's deputies and other police personnel, either.

In addition to Lucketts, the Loudon County Sheriff's Office is dealing with attacks down in Leesburg and over in Purcellville to the west as well as in the southeast of the county at the big Dulles Town Center shopping mall.

Dulles International Airport has also been attacked. An arriving international flight from Paris is shot down as it's trying to land. The four men leaping from an unremarkable sedan traveling on the state road running parallel to the runway have gotten near enough to the airport's perimeter fence with at least two Stinger missile-type man-portable devices to shoot the big jet airliner down. The massive fireball and column of smoke that erupts are visible for miles.

Of course, the men have tripped every security alarm possible as they position themselves to do their dirty deed, but according to eyewitnesses stopped along the state road after seeing them rush to the fence, they didn't seem to care.

After they complete their mission, they even drop to their knees to assume some sort of position of prayer, or at least it appears that way to onlookers, all of whom have quickly hidden behind their own vehicles for fear of being shot at.

Airport, as well as federal police and marshals and the facility's SWAT team, arrive in an amazingly short amount of time. They even manage to kill all four of the men after a short but vicious firefight. Though police had wanted to capture at least one of them alive for later interrogation, the quartet made sure they went out in a blaze of glory, or perhaps martyrdom.

Experienced law enforcement officers involved in the event are under no illusions as to just what the people with the MANPADS and M4 carbines were up to.

It was a long-threatened *jihad*, pure and simple. Fortunately, there was now time enough to gather intelligence from the remains of the dead attackers as well as their vehicle.

Victorious, the police approach the four dead men as well as their vehicle. At their moment of triumph, though, a remotely detonated explosive device consumes them all.

Seven police and SWAT officers are killed and a dozen more

wounded, some of them mortally. They won't last the hour because emergency medical services at the airport and surrounding it are overwhelmed. A van left in the airport's terminal area parking lot had suddenly exploded just as the jet airliner began its death dive.

Dozens of people are killed in the vehicle's blast. Others are so badly wounded by the shrapnel packed into the cargo area that there's almost no hope of saving them, no matter the level of medical intervention available on site, which is pitifully small in the aftermath of so much carnage.

The airport is a madhouse. Parts of it, out on the runways and in front of the main terminal, have been turned into a slaughterhouse. Those near the terminal who were fortunate enough to escape the blast's effects and who then went to give aid to people lying wounded are themselves killed by a second blast from yet another vehicle.

This twin-blast attack is a common tactic used by innumerable terror groups in the Middle East and parts of Southwest Asia, including Pakistan and Afghanistan. Detonate one bomb and then wait for rescue and emergency personnel to arrive, then set off the next bomb. It was Satan's own "buy-one-get-one-free" special.

Looking at the devastation wrought around his county, the Loudoun County Sheriff wonders if he even has a department anymore. To start with, there's been no word for at least two hours from one of his deputies who'd radioed in from Lucketts that he and Eric Simmons, another of his deputies, were under serious attack.

Before radio and cellular communications went down, the Sheriff and his dispatch people had received reports from still other deputies over in Leesburg. There, they'd responded to several seem-ingly innocuous calls as well as a series of routine traffic stops, and then they'd been ambushed. He knew some of his people were lying dead, others had been wounded, and still others unaccounted for.

This is insane!

The Sheriff didn't know what was going on and he was effec-tively blind. To fix that, he'd tried to take advantage of an aviation asset. Though he didn't have a helicopter, the Fairfax County Police Department did.

In keeping with long-observed agreements between his office and Fairfax PD, that department had freed up their chopper momentarily so that its pilot and airborne observer could fly an aerial reconnaissance mission over the big shopping mall. His deputies had been reporting an active shooter and mass casualty event at the site and were themselves slugging it out with several other people, all of whom were armed with M4s and even submachine guns.

As near as he could tell, though, the attackers had expected police helicopter support and were waiting for it to approach the mall. No sooner had the bird popped up near the place than a fusillade of anti-aircraft missiles struck it, knocking it out of the sky and killing the two officers on board.

Almost at once after the chopper was shot down, internet, radio and cellular communications also died. Those didn't seem likely to come back online anytime soon, either.

The Sheriff, a retired Army military police colonel who'd been elected to the office some years back, sighed deeply and sat down behind his desk. He rubbed his eyes and tried to wish it all away, but he knew he was wasting time. He needed information, wasn't getting it, and wasn't likely to anytime soon.

Taking stock of things, the chief law enforcement officer for Loudoun County, Virginia, knew he had nothing to throw into the fight and no way of doing anything about it even if he had the bodies.

Which I don't.

The Sheriff couldn't send any of his deputies anywhere because he now had no idea where they were or even if he still had any among the living.

Looking at the devastation sweeping over his county, he heaved another great sigh and slowly shook his head.

If the assignment of police officers and sheriff's deputies could be thought of as a medical triage exercise – one where you treated people based on the severity of their wounds and likelihood of being saved by doctors and their medical resources -- then his force was "Blue" or a non-priority.

Judging from everything he'd seen and heard before comms went down his department was probably fatally wounded. In medical triage – something he'd learned a great deal about as a military police commander as well as during his law enforcement career – there is no medical treatment or help for those classified Blue. To spend precious medical resources on casualties who wouldn't make it no matter what help they received would be a waste of time. Instead, death would be allowed to creep in and steel away the mortally wounded victim – meaning his department.

And there isn't a thing I can freaking do about it!

His county, from Lucketts down to Dulles and all points in between, as well as his nation – one he'd served for decades – was on its own and fighting for survival. In the hours to come people would live and die based on fate and perhaps any defensive skills, they could summon from whatever useful experiences they'd lived in the past.

The Sheriff lowered his head into his hands and silently prayed.

CHAPTER 12
REVELATIONS

"YOU HAVE 10 SECONDS TO START TELLING ME WHAT THIS IS ALL about, ma'am, and don't lie to me. I'll know it if you do."

Luke Ellis' voice made it clear his patience with the mystery woman he'd saved not all that long ago had ended. The former Delta Force operator gave the woman a look he used to reserve only for the jihadist hard cases he'd helped capture and then interrogate.

The woman returned his gaze with one of her own. She was clearly trying to come to a decision about what to do.

Luke knew he couldn't give her the time to formulate another lie or to dissemble in any way.

"Ten," he said.

"I don't-"

Ellis' voice – now as hard-edged and as razor-sharp as a samurai sword -- cut her off. "Nine."

"Believe me, Mister Ellis-"

"Eight."

Ellis looked behind him while he walked and talked. He was checking to make sure their pursuers were still far enough away that he'd have time to develop his play and convince the woman to confess just why she was being chased and why this crazy attack, which at minimum appeared to be region wide, was going on. He looked at her again, waiting.

Her eyes had taken on a slightly more fearful look after seeing the ex-soldier who'd been guarding her take a look behind him.

Very bad people are after me.

She knew it, and she could tell this ex-soldier Ellis knew it, too. If the men in pursuit caught her, she would likely live for some time – though probably not very pleasantly -- while the other people with her would be quickly killed without a second thought.

She didn't know if she could bear to have their deaths – or anyone else's death, for that matter -- on her conscience.

Too many people had died in the past, both as a result of government efforts to end any knowledge of what she'd created, as well as just "incidentally." Some of those deaths – meaning her parents' sad demise – were due to grief and mourning over her own supposed passing. A few others had died due to excess curiosity about what had become of her. Some science reporters and journalists had never accepted the story of her death, for instance, and so they began digging.

To a man and woman, they'd all died prematurely, either because of accidents or heart attacks, because her own premature death had just seemed too pat and too convenient to them. After all, her end had come so soon after she'd briefly published a small portion of the shape and scope of her work on a "virus" she'd told the scientific community might eventually be able to deliver to everyone a long life free of debility.

In a way, her discovery was a modern day version of Ponce De Leon's mythical fountain of youth, but one that would be accessible to the masses. She was certain she'd make sure of that.

And then it had all gone horribly, horribly wrong. And so, she'd taken immediate steps to prevent her creation from ever seeing the light of day. There was only a single 48-hour period, a mere weekend – a time when the government and its agents were paying little attention to her – in which to do it all.

She acted, though with tragic personal result.

The computer scientist who'd created her failsafe also took his own life at the end. He'd been her closest and best friend. To be honest, he'd been her only friend. She'd been his, too.

Jay was genius-level, an amazingly gifted programmer and AI designer. If he'd been able to publish how he'd done it -- by using a continually evolving AI and devilishly clever data transport program that lived everywhere and all at once on the internet -- but also nowhere at all -- he'd have rightfully been awarded the Nobel Prize and gained his own form of scientific immortality.

These days, the AI most likely existed in the Cloud – though she couldn't say with absolute certainty -- and it was Jay's ultimate human-thinking "ghost program." It was also completely undetectable and impervious to even the most stringent security measures. Unseen, it could worm its way into and out of any server and onto any internet platform. Jay's AI had also probably evolved far past quantum computing. God-like, it would be an unstoppable force if it decided action was necessary.

The woman knew her precious friend's design had been brilliant, and also brilliantly carried out in less than the weekend they had before both expected to be hauled in and interrogated or worse. They also knew there was no way the government could be trusted with what she'd brought to evil life. At minimum, government agents would destroy all knowledge of her non-organism organism's existence. The both of them would quickly follow once every piece of information about it had been extracted from them.

Barring that, the powerful might instead decide to try to tame her infernal creature and then turn it into a superweapon, the likes of which the world had never seen. Certainly, there were people running around in government who wouldn't blink an eye at the thought of wiping out hundreds of millions, or even billions, of people if they had to. Neither of those options were acceptable to her or Jay.

For one, she knew her creature could never be tamed, though the government would undoubtedly try.

No, what would happen instead is that the beast would break out and then kill them all as easily as stepping on an anthill during the course of an early evening's stroll through a park.

Her dear Jay had also been nobody's fool. He knew he was placing his neck on the chopping block by helping her, but he'd willingly done so nonetheless, such was the power of their friendship and love for each other, one which at the end of the weekend both knew would be ended.

They'd always thought there'd be more time. Time to take things slowly, to savor the sweetness of the approach and the ultimate joining together of two kindred spirits, both immensely gifted in their own way. But because of what she'd done, the world had to be saved no matter the sacrifice needed.

Jay instinctively knew this. He'd always been much more attuned to the down-and-dirty of human existence.

"I'm doing this for you," he'd told her, making it clear the world came second to saving her.

How could God have created such a man only to see him unquestioningly dash himself upon the rocky cliffs for someone else?

She didn't know and had been bereft at his loss. She'd also learned for herself -- through bitter, bitter tears -- that Jesus was right all along: No greater love existed than when a person laid down their life for their friends.

Jay cared about saving the world, of course, but she knew at the last that her best friend cared more about saving *her*. After all, saving the world was simply too big a task to conceptualize. Not even an intellect as finely honed as Jay's could conceive of such an enormity.

Saving his one true friend, though?

"That's easy enough," he'd told her as he completed the failsafe and then sent it out into the world, there to hover invisibly over everything -- every transaction, post, news article and calculation, every bit and byte of data stored no matter where it was.

Now, it awaited her regular interaction with it.

Coldly analytical and indifferent to whether it ended up killing or saving everyone – like all AI, it simply didn't care about such things -- it both responded to her commands and also sat in judgment of its interactions with the sole human it allowed to communicate with it.

If the AI discerned any duress emanating from her – and it would easily be able to -- and then figured out that she was being forced to respond by others intent on deactivating or controlling it for their own purposes it would dump all the knowledge it contained about the virus onto millions of servers all over the world.

Once it did that, the hellcat would be out of the bag and that which must never be known would, in fact, be known by one and all.

She and Jay had known this last-ditch tactic was a calculated risk. They had prayed – naively, as it turned out -- that with its release to the world, the promise of mutually assured destruction, or "MAD" (and never had an acronym been so exact as that one), would ensue. All nations would work together to ensure the destruction of the demon she'd brought to life so that none of them could have it. And everyone would live happily ever after.

The time she'd spent in government since she and Jay had set everything up ended her naivete on that front.

While most governments might quake at the thought of trying to harness this beast – and she knew her own had, and so it had done what it could to prevent it from breaking out while keeping her protected and among the living -- the same couldn't be said of a very small selection of outlaw regimes.

Given their ideological fervor, there was no bargaining with such nations. They also controlled an array of terror organizations through a collection of proxies, though they took great care to never get close enough to those groups to provoke the United States and its allies into finally attacking and destroying regime and terror group alike. Those regimes were patient, though, and they were biding their time, waiting for the opportunity to strike such a blow against the rest of the world that only they would remain in its aftermath.

Sighing internally, the woman knew the ability to wield her non-organism organism – her "virus" – would change the balance of terror, shifting it permanently to the outlaws. She'd long raged at the thought of some nation – eager to bring about the apocalypse its leaders believed was necessary to create a religious paradise on Earth – obsessively working to spark a global cataclysm that would kill them all.

Well, some of them also just want to watch the world burn, pure and simple!

And so, to protect her Jay knew he would have to die. Just what he could tell the world about her creation was enough to place all of humanity in mortal danger and to make him a target of not only his own government but any number of other ones if word ever got out.

Add in that a small army of terror groups will pay any price and kill as many as they have to so they can take what I know, and it's one heck of a mess I've made for everyone, haven't I?

She and Jay had quickly concluded that they were also a two-fer, a prize beyond compare. Any group or government grabbing them would gain an AI-based program of peerless design and endless uses as well as a weapon of mass destruction so terrible that no nation – no matter how many others allied with it – could stand against those that owned the virus just so long as they showed the will to use it, which they would.

Once Jay finished his work, he'd coolly and calmly walked into oncoming traffic and became just another sad fatality in a world already overflowing with them.

She grieved for her friend to this day. The price was much too high, and she'd long ago realized an ocean of blood might one day be spilled because of her.

Looking back once again, the woman understood on an intellectual level just why she'd taken the last step toward bringing her creation to life – or at least "life" such as it was when it came to her virus.

The economic, cultural, and human evolutionary implications that would be brought about by what she'd created had been staggering. It was nothing less than the reordering of the human genome. What she'd done would deliver a new and supercharged human species once her creation had completed its work.

Hah! So much for that!

Returning to the real world and acutely aware of the peril now threatening to engulf them all, she just didn't know who she could trust. She certainly didn't know anything about the man now demanding she confess to something so monstrously enormous as what she'd once inadvertently done.

Or maybe the end result hadn't been so inadvertent, huh?

She'd clearly seen the possibility of what might ensue as far as her DNA-altering organism was concerned. Starting at the molecular level, her virus would do amazing things for the world.

If it could be controlled, that is.

I thought I could control it. Or I hoped I could!

Fully knowing the risks, she'd chosen to go down one path – one promising much faster development, though with more risk than she knew she should have accepted -- rather than the other much safer one. It would take years of testing and experimentation, all done ethically, to travel that path while the riskier way promised a few weeks at most to obtain the glittering prize.

How completely and utterly selfish I was.

In her gargantuan hubris – hungry for godlike powers she wasn't equipped to control -- she'd convinced herself that humanity couldn't wait. For her, a Nobel Prize would be the least of the acclaim she'd receive. If she succeeded, she would reach scientific and historic immortality that would surpass even Einstein's.

The prize for humanity?

Healthy people receiving the virus would gain a vigorous life measured over the span of a century at minimum, and oftentimes longer than that. Much longer.

For those presently sick, they would at least be restored to a better level of health and then could expect an average lifespan when they probably would have died sooner.

Could anyone have looked into the eyes of a young child, knowing we had the means to give them a better, healthier and longer life? I couldn't have!

She remembered what her answer back then had been. In the face of such temptation, how could she refuse the opportunity to quickly see her work all the way through to the end? In this, there would be no failure of either nerve or imagination.

In her eagerness to help and in her hunger for historic achievement, however, she'd cut some corners.

And look how that turned out!

For years, in the still calm of the night she frequently wept over what she'd done.

In the aftermath of her great error, she'd had to create a prison for herself – gilded though it was. But it was one necessary to ensure that what she'd brought to demonic life could never be used by any person, government or group while she still lived.

It would all die with her. Jay's own awesome creation would see to that. It would *know* when the time was right, too. And then, once she was gone, it would, in turn, destroy itself.

I hope!

Self-destruction at the end was what Jay said it had been designed to do, but would it?

I'll be dead. How will I know and will I even care?

It was all just too much.

Tragically, she'd grown complacent and softheaded over time because she'd stupidly assumed it had all gone away.

Sighing inwardly, she now knew just how wrong she was.

The man Ellis just continued watching her and waiting. Her silent contemplation to this point could be counted in bare seconds so there was no rush just yet to deal with him.

Now she silently raged inside.

If only I'd been as courageous as Jay and just killed myself!

Stop whining!

It was her other self. The brutally honest one.

Great.

Face it. You were cowardly then and you're cowardly now, especially compared to poor Jay. Now humanity may have to pay the butcher's bill for what you did unless you fix it.

Though she was tired unto death at the thought of trying to fix this, she admitted the truth to herself.

It's time to settle all accounts and make things right!

Still, she trembled.

Luke noticed a small bead of sweat slowly building up on the mystery woman's forehead. Her hands also moved nervously and one of them crept up to brush away a scattered lock of sweat-soaked hair from her forehead and her eyes darted from side to side. All were classic "tells" or mannerisms revealing to the retired soldier man what he needed to know.

She's a player for sure, Luke!

"Lady, you should never play poker. You're no good at bluffing and I don't have the time to find out just why you're trying to bluff your way out of this mess. Now talk."

Ellis fell silent, waiting for the pressure to build. She raised her head again before she spoke.

"Look," the woman said, "there's nothing—

"Seven."

Ellis' voice was equal parts ice and doom. The woman beside him, whom he'd almost died protecting, was going to reveal the secret she was keeping. It was still clear to him that all of what had gone on so far was directly related to her. The deputy sheriff, Holman, had whispered to him that the shooters were taking great pains not to hit her with their rifle fire. It was also why all five of them hadn't been bum rushed and then killed by the attackers after nearly walking into the kill box they'd set up.

The woman stopped. Her arms dropped to her side and her shoulders fell in resignation. She'd clearly made her decision.

"You have to get me out of here and to some type of phone or radio communication, Mister Ellis. I'm begging you. Please just trust me on this." The woman's voice was low but urgent and intent and pleading all at once.

Luke wasn't buying what she was selling.

"Uh-uh. Not until you explain just why I and these other folks here should go to the wall for you. Or why I shouldn't just tie you to a tree and let those men have you." The soldier spoke with finality on that point.

The woman didn't doubt him for a minute. She was boxed in. Oddly, the relief of finding herself pinioned this way washed over her.

When you have nowhere to run, your choices become amazingly clear and stunningly binary, don't they?

She began speaking.

Just a few seconds before, Ellis had let his AR-15 dangle by its bungee-type sling for a second and then crossed his arms. The voices of their pursuers had angled slightly off their general route of travel for the moment.

The bad guys are probably stopping for a second to try to figure out just went wrong at the ambush site.

That they were willing to spend the time to do so also told Luke a few things about the forces they had in reserve as well as their general confidence in winning out in the end. It was clear that the Catoctin District, including Lucketts, had been effectively sealed off – at least temporarily -- from outside interference. Why the attackers had done, that was a mystery to him, but that also didn't matter right now.

I don't know if any police or military are on the way, but even if they are, they're not going to get here in time.

He faced the woman once more, an intense look on his face.

"Things have gotten hairy and they're going to get hairier still before this day is over, lady. If you want to survive, you need to trust me on that point."

He kept his gaze fixed on the woman, willing her to spill her guts. Soon enough, enemy fighters would begin firing into the trees, hoping to panic them all into revealing their position.

"Mister Ellis-"

"Six."

Yet another resigned sigh escaped from her lips.

"Five."

The woman's whisper was harsh.

"Okay, you win, Mister Ellis!"

I knew she'd break!

For a second, he had a hard time keeping a triumphant look off his face.

Luke was no more ready to believe anything she was about to tell him than he'd been before but he knew it was time to give her at least the illusion of some breathing room. Naturally, she grasped at the life ring he tossed her.

"Can we get moving again first before I tell you what's going on?" the woman asked plaintively. Her near-atavistic need to flee was almost at the breaking point. She was afraid she'd soon enough run screaming deeper into the forest like a madwoman intent on throwing herself off a cliff and into the deep, bottomless ocean beneath it, all to be delivered into a sanctuary she knew she hadn't earned nor deserved.

At least not yet!

Luke interrupted her reverie one more time.

"Once you start talking, we'll start walking, ma'am."

Time to deliver the final push.

"Four."

Luke looked down at his watch and then up at the quickly darkening sky. Nightfall was nearly upon the good and the evil alike and he knew it would hold its own terrors for her if he left her alone in it, hogtied on the ground or lashed to a tree. She knew it as well.

It's time to tell him!

"If you don't get me away from here and from the men chasing us, and to a cellular or satellite phone or a radio of some kind, we're all going to die."

Luke wasn't all that surprised, given they were currently being pursued and had been vigorously shot at only a few minutes ago.

"I like my chances against those men, ma'am."

The ex-soldier looked behind him and at the surrounding forest. He wasn't going to let her dictate the terms of this engagement. He had to admit her response, however, was a bit surprising. The woman's eyes widened and she shook her head at him, as if he'd said something profoundly stupid.

"You're not understanding me, Mister Ellis. Believe me, you're really not getting what I'm saying."

"How do you mean? Now that we know those boys are coming and that they may have a few surprises for us, I think I can steer us out of the way of trouble well enough."

Luke was serious. He really thought he could handle it all, just as he'd done a thousand times before.

It was the woman's turn to deliver a revelation, though, and now she did.

Summoning her reserves, she spoke in a clipped, matter-of-fact voice, as if she were delivering a biology lecture to a group of college freshmen.

"Once again, you're not understanding me, Mister Ellis. That's not surprising because you're thinking of just our little piece of the Devil's own pie right now."

"Go on, ma'am. I'm all ears."

Luke projected an aura of confidence. Inside, though, he was mentally taken aback at this strange woman's sudden change of behavior. Fortunately, he was skilled enough not to show it. What could she be talking about?

"I don't mean that we – meaning you and me and the others with us – will be the ones to die, though we, of course, would, but that wouldn't matter in the least at this point." Pausing for a second, she looked down at her own watch before raising her head once more to speak. "No, I mean that the entire world will die if you can't keep me safe and get me to some form of communication before it's too late."

The woman stopped talking and looked Ellis firmly in the eye. Time was running out, not only for her and the people she was traveling with but for all humanity. If she couldn't contact her failsafe before it decided she'd been captured or killed – and much of the internet suddenly going down had to be making the program highly suspicious -- the planet was doomed.

Or at least 97 percent of humanity was. There wouldn't be nearly enough people left to reconstitute the species given her little creation's penchant for killing off more females than males. At minimum, 99.9 percent of women and girls of every age would die in the first wave, with a slightly smaller percentage of males meeting their doom right alongside them.

There would be no recovery at that point. War and conflict, disease, pestilence and the singular bloody minded human determination to compete for every single resource would quickly do in the rest. The lady scientist's little virus also wasn't susceptible to any form of genetic manipulation to reduce or attenuate its virulence. It had been tried before with absolutely no positive result and now there was no time left to try yet again. No matter what any government or scientist could do, it would simply remain the same world-wrecking killer to which she'd given "life," if that were the right word to use.

Inside, she laughed briefly at the thought of calling herself a "scientist" ever again. She and her creation were killers. They were Shiva, destroyer of worlds. Her creation would sweep across the planet in the relative blink of an eye because it was the ultimate highly transmissible agent. Once it did its work, it would stand triumphant atop the ruins.

Of course, I'll be long dead before then, so I won't have to live with what I've unleashed.

That fact was of absolutely no comfort to her. The surviving remnants of the human race would die off, just as the Denisovans and Neanderthals of prehistory did. This time there would be no other higher-order human species to step in and step up, so to speak.

She'd truly grabbed a devil by its forked tail, hadn't she?

Looking back at what she'd done, she remembered that she'd almost at once understood what she'd done and then tried to destroy all evidence of its creation. Tragically, her paper trail had betrayed her and parts of it were out in the wild due to her own stupidity. So, she'd done what she could to keep Pandora's box firmly shut, meaning Jay and his brilliantly designed failsafe, which was her ultimatum to the powerful above her: Destroy her virus, as well as her notes and records, and also keep her safe, or suffer the consequences. The data contained within her failsafe, which would guarantee her survival, would make sure of that.

In the end, those above her – far, far above her – had done the right thing, though she'd had to use a pretty big stick to convince them to do so.

What was that old saying? Oh, yes. "If you want to make an omelet, you have to break a few eggs" or words to that effect.

She didn't care at this point. What mattered was keeping the box firmly shut. Of course, it was now all for naught. She'd been too clever by half. Until just a few hours ago, her plan had been working, but now it wasn't.

On some level, she'd always known this day would finally arrive. Her failsafe wouldn't make allowances nor draw a distinction for something so mundane and prosaic as a nationwide or even global terror attack and her death or capture during it.

No, it will do what I set it up to do, meaning we're all doomed.

The AI – which was always listening and waiting and watching -- would do what it had been designed to do. Tragically, whoever had decided to make a play for her and what she'd made probably hadn't known enough – or at least hadn't been filled in enough -- to make sure she wasn't cut off from communication.

The woman paused for a moment and thought things through. Maybe they actually did know and figured they could scoop her up in time to prevent her from activating her failsafe in retaliation as well as convince her – using whatever means they desired -- to then deactivate it. Once that was done, they could take their time peeling her layer by layer to gain the information she held. Maybe they would be nice about it at first, and even try to persuade her to work for them, but once she refused, they'd undoubtedly do whatever they needed to do to convince her to give up her secrets.

Too bad they didn't realize the AI wouldn't fall for such a patently obvious ploy. Too bad, as well, that she'd probably be unsuccessful in convincing them otherwise.

Inside, she shook her fist at the sky and the injustice of it all. She had some educated guesses about just who wanted her, and none of those people were nice in the least.

Then again, anyone wanting to know what I know are, by definition, pretty bad people, aren't they?

She stared at the man Ellis, accepting that the kill-all-of-humanity trick employed by her virus was something she hadn't really and truly expected.

Face it. It's been pretty much the complete opposite of what you anticipated, hasn't it been?

Her virus didn't save life – which is what she'd been striving for. It took life. It stole it, chewed it up and spit it out. It did all those things and much more. It was implacable, unstoppable and totally indifferent to what it left in its wake. She had to admit that as far as weapons of mass destruction went, she'd created the one to rule all the others.

Bile grew in her throat as she thought of what she'd done and also what she'd become. She was about to easily surpass J. Robert Oppenheimer, the father of the atomic bomb, in terms of giving humanity the power to destroy itself.

"Now I am become Death, the destroyer of worlds," she whispered aloud, looking at the man looming over her.

Luke froze.

He stared intently at the mystery woman, knowing that particular phrase and what it had meant in his old line of work. He'd once thought of himself as a destroyer – though only of those who'd sorely deserved it -- but nothing on the scale this strange lady was claiming. Ellis suddenly realized he believed what she was confessing to him. Everything taking place around him, all the efforts to capture her, the attacks not only in the local area but the huge plumes of smoke in the distance that rose thousands of feet into the air – obviously from other terror attacks – told him one thing:

Things are very, very bad, Luke. Beyond hairy, in fact.

The former Delta operator looked closely at the woman once more.

She was absolutely still and her eyes were now fixed on him. She whispered the phrase yet again, and again, and again, and yet again. *On and on and on, world without end, Amen.*

The irony in his last thought was just too insane for him to contemplate.

The woman stepped outside herself. The line she was reciting from the *Bhagavad Gita*, the most well-known of the Hindu holy texts, reverberated over and over in her head and also between the two of them, woman scientist and ultra-hard special operations warrior.

Ellis snapped his fingers in front of her face.

No reaction.

He had to stop her from descending into madness because she was right on the edge of the Abyss. One more inch and it would be over for her.

Grabbing her shoulders, he violently shook her. Once, twice, a third time.

"WAKE UP!" he ordered, using his command voice.

The mystery woman's hazel eyes slowly refocused, but only for a second. Ellis could tell she was working hard to kick to the surface of the deep, deep water into which she'd thrown herself.

"You don't get to escape like this, ma'am!" He understood the mortal threat – both in the here and now and in the near future -- they were all facing.

Her eyes lost focus once again.

She floated in the air over her corporeal self and considered her choices.

Would it be the sweet release of the Abyss and the oblivion she once thought she'd craved, or the much more difficult – nearly impossible, in fact – path of return and possible redemption?

Long odds, indeed, aren't they?

She knew what it would now take to disarm her failsafe. Time was rapidly slipping away. Minute by minute, second by second, micro-tick by micro-tick. She felt as if she could see even the most minute movement of the hands of the world's finest atomic clock. At the subatomic level she was occupying at the moment, it would take eons for the minute hand to complete even a single sweep second.

That was comforting, wasn't it?

"Such folly," she said to herself reprovingly. Even that clock was showing almost no time left.

A heavy sigh escaped her lips once more.

No matter what she did, it would be fruitless.

We're all doomed, so why should I even try?

But she had to, didn't she?

I'm not so far down the rabbit hole, am I? I can't just doom everyone, can I?

The questions echoed over and over again in her mind. She was in superposition and could see all coincidences and all possibilities, but not all outcomes.

"Such sight is not for you to have," she heard a distant, deep voice say to her.

Suddenly, she made a final, decisive choice.

I have to try!

For a second, she thought she could hear a sigh of satisfaction, perhaps from her more honest self. At any rate, she took pleasure in seeing her incorporeal form rush back into her body. .

"It's about time you did the right thing," she thought; she heard that same distant voice remark before it faded into nothingness.

Still in superposition, she watched as her eyes refocused.

The man Ellis, who was still shaking her and snapping his fingers annoyingly in her face, was right.

She had no right to cop out so easily and choose oblivion, at least not yet. There was a penance to pay, after all, and she couldn't begin to pay it until she made right what she'd first made wrong.

She had to disarm and forever end her failsafe and then also remove herself from the chessboard. It was the least she could do, and it was the only way to save the world from the Destroyer she'd unleashed upon it.

Finally, a sense of peace came over her. It was like a cool, gentle mist of rain on a hot summer day.

Time to wake up, girl.

She returned to real time and space and inhaled deeply, tasting the sweet, late-summer air around her, then she looked up at the nearly dark sky.

"What stars are now visible in the gloaming?" she asked aloud.

She'd never felt more alive than at this moment. The man Ellis just looked at her, demanding answers on far more mundane matters.

Such a pity.

She looked back at the man. He at least had the good manners to stop that awful finger snapping.

Speaking to him, she used her own version of the command voice.

"Listen carefully to me, Ellis, and do what I say or the world is dead. Do you understand me?"

Luke fell silent, looking at her and deciding. He knew when to talk and when to shut up and listen.

It's time to listen, Luke.

"Go on, ma'am." He realized he was slowly nodding his head.

Looking about him, he saw that the deputy sheriff, Holman, and the two kids had returned to where he and the mystery woman were standing. She spoke to him once more.

"Well, Ellis—"

Suddenly, bullets snapped and popped over their heads. The men chasing them had decided to flush their quarry.

As one, they all started running toward the nearby county road. A little beyond that, on the other side, lay Ellis' homestead and the hope of relative safety that it offered.

I hope we make it, was all Luke thought to himself as he and the others began their desperate journey.

CHAPTER 13
RETRIBUTION

Hasan Baradar had had enough of Americans.

The Afghan terror chief wanted to kill every single one he encountered, in fact, and he intended to do so, starting with the woman he'd been sent to capture as part of the great strike against the United States, a profoundly evil nation his funders and trainers had always referred to as the Great Satan.

He looked down and a red haze settled over his vision.

At his feet lay even more of his fighters. They had all been shot, with most receiving two bullet wounds just above the body armor he'd demanded they wear. There was also a single shot to each man's head.

"How can this be?" he exclaimed, swearing loudly at the men around him. "These are the marks of a professional soldier or a very experienced military contractor, not of some Virginia gun nut enthusiast and pretend militiaman!"

Baradar had seen enough of killing and fighting – mostly against American military forces, but sometimes beside them – to know the truth of things.

The Taliban member and phony Afghan refugee thought about the scene in front of him. All those killed had originally been in an excellent ambush position. It should have just been a matter of killing the man protecting that infernal woman and then capturing and delivering her into his masters' hands.

Something had gone terribly wrong, though. It had happened, in fact, even as he and his fighters were moving through the woods to support these now-dead men.

"How could a single woman and a lone man – armed with a rifle or carbine, likely an AR-15 of some type – have done all this?" he asked his men, not expecting any of them to give him an answer. He was the thinker and planner, and they were mostly bullies and brawlers.

He decided to answer his rhetorical question.

"This woman is being protected by more than just a civilian with a rifle!" he exclaimed. They nodded their heads in return, eyes darting about, suddenly afraid. There was a devil in the woods waiting to drag them into hell.

The men, all except for Baradar – who thought such superstitions to be idiotic -- could feel it.

The terror cell leader knew his fighters – nominally "refugees" like himself -- were mostly barely literate at best, though they were certainly cocksure in their dominant ideology. Still, they were easily spooked, especially when they had no access to the *chars* – which was the Pashto word for hashish – they regularly used to calm themselves.

In Baradar's country, these men were denigrated as *charsi*, or hashish users, and were often thought of by wider Afghan society as lazy and even unhinged. It was one reason why almost all of them had been kicked out of their clans and tribes, with most ending up in Afghan national army positions and sometimes even in the civil service.

The Americans – who loved to play at tolerance, but who were more interested in buying peace than in doing what it took to bring it about and then brutally enforce it – had encouraged the integration of these men into the formal military and civil service structure of

Afghanistan. There, they'd received salaries and, more importantly, weapons training in the case of army enlistees.

Naturally enough, being *charsi*, none had managed to last in their jobs, with even the Americans finally tiring of their act and booting them from their positions. Of course, doing so left men like them with a more virulent hatred of Americans than even he'd thought possible. The upside for the Taliban was that the general dismissal of these men by Afghan society and also by the American power structure made it easy to recruit them for the final clash.

It was one reason, he surmised, why there were so many widespread terror attacks going on across America at present. A great many of the attackers had felt aggrieved in one way or another and they meant to take it out on their new country.

He looked at them all, standing around in the deepening twilight, and could see the fear in their eyes at the thought of confronting whoever had killed their compatriots. They might even melt away in the full dark of night and he knew he had to prevent that from happening.

The cure, he knew, was the death of the woman at their hands as well as anyone who was aiding her.

Everyone in this town must also die, of course.

Baradar was comforted by the thought of the wholesale killing to come.

He looked once more at his men. They were shuffling their feet and nervously licking their lips.

"Brothers, we will kill this woman and the ones giving her protection!" His voice was a sibilant hiss.

"Then, we will do the same to every person, no matter how old or young we find here!"

He swept his arm around the forest, showing through his gestures that they were to kill everyone they met tonight, and knew he'd struck just the right tone.

A killing gleam stole into his fighters' eyes and their bloodlust rose like a flood, something glaringly visible in the flush of the skin on their faces. They nodded their heads vigorously and a growing murmur of approval escaped their lips. They wanted to kill and loot and plunder and commit every sin against the Americans that they could think of.

All I have to do now is point them in the right direction and let them act on their own worst impulses.

Baradar was ecstatic at the thought of what would soon occur.

If some or even all of them die tonight, killed by Americans wielding their own rifles and pistols, who would care other than Allah?

He knew he wouldn't.

The only thing that mattered now was the woman. She had to die, preferably at his hands. After she was dead, he and his remaining force would kill everyone they could and then slip away and prepare for the inevitable downfall of this God-cursed nation.

He also knew revenge by those nations that had believed themselves badly treated or insulted by the United States would be swift and sure. They'd fall in on the wounded American beast and then finish it off.

The terror leader nodded at his men in satisfaction.

Turning, he looked off in the distance and then faced the direction the woman and her protectors had to have fled. He could even hear them several hundred yards ahead, foolishly carrying on a conversation.

"They're complete amateurs!" he hissed once again. "We are dealing with complete amateurs who somehow got lucky and killed our brothers!"

Baradar saw agreement in the eyes of his men. Their fear of devils and demons had been washed away by the excitement of the hunt and the retribution to come.

"Are you prepared to let your brothers go unavenged?" Well, ARE YOU?"

His voice cut through the men like a knife.

Baradar brought his M4 up to his chest, finger resting alongside its trigger guard. He aimed his carbine to his front, at where he thought he could make out voices, then gave a great victory shout, and began firing.

"YAAAAAAAH!"

"BLAM! BLAM! BLAM! BLAM!"

The crack and report of Baradar's weapon was a siren call to the murderous thugs he controlled. Seeing what he was doing, his men began to fire their own weapons, all trying to direct their fire into the bodies of the Americans ahead of them. Those people were among the many who'd killed their friends and brothers over the years and they didn't deserve to live.

"After them, my brothers! After them now!"

To a man, his fighters took off into the forest, using the tactical flashlights attached to their rifles while they fired them for all they were worth.

Seeing his men rush deeper into the woods, Hasan Baradar waited several seconds before he trotted after them at an easy lope.

No sense in me catching a bullet during all this.

Looking ahead, he knew that a general melee between his men and the fleeing American woman and her protectors would take place.

Hopefully, I'll be the one to kill the woman. It's the least I deserve for all the trouble she's given me!

CHAPTER 14
NIGHT FLIGHT

THEY'D ALL HEARD THE WOMAN'S VOICE. IT HAD BEEN FIRM AND
confident -- as if she had made a fateful decision and was now determined to see it through to the end no matter the cost to herself or even
to them.

Annie and Darren – frightened of what they'd learned and what
they knew was coming, could only stare at each other in disbelief as
they fled toward the county road and to Mister Ellis' place. Both were
young and in great health and could run all night if they needed to,
though knowing that fact wasn't helping them deal with their
growing fear.

"Come on, Darren!" Annie exhorted. She willed her feet to run
faster.

"I'm here. I'm here! Just keep running, Annie!"

The boy's breath came in little gulps, more from fear than any
sort of exhaustion. His satchel banged at his right side, rhythmically
striking his hip each time his feet got too far out in front of his body.
For some reason he couldn't remember at the moment. He knew he
needed to keep it with him even though it was probably slowing him
down a bit.

Maybe it had to do with something the lady with them had

hurriedly confessed? She'd told them she was some kind of scientist and that she had to communicate with an artificial intelligence program only she controlled.

He didn't know, though, and the need to survive long enough to get to Mister Ellis' place and then see the next sunrise kept him from remembering.

Darren looked around and turned to matters confronting him right now. He was keeping up with his older sibling and though he didn't know it, he was proving out the old observation that the threat of impending death often motivated people to undertake super-human efforts to avoid it.

Keep running!

He looked over at his sister again.

"Run faster, Annie!"

No way, no way, NO WAY!

Alec Holman's thoughts were one long exclamation at this point.

There was no need for quiet now. If the woman was telling the truth about everything, and they were in it up to their necks, then the racket they made as they bulled their way through the forest really didn't matter anymore.

It was now a race against time, and he knew they were losing it. Her story might sound crazy, but everything around him screamed at him to believe, believe, believe.

He looked down at his watch, its luminous face counting down to the end of the world.

Five seconds had passed since he'd last checked. It was time to look behind him again. He couldn't allow the people chasing them to catch up. Flashlight beams were hungrily devouring the dark night as the men in pursuit grew ever closer.

Alec knew he'd soon have another decision to make. This time, what he did might save the world or he might doom it if he failed. He couldn't wrap his mind around that fact to tell the truth.

When they took flight, the lawman made sure he was in the rear-guard position, with the two kids between him and the ex-soldier Ellis – who was escorting the mystery woman or scientist or whatever she was.

All he was sure of was that the people chasing them badly wanted her. Or they once had. Now he wasn't so sure they weren't just trying to kill her.

Something had changed, and now with bullets whizzing all around him he could sense they were on a different mission. Now, it looked like they wanted to kill everyone without exception, even the lady scientist.

That woman was now the most important person in his and everyone else's life. He knew it, the bad guys knew it, and Ellis – who Alec could now tell was clearly more than just a retired soldier -- certainly knew it.

Alec took a deep breath and thought back to just a few minutes ago.

What the woman had confessed stunned him and everyone else, and there was simply no denying the underlying evidence supporting her words.

For one, they were now racing through the woods and throwing caution to the winds. They were also desperately trying to avoid getting shot as they made their way to the ex-Army man's place. Plus, the whole county looked to be under attack – meaning this wasn't just some local group of criminals deciding to take whatever they could get. If it was indeed a terror attack, it sure didn't seem to be an isolated or local incident.

No, this one was much more than that.

If the many pillars of smoke on the horizon, in every direction he looked, were any sign, Washington, D.C. had been put to the terror torch.

The whole country's probably been attacked!

Holman wasn't aware he was voicing his inner thoughts at the moment and wouldn't have cared even if he did. He was more than motivated enough to keep himself and the others with him moving quickly. From what he could understand, the woman needed a radio or a satellite phone or even just a regular cellular phone that worked. If a radio, it had to be able to send on a certain frequency range and also receive a transmission in return.

"I could even use a computer if there's internet access," she'd told them all.

Unfortunately, all networks seemed to be down and so was everyone's cellular service. Radio appeared to be out as well, though that wasn't precisely true. Rather, the frequencies used on police bands – which were the only ones on his radio – were being scrambled or interfered with.

"I don't need police bands," the woman reassured them. "If I speak the correct words into even a simple walkie-talkie radio with the right frequencies, we might have a chance."

If she couldn't get to a radio, though, Armageddon would be the end result. Worst of all, they had less than an hour to do it, or whatever it was she controlled would turn into a dead man's switch and act on its own.

Scenes from a Stanley Kubrick movie he'd once seen on some cable movie channel – one in which the world ended in a nuclear holocaust because of a demented Air Force general obsessed with his body's vital fluids, along with a crazy B-52 bomber pilot named 'King' Kong who was just doing his job, as it turned out – played in his head. Atomic bomb after atomic bomb tore up the world until the entire planet was a nuclear fireball.

Alec caught his breath and shook his head.

That's minor league, buddy.

"This will be much worse," the lady scientist told them, and she hadn't spared the girl Annie or her little brother Darren from the imagery, either.

Just before they all started running from the men chasing them –

bullets flying through the trees on all sides -- the lady confessed she'd created some sort of unstoppable virus – she called it a "non-organism organism" – that would eventually kill off all human life on Earth, and in not all that long a timeframe either. So she had to contact what she called her "failsafe," and pretty soon, too, or it was all over.

Of course, it would also be the end if she got herself killed before then.

Alec considered his options. From what he could glean from the woman's short explication in the very few seconds they'd had before chaos had erupted once again, her failsafe was some sort of AI program. Amazingly, it was so powerful it could actually tell if she'd been captured by bad actors, murdered, executed or otherwise died from anything but natural causes, even if she was completely isolated from its electronic presence.

Holman – a man educated at the University of Virginia and intelligent in his own right – had no idea how something existing only within the electronic world could discern what was going on in the real world when it came to the mystery woman, but she'd assured them all that it indeed could.

After everything he'd gone through today, he had no reason to doubt her. Besides, even if he did, there was little they could do except getting her to the Ellis' place.

"I've got more than enough comm gear there," the retired soldier told them. "A couple of satellite phones as well as a shortwave radio and a set of walkie-talkies and tactical radios, for starters."

Alec saw relief wash over the woman in waves. To tell the truth, he was mighty relieved as well. Looking at the two kids, Annie and Darren, the lawman could see they were, too. Only Ellis was unreadable. Holman wasn't shocked in the least at that.

"I've also got another four-by-four gassed up and ready to go," Luke told them just seconds before they had to take flight. They were running for their lives once again.

The woman huffed and puffed slightly, with Ellis' callused left hand under her arm helping her along and supporting her whenever she appeared in danger of falling.

"Mister Ellis," she wheezed slightly.

"Yes, ma'am. Look, I know you're afraid, but I'll get you through this. Trust me."

Luke had been through more than his fair share of firefights, jihadist takedowns, raids – you name it. He'd been there, done that, and had the t-shirt to prove it. He also had a plan for turning the tables on the people chasing them. He thought the mystery woman he was trying to protect was afraid of dying and looked to reassure her.

He was mistaken.

"You can't allow me to be captured, Mister Ellis. I'm a danger to the world now even if I do manage to permanently deactivate my failsafe."

Luke had already come to that conclusion, and he knew what she was getting at. His tactical senses were telling him, though, that the men after them were now more interested in killing everyone, including even her.

Something had changed in the last hour, he knew.

Perhaps they were enraged at just how many of their number he and the deputy, Holman, had already killed, or maybe they'd even been given a new set of orders by whoever it was controlling them.

Right now, he didn't know and he didn't care. All he knew was that they needed some form of communication and they didn't have it. If they all were killed AFTER he'd gotten the mystery woman across the finish line, then it was what it was.

"It's a cold, hard world," he'd told his troops on more than a few occasions during his military career.

Well, the fix they were in certainly qualified as "cold and hard," didn't it?

Right now, though, the woman simply couldn't die. That meant he couldn't die, either. At least, not until he'd made sure she'd made things right.

As Luke saw it, his current job was "avoid holes, plug holes, make holes." That meant no holes in the woman – and himself if he could avoid it. If she did develop a hole, he had to plug it and keep her alive long enough to matter. Lastly, if he had to, he needed to make holes in every bad guy that came their way.

Whatever!

The ex-soldier shook his head, willing away all thoughts except those related to the tactical situation at hand, which meant fighting off the bad guys – and maybe even killing all of them if he was lucky – so that his mystery woman scientist could reach out and shut off the thing just waiting to kill all of humanity.

As if that wasn't daunting enough, they now had less than 45 minutes and his place was still off in the distance, through heavy forest and rolling terrain and with the enemy circling all around them.

He also didn't doubt that some of them were waiting just up ahead at the county road.

Cold realization struck him.

We're not going to make it to my place in time. Not unless I bring the fight to them.

It was a desperate move, but what options were left?

Answer: None.

Luke made up his mind. He breathed in deeply and then exhaled and grabbed the woman by the wrist, bringing them both to a sudden stop.

"What are you doing?!?" she exclaimed, eyes wild. "We have to run!"

Ellis shook his head and put an index finger to his lips, shushing her. He pulled them both down low to the ground.

"What are you doing?" she hissed at him, trying to rise to her feet and take flight once again.

Luke's iron grip prevented her from fleeing. Right now, to run was to die. Either they'd be shot trying to cross the road or they'd catch a bullet in the back, so thick was the air with lead.

He was no fool. To stand and fight might also bring about the same result – meaning an ugly death -- sure enough.

All his years of experience told him, though, that there was a better chance of success right now in sneaking up to the county road so that he could do Part Three of his job: Make holes.

A bright, shining thought now slammed into his mind and it was crystal clear how to do it.

His eyes locked onto the woman's. She snapped her mouth shut and waited for him to say something.

Luke spoke two words:

"Seek battle."

CHAPTER 15
SEEK BATTLE I

"I've had just about enough of this crap!" Alec Holman swore aloud.

He was frustrated, scared and enraged all at once and the need to do something – to strike out at the ones trying to kill him and the other people he was charged by law with protecting – was now enormous. Looking ahead, he saw the kids, Annie and Darren, and beyond them the cause of all the insanity. She was practically being carried by the man Ellis.

That guy's hardly breathing hard!

Alec was panting and slightly out of breath. He was glad the man was on his side in this fight.

Suddenly, the hairs on the back of his neck stood up.

Duck! Duck! Duck!

He threw himself to the ground. A bullet passed directly overhead, in the space where his head had been just a second ago.

"PEW! PEW! PEW!"

The sound of lead flying through the air and hitting tree trunks and rocks in every direction grew cacophonous. It was now as chaotic and as loud as a fighter jet going to afterburner.

Alec got up and ran once more, now gasping for air. He pulled in a desperate breath and then almost immediately let it out, doing it over and over again until his head began to swim and a reddish cloud threatened to descend over his eyes. He knew he was on the verge of hyperventilating and he couldn't risk passing out from oxygen deprivation and way too much CO_2 in his bloodstream. If he crashed now, he was dead and so was everyone with him.

I know what I have to do one more time!

The people he was with had to be saved, first because they deserved to live and, second, because the world especially did.

Realization and acceptance now rushed at him.

Ellis and the others are counting on me to guard their rear!

That was going to be a serious problem for him because the men trying to kill everyone were close, so close.

Too close.

The glow from the flashlights they were using lit up the night with increasing intensity. They were now only about 75 meters away.

Their lights would expose first him and then the others.

After that, things would really go south and the dozens of bullets flying through the air would soon start finding their mark. One by one, he and everyone else would fall to the ground, either wounded or dead.

Holman knew his mind was threatening to run away from him, and so he raised his left hand and slapped himself hard in the face.

STOP IT!

Strangely, the blow calmed him somewhat, and he saw things just a bit more rationally, even if only for a moment.

A minute's all I'm going to need.

He came to a stop, turned around and then crouched down.

Alec steeled himself to once more charge into a group of men with rifles, all of whom were trying to kill him.

"It's the only tactic I have in my playbook now, right?" he whispered aloud.

Sure, it is, he heard the night answer in return.

The lawman knew on an intellectual level he was just trying to convince himself his desperate play would work.

It just might, too.

Or it might not.

To tell the truth, I really don't care at this point!

Finally, he went deadly silent. His need to kill the men trying to murder them all grew and grew and threatened to wash over him like a tsunami of death and destruction.

Though he knew he was a cop and not a soldier, Alec also knew he'd just experienced more than his fair share of violence. Probably more than most any lawman – and even many soldiers -- would ever experience in their lives, even.

I'm still no super-soldier like that guy Ellis, and this is honest-to-God combat. Plus, the numbers are against me!

He slapped his face once more, this time harder still. The sound echoed in the still night air.

The blow energized him and encouraged him to let his inner Berserker run amok.

He looked down at his carbine one last time and slammed a fresh 30-round magazine – the last one he had -- into his M4 before he pulled back the charging handle. A 5.56 mm round moved up and into his weapon's firing chamber.

He was ready to start killing his enemies.

Now peering into the dark night that had wrapped itself around the woods like a funeral shawl, he had but a single thought.

Where were the bad guys?

Of course.

They're where the lights are at.

Leaping to his feet, bullets whizzing all around him, Alec charged forward.

There!

Shoot him! Shoot him! Shoot him!

And so Alec did.

The man went down and howled in agony. Almost at once, he became as still and as quiet as the grave.

Over there! Another one! Another one! Fire! Fire!

Holman heard rather than saw another bad guy go down hard. He shot him once more to be sure. The man didn't move.

Good!

A bullet suddenly grazed his cheek and burned his flesh like a hot poker. Another one nearly slammed into his side, missing him only by a millimeter as he turned slightly in reaction to the wound on his cheek.

Strangely, the agony he should have felt from taking one to the face was nothing to him. Adrenaline coursed through his veins like nitrous oxide injected into a street racer's engine. It powered him like an unstoppable force. He shook his head and then raced headlong, firing his M4 and willing his bullets to find the men trying to kill him.

Two of them!

He screamed and fired. He could see the fear in their eyes as the devil in front of them seemed to dodge their own bullets with ease and then moved in to kill them both.

They turned and fled, desperate to find safety in the dark woods.

He shot them both, feeling nothing as he killed them.

Dispassionate, he could see he'd hit them in the backs of their heads. This time, he didn't waste another bullet to make sure they were indeed down for good, not with the mess he'd just turned them into.

"YAAAAAAAH!"

Alec screamed even louder and took off deeper into the woods, shooting at every flashlight beam he could see. He was having trouble focusing his eyes because a red curtain of death had descended over them.

His rage at the possibility that everything might end if the woman they were guarding failed in her mission created a bloody mist in the air around him. It was a mist of his own making, he knew, at once ashamed of what he'd forced himself to become yet also immensely proud at the same time.

"DIE! DIE! DIE! DIE!"

Now he was screaming at the enemy, firing at every target of opportunity he could find. He lost count of how many men he'd shot during his insane charge.

How many are left to kill? Who cares! Alec continuing firing, moving to a new position after each aimed shot. He desperately hoped they wouldn't zero him and let him have it.

That wasn't to be, of course. What felt like a ton of bricks suddenly hit his leg and dropped him in his tracks.

"AAAAAAAAAH!" he howled and then rolled over, gripping his left thigh.

Looking at his side, he saw his M4 on the ground near him and then slammed his hand over his mouth to keep from screaming again.

You'll give your position away if you do! he imagined Luke Ellis yelling at him.

Two men out in the dark were now shouting at each other in a language he didn't understand. The sound came from the same direction the round that hit him had.

Probably fighting over who gets the honor of shooting me in the head!

Alec fought through waves of pain and concentrated on staying conscious.

I hope I killed enough of them to give Ellis and the others a chance. I'd die happy if I did!

Looking down at his thigh once more, he saw a nasty, ragged bullet hole in it. The round had passed through the meaty outer part and left a noticeable gouge. It looked to him like it was a clean wound, though.

Really, dude, it's hardly even bleeding. He was relieved at the thought. Then a string of nonsense words ran through his mind.

Am I going into shock? Maybe just a little. Well, at least it's keeping me from thinking too much about my leg!

The two men arguing over who would have the pleasure of killing him suddenly fell silent.

Looks like they've decided who's going to kill me. He felt a little sad at the thought but also weirdly satisfied.

Two flashlight beams passed over his position and continued moving, seeking him out. They swept back over the spot where he lay and then kept moving once again, this time in the other direction. The sound of the men tramping through the woods moved off to his left.

They're going in the wrong direction!

The thought of their stupidity gave him great pleasure. It was almost enough to deaden the pain coming from his leg, in fact.

Alec wanted to shout at the night sky in triumph. Instead, he bit down hard on his lower lip to force himself to concentrate. When he'd been felled by that bullet, he'd landed in heavy underbrush in a depression lying slightly below the rest of the forest floor.

From the top of the brush, though, everything looked even and symmetrical. Once shot, he'd rolled himself into this hiding place and it was fully obscuring him from the men working to find him.

I just might get out of this with my hide intact!

Suddenly, a beam of light stabbed at the brush surrounding him and fixed itself in place, this time just slightly off to his right. They hadn't found him, but they were close.

He froze, not daring to move nor draw a breath or even blink his eyes.

His sadness returned. This time it was much stronger than before. But it was quickly replaced by adamantine determination mixed with white-hot molten steel.

If it's the end, it's the end, but I'm going down swinging!

His M4 was by his side. There were still a few rounds left in the magazine.

Alec closed his eyes one last time and said a silent prayer. He was going to pop up and start shooting.

It's time, buddy.

He silently began counting down, his lips moving in response.

Three, two, one... wait!

What was that?

A different and far angrier man's voice cut through the night air and froze the two men hunting him dead in their tracks. As near as he could tell, it was in the same language as the one the other men were speaking.

Hope bubbled up.

Can it be?

Lying in the underbrush, stuck in place as if he'd been encased in resin, he heard the duo answer the angry man. From the sound of things, he had to be the one in charge of all this mayhem. It was also clear those men were afraid of him.

Suddenly, the flashlight beams moved away from his hiding place.

The men, including the one doing all the shouting, moved rapidly off to his left and towards the county road.

Alec lay deathly still and listened for the footfall of anyone else hunting him. There were none, though that didn't mean there weren't other bad guys out there somewhere.

Now that the coast seemed to be clear. His next thought was more exuberant.

My banzai charge worked again! I put 'em down and thinned 'em out!

The euphoria of survival made him a bit light-headed. Now, maybe the man Ellis and the woman – and Annie and Darren – would have a fighting chance, both for themselves and for humanity.

That's good enough for me!

He was ecstatic that he was still drawing air, at least for the moment. But then he was seized with dread realization.

That guy leading them definitely has the county road covered!

Taking a breath, he steeled himself and looked down at his leg. He slammed his hand over his mouth once more as waves of agony erupted when he flexed it.

Not good! Not good!

Gritting his teeth, he took his M4 and extended the butt stock to maximum length. He'd have to use it as a cane, even though one part of him wanted to just remain hidden in this safe spot.

No one's looking for me now, and I can just ride all this insanity out, right?

Alec was ashamed of himself, and he instantly regretted even thinking about laying low until this entire mess sorted itself out.

His thought was stern and unyielding.

Get up and get moving, dude! The county road's just ahead. Your friends need help!

As if in response to his thinking, he heard gunfire come from near the road, which was less than a thousand feet away. The sound of a carbine echoed in the air and was answered in return by other ones.

Alec heaved himself to his feet, almost fainting from the pain ripping through his leg. He had to get moving.

He leaned heavily on his makeshift cane, butt stock on the ground and muzzle in his right hand, now cool to the touch after he'd fired it so often and so quickly. Sucking in his breath, he took as much weight as he could off his wounded leg and began limping toward the county road, biting deep into his lower lip to keep from fainting.

Cold reality quickly slapped him in the face just then. Looking up at the night sky, the lawman felt sorrow and pain and rage all at once.

I'm not going to make it in time!

CHAPTER 16
SEEK BATTLE II

"GET DOWN!"

Though harsh, Ellis' whisper was still nearly inaudible. It brought all of them up just short of the county road. He still held the mystery woman's upper arm in the iron grip of his free hand.

Annie, her brother Darren, and the woman they all had to protect knew not to say a word in response. There could be men waiting for them to step out into the road and give their position away, for one, or those same men could be lying in wait in the thickly forested woods just behind and ahead of them.

Luke knew they were still being pursued by at least several men, killers who were closing the gap on them pretty quickly. Or they had been until a moment ago, when what sounded like a heck of a fire-fight erupted in the woods just behind them.

I know what all that shooting was about. It has to be Holman.

Taking a second, he sized up the tactical situation and their odds of crossing the road unscathed.

One: He'd lost contact with Alec Holman, the sheriff's deputy who'd been guarding their rear.

Two: Less than 10 seconds after that, there'd been shooting

involving at least a half-dozen M4s. He'd given the young lawman one of those – taken from one of the men he'd killed earlier in the day – and he knew Holman had put it to good use.

Three: The pace of fire coming from the woods to their rear slackened greatly after that firefight.

Yet again, Alec Holman showed me he was a good man to have in a fight!

His thought on that matter was sorrowful. No way the deputy had walked away from it at the end.

Worse, he knew he couldn't spare the time to go back down the trail to help him.

The hard truth was that he just couldn't afford to leave the woman, Annie and Darren. They were all on what had now become a Doomsday clock. Fail in getting the lady scientist to some form of communication in time, and it was all over for everyone, good and bad alike. Game over, end of story, no sequels or reruns.

Never one to quake or quail and as hard a man as they came, Luke felt a momentary chill run down his spine at the thought of the coming annihilation if they failed in their mission.

This is counterproductive. Focus!

Snapping back to the here-and-now, the retired Delta Force operator slowly gathered his three charges around him. He wanted to make sure that only they could hear what he was saying. No sudden movements, no loud speech, no standing up and 'sky lining' themselves against the star-filled night, no nothing.

He slowly reached down into his daypack and pulled out a pair of night-vision optical devices, the ones his battle buddies at Joint Special Operations Command had given him upon his retirement. They were of outstanding quality and highly capable.

Luke didn't have time to train his three charges in rudimentary tactical hand signals so he had to risk whispering to them all.

"Don't move and stay low while I take a quick look around," he whispered to the mystery woman and the kids.

None of them said anything in return. Wide-eyed, the teenage girl just nodded her head very slightly for all three of them. Ellis noted with satisfaction that the woman and the boy had frozen themselves in place, awaiting his commands. He also saw that the woman was counting down the minutes until all of their efforts came to naught. The urgent need to get to his place and all his comms gear weighed heavily on them both.

Suddenly, there were running noises once again in the woods behind them and beams of light began piercing, though those quickly died. The three civilians all prepared to start running once again.

"Calm down," Luke whispered. "They're trying not to give themselves away while they hunt for our trail. There aren't that many of them left, either. Looks like Deputy Holman did good."

The ex-soldier dipped his head slightly at this last observation. He barely knew the lawman, but he also knew that a good man had done what he could to help them and that he may have willingly given up his life in the process. Annie and Darren both looked stricken as well.

Only the woman, who barely knew any of them until just a few short hours ago, remained largely unaffected at the realization that the sheriff's deputy might not have made it, though that wasn't actually why she appeared so stoic.

Time enough for sorrow after I contact my failsafe. Right now, we can't afford to fail!

She almost heaved an audible sigh of relief at the man Ellis' pronouncement that their pursuers had lost the trail. Fortunately, the girl Annie squeezed her forearm just in time and looked at her, warning her into continued silence. She nodded at the girl in return.

Now reminded of the need to stay undiscovered while Ellis looked for a way to get them across the road, she took a second to look at the 12-year-old boy with them. His name was Darren and he was the girl's brother, she knew.

In imitation of his adult mentor, she saw the boy was also craning his head slowly around – never making any sudden movements that would catch the eye. Apparently, he was trying to help the man spot anyone hiding in the dark night. No doubt, they were waiting to shoot everyone but her. Sadly, she couldn't help but think that a quick death for the three people with her would be preferable to what she'd most likely go through if she were captured. Those men had to have radios or working cellular or satellite phones and she knew she'd have to beg them to allow her to use one, in the process revealing just why she needed to.

She had to buy the world more time while she either worked something out with her captors as far as an exchange of information went or somehow managed to kill herself once she'd deactivated her failsafe.

No good options, and I'm dead no matter what.

Oddly, the idea of her impending doom no longer frightened her. Earlier in the day, before all this insanity, a premature and unnatural demise chilled her to the bone. Now, though? She would welcome it as long as she could first atone for her manifest sins.

Luke saw the terrorists.

There were a pair of them, one on either side of the road. They were waiting for him and his people to cross. There were also two in the woods on the other side of the road, waiting to spring the trap in case they made it across. All of them were set up in positions that would ensure they didn't fire on each other when they let loose. He could also hear at least two more men running through the woods on his side, rushing to catch him and his three charges and then take them all under fire.

He had to come up with a plan fast.

He looked once again at the woman, the boy and the teenager Annie. They were all ears as he leaned in to speak to them.

"There are a couple of men out on the road waiting for us and two men in the woods across the road, plus at least two more on the hunt for us on this side."

The woman whispered back at Luke. She couldn't keep the despair out of her voice.

"How do we get out of this, Mister Ellis? We're running out of time!"

Annie placed a hand over her brother Darren's mouth to keep him from saying anything and looked closely at him, willing him to remain silent.

After a second, the boy nodded in return, and she removed her hand. She refocused her attention on the whispered back-and-forth going on between the two adults. Ellis spoke once more.

"I know we're on the clock, ma'am. And here's what we're going to do."

Leaning in even closer, Luke gave them the plan.

After a moment, they all nodded at him and got ready. His own voice, even as low as it was, had held nothing but commands and directives and they were determined to follow them.

The retired Delta Force operator slowly pivoted, taking care not to upset the high weeds and underbrush concealing their position. He dropped his eyes to check out his weapon as well as its sound suppressor. The optic on his carbine was also far more than just a red dot. It supplied better-than-fourth-generation night vision – which was the latest capability available on the civilian market -- and it had a clarity that just couldn't be beaten. Nothing that existed in the night could escape its notice.

Now, it was time to use it.

He selected from among his optic's various choices and then slowly – ever so slowly -- brought his rifle up and sighted in on the two men off in the woods across the road. Like the first two of them he'd shot earlier in the day, this pair had also foolishly positioned themselves too close together and hadn't taken the time to find good cover or concealment. His brow wrinkled slightly as he put the optic's reticle on one of the men. He let out a long, slow and inaudible breath.

Those two guys reminded him of a few of the dumber Taliban fighters he'd dealt with over in Afghanistan during his time there. He wasn't too surprised at the revelation, though, not after hearing both Dari and Pashto spoken on the radio he'd taken off the first pair he'd taken out. Not long after, though, the bad guys activated some sort of self-destruct mechanism and the circuit board inside fried itself with an audible hiss.

Concentrate, Luke.

"POP!"

The report from his carbine was barely audible in the night and there was no muzzle flash from his weapon to give his position away. The first man flopped over on his side, shot through the throat and either dead or paralyzed and useless.

Grunting silently in satisfaction, Luke quickly took aim at the man's partner. Like every poorly trained Taliban fighter he'd ever come across, this one was dumbfounded by his partner's unexpected demise and just stared stupidly at his body rather than launch himself away in search of better cover.

Luke didn't have time to draw another breath. He was still exhaling his first one.

"POP!" once more.

He'd just made the man pay the ultimate price for his lack of tactical awareness by putting a 5.56mm round in him. The man fell backwards and into a position not anatomically possible for humans except in cases of complete brain and nerve death.

Almost at once, the two men stationed on either side of the road began firing. One or both of them were likely equipped with some sort of night vision device and they meant to zero in on Ellis and shoot him in return.

He'd expected just such a response, though. Going to ground quickly but silently, he moved away from where he'd just fired his weapon. To him, the surrounding night was as clear as day and he could see everything and hear everything, the violence in the night air giving him a kind of supersensory ability.

"PEW! PEW! PEW! PEW!"

The return fire from the terrorists' M4s sailed harmlessly over his head. He was already several feet away from where he'd been when he started the firefight and he planned to be even farther away in the next couple of seconds. Not coincidentally, he was also going to be closer to the enemy pair as well. That was something he fervently hoped they wouldn't realize in time.

Now on auto-response as he serviced targets, the ex-soldier worked his way through the high weeds, ever closer to the two shooters still sending rounds in his general vicinity. He couldn't worry yet about the ones running through the woods on his side of the road. Doubtless, they'd be attracted by all the shooting.

Luke was traveling light at the moment. He carried only his carbine, while his front pocket held a single 30-round magazine. He wanted to be able to get as low to the ground as possible and didn't need magazines and other items adding inches to his profile if he had to flatten himself as much as possible. Annie was safeguarding their last spare M4 and his daypack. It had been greatly lightened by his efforts up to this point.

If worse came to worst, she'd have to use the Glock pistol the deputy, Alec Holman, had left with her. She might even have to give her brother the Glock and use the M4 herself if things really and truly went sideways. All three of them were still hunkered down in the underbrush, under camouflaged thermal blankets he'd distributed to them after showing them how to drape the things over themselves.

Darren's eyes were wide, as if they were trying to take in every bit of audible and visual clue he could find. His heart was also racing and he was fighting to be brave for his sister, Annie. So far, he was succeeding, though he didn't know how long that would last. Annie was under the thermal blanket with him, and her free hand – she had that pistol the deputy sheriff had given her in the other – reached out to him in the dark, looking to comfort him. Personally, he wasn't so sure everything would turn out well, but he had no other choice but to trust his sister and the two adults with them.

I'm not going to run off screaming like a little baby, he vowed, determined to show his sister that she could count on him.

He paused for a second to reflect on the moment they were living.

He knew what the plan was.

Mister Ellis -- who'd now risen to Olympian heights in his eyes -- was shooting at the bad men and they were shooting back at him, that much he was sure of. That was their signal to start counting down from 30. Once they reached zero, they were supposed to run across the road and not stop for anything no matter what. Mister Ellis had told them all that he needed 30 seconds to do what he was going to do, which was to make sure it was safe enough for them to start moving.

Once they got to the other side, they were supposed to duck down and wait another 30 seconds to make sure no one was after them and then make a beeline straight ahead until they came to Mister Ellis' property. They'd also have to use the gun and the rifle their ex-Army friend had left with them if someone did manage to track them down.

Darren was afraid he wouldn't have the courage to do that, and so he prayed to find some.

After explaining his plan, Mister Ellis had reassured them all. "I'll join up with you as soon as I can." Darren fervently hoped his big ex-Army friend's pronouncement would come true.

"Right now, we just don't have enough people to find a safer, surer way of doing all this," Mister Ellis had said to them. "If for some reason I don't make it, get to my place as quickly as you can and then enter the security code I gave all of you. Once you're inside, go down to my basement. The communications radios and my backup satellite phones are on the big workbench you'll see right in front of you at the bottom of the stairs."

His big ex-Army friend's voice had been almost nonchalant, as if what he was getting ready to do amounted to nothing more than an early evening stroll to the local convenience store in town.

Darren knew better, though, even if he was only 12 years old. He'd seen plenty of war movies.

Mister Ellis isn't sure he's going to make it.

For a second, the thought made him want to cry, but he knew if he did he might never stop, so he squeezed his sister's hand even tighter before he let it drop away. For just a half-second, the night air became completely still and silent, like the world around him was taking a deep breath, with all struggle and strife halted for just that instant.

Then the sounds of combat erupted yet again.

The air around the trio echoed with the roar of gunfire. They remained hidden in the underbrush, counting down the seconds before they could race across the road. First, a few pops came from a rifle fitted with a sound suppressor. After a second, those were answered by much louder rifle reports.

Darren thought he could almost hear angry exclamations coming from the men who were firing the much louder rifles.

"BLAM! BLAM! BLAM! BLAM!"

Bullets tore into the ground where Luke Ellis had been kneeling just a second before. He'd avoided them just in the nick of time. One of the rounds might even have gouged a line in the sole of left assault boot.

Well, it certainly feels like it, Luke thought, somewhat laconically, *but I'm not about to waste time checking it out.*

He was always amazed by the stray thoughts that often ran

through his mind at a sub-level whenever he found himself in a firefight.

That shot had been close. Way too close, in fact. The bad guys were on the verge of catching a lucky break, maybe, and he knew he couldn't allow that.

It's time to end this dance, Luke!

One second he was shooting and moving and in the next rolling out of the path of a stream of bullets that were striking the ground all around him.

Suddenly, he found himself kneeling and looking directly at one of his tormentors. The man hadn't registered him yet, fortunately.

There you are!

He shot the man three times. His body jerked and danced like a puppet on a string before it fell to the ground in a lifeless heap.

Luke quickly looked behind him before he moved again. Thirty seconds had passed since he'd shot the first two men concealed in the woods across from his initial position.

Ellis picked out sudden movement in the night.

There was the other shooter who'd been guarding the road!

"POP! POP!"

Two shots from his suppressed carbine finished the man off.

Still more movement! Who were they?

Ah, yes.

Three figures, one shorter than the other two, ran across the county road and into the shady dark forest he'd just cleared of terrorists.

Shoot and move, shoot and move!

The refrain ran through Luke's mind as he maneuvered to cross over the road himself. He wanted to angle his line of march inward and toward the three people he was protecting as they made their way to his homestead. If all went well, he could get the lady scientist on the air or on a sat phone or whatever with a minute or so to spare before Armageddon occurred. He also briefly considered doubling back and trying to catch the remaining bad guys unaware but then quickly decided against it.

Time has priority on this mission, Luke. We're going to have to hustle now!

He started running across the county road and into the woods he'd just cleared of enemy. Rifle fire erupted around him as he took off.

The voice in his head screamed: *It's not over yet!*

CHAPTER 17
BARADAR

"SHOOT HIM!" HASAN BARADAR LOUDLY URGED HIS TWO remaining men, heedless of attracting the rip and roar of gunfire coming from the road just to his right. He didn't think the American who'd just killed four more of his own men could see into the stand of trees in which they'd all hidden themselves, and so he felt safe in having his fighters direct their rifle fire at him.

Alone among the survivors in his terror cell, Baradar still had a pair of night vision goggles -- in addition to the AT4 anti-tank rocket he carried on his back, of course. He now knew just why he'd ordered it brought to him by one of his fighters, a man who'd been killed not ten minutes ago in the woods to their rear. That had been in a separate clash with some sort of American police officer who'd charged them all, firing with abandon and striking and killing several of his men before they'd finally managed to shoot him down like the dog he was.

I'll never understand Americans! They fight like demons sometimes, but then at other times they surrender like lambs being led to the slaughter!

Baradar vigorously shook his head, as if trying to empty it of the contradictions almost all Americans presented to the world at large.

Head clear, he took stock of his personal equipment. He intended to make good use of both his night vision goggles as well as his anti-tank weapon, not to mention his M4, when it came to running down and then killing the woman he was hunting as well as that evil man protecting her. The thought of their deaths sent a tingle down his spine. He'd killed before but never out of spite or to seek pleasure.

This time was different, though. The deaths of the two Americans, in fact, had become his sole reason for being at this point and he knew he would gladly sacrifice both of his remaining men if it meant the woman and that filthy man would finally die.

The terror cell leader looked around, first at his own troops and then at the retreating back of the obviously deadly American who'd just easily killed four of his better-trained fighters.

"That one has had a great deal of military training," Baradar said in a frustrated voice to his men, capping it off with a loud exhalation.

Both his men nodded knowingly. They'd all seen American Green Berets, Delta Force, and Navy SEAL units in action in the past back in their own country as well as in the training films they'd studied closely. Those American soldiers were devils, pure and simple, and wherever they fought, they killed and they won. In fact, they made the Soviet Special Forces troops their own fathers had fought against in the 1980s – the fabled Russian *Spetznaz* – look like rank amateurs.

Baradar was honest enough to admit to himself that even though much of America had become soft and had always been ungodly, such weakness hadn't yet infected the special operations forces of his hated enemy's military.

No, those American soldiers are as near to being stone cold killers as it's possible for Allah to make when it comes to infidels.

Fortunately for them all, and as near as he and his men could tell, there was only the one lone man standing against them and even if he'd once served in one of the American military's special forces units, he was still only just a single man. Baradar looked at his own men, examining them carefully for any sign of fright or unwillingness. He was satisfied by what he saw.

They were killers, both of them, and they'd carry out any order he gave.

That's good enough for me.

He spoke to them now, speaking in a voice designed to urge them on to great things.

"I don't know why the American man is fighting so ferociously on behalf of that cursed woman, brothers, but he is spitting on the noble efforts of our people all around this country who are even now taking the fight to America!"

"Yes, Commander!" both men exclaimed, their bright eyes avid to move in for the kill. They cared little for the woman who seemed to be the source of their leader's fixation but would gladly kill her if it meant throwing the man who was protecting her off his own game. They both knew doing so would make it easier to outflank and then kill him.

Hasan Baradar had been briefed – well, mostly briefed, though his own masters had been a little coy, no doubt for operational security -- about the mystery woman's "special" status. He knew he was supposed to treat the damnable female as a high-value target and that he was to capture, not kill, her if at all possible. However, his own rage had long ago caused him to obsess about her death at his hands, if only because of all the trouble she'd caused him, including the loss of nearly all his men.

*Besides, my masters didn't tell me I **couldn't** kill her, right? Or that I absolutely **HAD** to take her alive? No, they did not!*

Baradar had now settled once and for all the dispute in his head about what action to take concerning the woman.

He recalled that the men who ruled him had left the distinct impression that if they couldn't have the woman and whatever it was she knew then no one could. And so, they'd implicitly left it up to him to do what they knew he would do without hesitation, as he'd demonstrated throughout the warm Virginia summer's day and now evening.

Baradar considered his options. Neither he nor his men had any desire to stand toe-to-toe against the man who'd just melted away into the woods.

"Surprise is the key," he told the two men with him.

"Yes, brother," the taller one said. "We can tail him from a distance and then move in and strike just when his guard is down."

The shorter of his men, ratty of face but also as cunning as any flea-infested rodent who'd ever scuttled along the streets of his dusty little village, also nodded his head in agreement.

"That devil of a man doesn't know where we're at, brothers. If we cease firing, he'll think we've given up and will become incautious and careless in trying to link up with the woman, who he's obviously told to flee and then hide somewhere else."

Baradar stopped talking and then reached around to his back. He brought his anti-tank weapon to his front.

"Once we see the woman, I'll use this to turn them both into pink mist!" The Afghan caressed the rocket for a second and made sure his men could see he was serious about using it and ending both her and the man guarding her.

He could see that his men were excited.

"Yes!" they both exclaimed in unison. They could tell that their leader – who spoke so confidently about the end game to come – was eager to move back into action.

Hasan Baradar quickly turned on his heels and took off at a trot.

Both fighters looked at each other, each eager to help kill the man and the woman who'd bedeviled them so, and quickly set off after their master.

CHAPTER 18

ENDGAME I

ANNIE WAS JOGGING BESIDE THE WOMAN.

"Faster, ma'am! We have to move faster!"

The teenager could tell the older lady was clearly flagging. The short, sharp gasps coming from her showed she hadn't exercised so strenuously in years, if ever.

The woman also kept looking at her watch and pointing up ahead at Luke Ellis' home. His unpretentious single-story ranch house stood on a slightly elevated piece of ground, as if the ex-soldier had deliberately built it on a small hillock to make it more difficult for enemy invaders to storm it.

That's just too paranoid, even for me, isn't it?

She struggled to catch a breath. In and out, in and out. Each tortured gasp followed by another one. "Pick 'em up and put 'em down!" she recalled some of her security people exclaiming to each other as she watched them do laps on a large indoor track in the underground facility she'd lived in until today.

No sense going there now.

She didn't want to think about her two security men, who'd been friendly to her whenever possible, lying dead in a parking lot. Instead, she looked over to her right, where the girl trotted alongside, exhorting her to speed up.

God, how I hate that young lady right now. She hardly looks like she's breathing hard!

She swore to herself petulantly, knowing she was just jealous of the teenager's youth and strength.

If she knew what I know – all of it – she'd probably curl up in a ball on the floor and suck her thumb!

The woman followed this exclamation with several choice swear words, though she was careful not to speak aloud for fear of the men pursuing them finally capturing or killing her before she could get to her failsafe.

The thought of all of them – the man Ellis, the girl Annie and her brother Darren – lying on the ground sucking their thumbs gave her pleasure, even though she knew they were just trying to help her carry out a small, insignificant task called "Saving the World."

She sighed in resignation.

Okay, okay. Let's get this over with!

She tried to run a bit faster, though what she thought of as a "run" was more of a shambles of a trot at this point. Inside, she prayed her heart wouldn't give out until after she'd completed her task.

After that, a massive heart attack would be the least I deserve!

She looked at the teenage girl accompanying her. She was still easily loping alongside, urging her on to even greater athletic feats.

I really, really hate that girl!

As if the teen had heard her wailing, Annie urged the woman on once more. "Lady, I hate to keep nagging you, but we have to pick up the pace some more!"

The woman just rolled her eyes, looking up at the heavens for succor.

She's like some demented running coach trying to kill me before I can kill myself!

As if to defy the fitness gods she just knew were swarming around them, laughing uproariously at her ridiculous effort, the woman instead smiled at the teenager, raised her hand and gave her a thumbs-up sign.

That'll show you!

The woman's thought was more a grunt of pain than anything else, though she was desperate to prove to the girl that she could pull her own weight.

Annie gave her yet another thumbs-up, encouraged by the woman's effort.

Soon, we'll be safe! The girl was thrilled at the prospect. She had to admit.

"WOOF!"

The woman's cry was loud. What felt like a sledgehammer had just struck her in the back, and she stumbled forward as the air was forced from her lungs.

She lost the fight to stay on her feet and instead tumbled into blackness.

Seeing the thumbs-up and smile the woman had given her, Annie smiled broadly in return, white teeth visible in the night, and gave her a thumbs-up of her own.

Both of them were on the verge of laughing out loud.

It's going to be okay after all!

Annie's joyous mental shout fizzed and bubbled in the night air. They had several minutes to spare and Mister Ellis' home lay just ahead, not more than 100 yards away. Plus, the both of them knew the security code to get inside as well as where his radio and satellite phone were at.

After that, it's up to the lady to do her magic, isn't it?

Annie imagined the woman talking to her AI program and convincing it to stand down. She didn't know if Mister Ellis was even now trying to catch up with them or if he'd decided to sweep the surrounding area to make sure they were all still safe, but she knew one thing: There was no way he'd been killed getting them across that county road.

That's because he's just too strong!

In her eyes, Luke now ranked just below her father as the man she most respected and believed in. Someday, she hoped, her brother Darren would be there with those two men.

He certainly has the potential, doesn't he?

Thinking about her little brother for a second, the teenager glanced behind her to see where he was at.

There he is!

She was ecstatic that he was still hanging in, at only about 25 yards behind her and the mystery woman she was escorting. His shorter legs, though, were preventing him from quickly making up the distance she and the lady scientist had created when she'd forced the woman to pick up the pace. She also saw that his satchel was still banging against his side. She frowned a little at the sight.

I don't know why he hasn't just dumped that thing, because it looks like it's slowing him down.

Whatever.

She could worry about Darren – who, to be fair, was also carrying Deputy Holman's pistol while she ran with the black rifle Mister Ellis gave her -- once she and the woman made it to the house, which was now only about 50 yards away.

Annie fingered the rifle's trigger guard nervously. Personally, she didn't know what the guard was called. She only knew she wasn't supposed to put her finger on the trigger it was guarding until she was ready to shoot someone. Mister Ellis had made sure she understood that much after he'd loaded it with a fresh magazine and made it ready to fire.

She fervently prayed she wouldn't have to use the rifle – because she was no fighter -- but she also knew she'd do it if she had to. The day's events had shown her she had it in her, something that surprised her greatly.

Pausing for a second, the teenager remembered what the ex-soldier had shown her and told her about the rifle and how to use it before he'd moved off to attack those men lying in wait alongside the road. She also knew he had a very scary looking knife he'd pulled out of his backpack and then also attached to his waist just before he left them to make their headlong rush to his house.

The look on his face was vulpine, which was a word she'd learned in her AP English classes. It was also hungry, as if he was born to hunt other predators like himself, with some of them being more numerous or even stronger than him.

Nothing seems to frighten Mister Ellis, though you'd never know he was such a serious man unless he was forced to reveal it.

Like he'd had to do today.

A chill ran down her spine for just an instant as she thought about how quickly her ex-Army friend had gone from friendly to ferocious.

I'd sure hate for Mister Ellis to be mad at me!

Returning to the present, she looked over at the woman she was urging onward, ever onward toward their final destination.

The lady was flagging now, and badly. She could hear her painful gasps.

Time was a relentless, remorseless and cruel master, though. If they were to have a chance of avoiding Doomsday, she knew she had to be equally as cruel.

She looked once more at the woman and then spoke to her.

"Lady, I hate to keep nagging you, but we have to pick up the pace some more!" Her voice was filled with equal parts regret and steely determination. She was pleased to see the lady give her a thumbs-up in return.

Annie felt a bit sorry for her. She also knew the world was simply too vast for her to wrap her arms around and protect, though, and so she concentrated on the four people in her life that were now of the most importance to her: Her brother Darren, her mother and father – probably frantic with worry and trying desperately to find them both -- and Mister Ellis, of course. He'd saved her life more than once today and so she carefully filed away the memory of his many deeds on their behalf so that she could consider them later.

If we make it out of this mess alive, that is!

To take her mind off their predicament, she looked over at the woman again. Now she was huffing and puffing and clearly winded, but also didn't seem like she was going to give up despite her fatigue.

"There we go," Annie said encouragingly as the woman gave her another thumbs-up. It was easy to imagine them both about to cross the finish line together, hand and hand, arms raised in tandem to celebrate their joint victory. Gratified, she smiled broadly and returned her thumbs-up with a final one of her own as they moved ever nearer to the Mister Ellis' house.

All of a sudden, the woman grunted with a loud "WOOF!" and then pitched forward face first, collapsing unconscious – or worse yet, maybe even dead – to the ground.

Annie was stunned and didn't know what to do.

Watch out!

Without thinking, she dove into the nearby shadows in hopes the men doing all the shooting would miss her as she lay absolutely still. She struggled to keep from hyperventilating and forced herself to take stock of her situation. Maybe doing so would convince her heart to slow down while she focused on not crying out.

She looked down, this time very slowly. Mister Ellis had come through once again. He'd told her that the eye picked out sudden movements far more easily than it did slow, steady ones.

Come on, girl! You've got a rifle! Think!

She wasn't sure she had the skill or courage to use it well enough to matter, was her thought at the moment.

That's one strike against me.

As if in response, Mister Ellis' voice raced into her mind, supporting her and willing the fright away.

Buck up, Annie! You have a lot going for you, and not just because you have a rifle and those two men don't know you're here lying in the shadows.

The doppelgänger of her ex-Army friend had confirmed her suspicions.

They don't know I'm here!

Desperate hope made her feel just a bit more confident about her predicament, though the more rational part of her didn't know why and chose instead to war with her.

Oh, really, Mister Ellis? Just what am I supposed to do? I don't know how to fight, I'm not a soldier, and I'm SCARED!

Annie feared she was losing it just when she couldn't afford to.

Seriously, Annie?

Her adult friend's voice chided her.

You should take stock of your situation. Start with your clothing and just where you're lying on the ground.

She looked around, realizing she was at least partially concealed by the night and that whoever had shot the woman probably didn't know she was there. The woman was still lying motionless, not five feet away, though there didn't seem to be any blood on her, which was curious. Then another despairing thought crashed into her head.

They won't know about me until they get nearer, that is!

Annie fought for control. The desire to get up and run away – an act that would surely get her killed – was nearly overwhelming.

Mister Ellis spoke to her again.

Breathe, Annie. Concentrate on your strengths!

She took another slow but deep breath and slowly let it out, thinking.

Well, I've got this really serious-looking black rifle, don't I? Also, my clothes are a big help.

The teenager stepped outside herself and sized up what she was wearing.

I'm wearing black denim jeans, right? Plus, I've got my favorite black high-top canvas sneakers on my feet, right?

So far, so good, Annie, she heard Mister Ellis say to her.

Lastly, she was wearing a black t-shirt with the market's logo on it. On days when she worked there, Annie always wore clothes that would hide the dirt she was bound to pick up as she helped unload fresh produce or swept up or performed other tasks. Today's ensemble had been dark to begin with, she knew, but all the dirt and underbrush she'd fallen into had probably made everything even darker still.

If you count the dirt on my face and arms and the grass and twigs in my hair, I'm practically in Army camouflage, aren't I?

She could almost imagine Mister Ellis smiling and giving her a big thumbs up. And then she became terribly frightened yet again.

Please God, please God, please God let it hide me, the teenager prayed silently, willing the darkness to conceal her.

Focus, girl! Mister Ellis' voice was as cold as ice and twice as hard now. It was nearly time.

She could hear at least two men out there in the dark. They were celebrating in some weird language as they got closer to the woman lying motionless only a few feet away. Annie wasn't sure she could do anything to help the woman nor do much about the men, either. She also wasn't sure the shadows were concealing her thoroughly enough.

The moon seems awfully high in the sky, doesn't it? But...

But its glow lay only over the woman and definitely not on her. The shadows cast by the nearby trees were like a black curtain lying over her own hiding place, in fact. If she'd been just a foot closer to the lady scientist, though, she'd have probably been shot as well.

The teenager forced herself to go completely still once more. Those voices were nearer now, even more jubilant than before.

Movement suddenly caught her attention.

The woman's arm twitched slightly, undetectable to anyone but her.

Was she still alive?

The teen focused all of her senses, hoping to pick up any other sign of life.

There it is! She's still breathing!

Her breathing was shallow for sure, but it was there, nonetheless. Annie was stunned.

No way that lady's still alive! She was shot in the back!

Annie looked at the woman again, straining her eyes to pick out details.

There isn't any blood, is there?

She tried to make sense of the situation. There was a bullet hole in the back of the lady's light windbreaker jacket, standing out clearly as the moonlight danced across her back.

How could that be?

Okay. Who cares? She's alive!

Hope once again dared to rush in. There was still a chance for her brother and her parents to keep on living. If only she could remain silent and let the men get closer.

That's crazy, Annie!

The more rational part of her mind was speaking to her, making its feelings clear about the whole debacle.

You have to run, girl!

Annie could almost imagine her earlier self, the 17-year-old teenager headed to the University of Virginia this coming weekend. This was the version of Annie that existed before the day had exploded so violently.

That one's arms were crossed and she was staring intently at the New Annie, as if the logic of running away and hiding rather than fighting was so clearly self-evident only a fool could fail to see the truth of it all.

Get out of my mind, Old Annie!

It was clear what she had to do: Stay and protect the woman long enough so that she could get into Mister Ellis' house.

Crying, Old Annie ran off to hide on her own.

Good riddance!

Returning to the real world, Annie once again listened intently to the night.

The men were now conversing normally as they approached. The fact they'd just shot a woman in the back didn't even seem to matter to them.

That's because they think she's the only one around!

She didn't know where her brother was at, but she hoped he'd had the good sense to run away and hide in the woods and not come out until after it was over.

Please, God. Help me with this!

Taking in a low, slow breath, she slowly put her finger on the rifle's safety to make sure it wasn't engaged. Mister Ellis had shown her just where it was and what it did. Satisfied her rifle was ready to go, she steeled herself for what was to come.

Her right hand moved very slightly, this time making sure her index finger was on the trigger. She intended to shoot those two men if she could and was slightly exhilarated yet also immensely depressed at the thought, mainly because of what taking such action would mean to her personally. She also desperately missed her brother and parents and all she'd known and all she'd been until just a few hours ago. A depressing thought intruded for just a second.

Maybe we'll all meet again someday.

Suddenly, she was filled with a terrible sadness at the fact she might be leaving behind everything she knew and loved. Now on the razor's edge, she froze, half-expecting the men approaching her position to spot her and kill her before she could do anything about it.

A small thrill of relief made her scalp tingle just slightly.

The men hadn't seen her and were instead moving up to the woman, all while still animatedly talking to each other.

Probably celebrating their great victory in shooting a poor, defense-less woman in the back!

Her eyes hardened and her lower lip stopped quivering. An icy calm settled over her as she slowly moved the rifle slightly to improve her firing position.

Take a breath in and then let it out slowly, Annie, she heard Mister Ellis say. *You can do this!* His voice was big and strong and confident.

The teen breathed in, then let her breath out slowly, her index finger pressing slowly on the trigger.

You should be a little surprised when the rifle fires, she heard her ex-Army friend remark, like they were both on one of those rifle ranges her brother and father had told her about while they were watching that Tom Cruise movie about some nomadic detective named Jack.

Don't worry, Mister Ellis continued, *there's barely any kick – any recoil – when these rifles fire. Just shoot, then point it at the bad guys again and keep shooting at them until they fall down or run away.*

Luke had, of course, left out the part about getting shot at in return, and there wasn't time to impress on Annie the need to shoot and then move, but desperation had driven him to send the three of them – the woman, the girl, her little brother – on while he dealt with the men by the road and then tried to catch up. There was no time to hide the trio in the thick underbrush and then go back and retrieve them, he'd known.

Waiting there in the dark and lying as still as she could – hoping her heart wouldn't explode from anxiety and an overdose of adrenaline – Annie knew there was nothing any of them could do about it now.

For one, Deputy Holman had already done what he could to delay the bad men chasing them. Sadly, he was probably lying dead somewhere back in the woods through which they'd fled. She paused to reflect on what had gone on before Mister Ellis had set off into the night to kill still more of the men chasing them. They had all known how important it was that the lady scientist survive.

Finally, Annie accepted what had to be.

Time now slowed down greatly for her. Everything began to move in slow motion.

Thinking back and reviewing what had gone on back at the road, she realized she'd been so deep in concentration -- trying to memorize everything Mister Ellis had told her about the rifle he'd given her – she hadn't noticed he'd removed the camouflaged vest he was wearing and then put it on the woman they were guarding.

Now that she thought about it, she could even remember the ex-soldier cinching it up and adjusting it to fit snugly over the part of the woman's chest where her heart lay as well as over the upper part of her back.

"Put your jacket back on, ma'am," Annie now recalled him telling the woman. All the better to conceal the fact she was wearing his vest.

Lying there in the dark, counting down the seconds and awaiting her fate, she thought about the incident. Earlier in the day, during the first part of their flight through the woods, she recalled Mister Ellis telling her his vest was able to stop the kinds of bullets the men chasing them were using. She now knew it had saved his life at least once during their desperate run through the forest, too, back at the ambush they'd nearly walked into.

Mister Ellis saved us there, too, and so did Deputy Holman.

Annie heard her voice rattling around in her head while she counted down the seconds until the men got close enough.

At least I've solved that little mystery, haven't I? She now knew why a woman with a bullet hole in the back of her jacket – who she was trying so desperately to protect -- was still among the living.

Enough!

She was trying to concentrate, she really was, but it was so hard. And everything was moving so slowly!

In her mind, she saw herself reaching out and hugging her mom and dad and little brother.

"Goodbye," Annie said to them as she continued to slowly press her finger against the M4's trigger.

She was indeed surprised when the rifle went off. The bad man she shot was even more surprised, though.

"BLAM!"

She didn't have any earplugs, and the M4's report was deafening.

The man went down in a heap, clutching his chest and kicking his legs.

For a brief, shining moment, he stopped kicking and went still.

Please, God. Let him be dead!

He began to sit up.

Wave after wave of disappointment rolled over her.

Oh, God!

He was wearing body armor as well.

She fired at the air over the man's head, trying to lower her rifle's muzzle enough to draw a bead on him and put him down for good.

It wasn't to be.

The man threw himself back down, rolled over on his belly, and began quickly low crawling out of her line of sight, rifle in hand.

She wondered briefly where the other man with him had gone but only up until a bullet slammed into the ground in front of her, kicking up a fountain of dirt. It had come from the one she'd shot.

Now she rolled quickly to her left, both out of a sense of pain and fear as well as out of instinct as she fought to avoid the return fire sent her way. She even remembered to raise her black rifle again and fire once she'd repositioned herself.

It was clear, though, that at least one of the men would soon find her, if only from the flashes coming from the end of her rifle's barrel. Then they'd put her down for good. A tsunami of regret passed over her as she reconciled herself to her fate.

She could hear and see herself still firing her black rifle, of course, but the deepest part of her realized she was nearly done. She was trying hard but knew it was pitifully small action on her part. She just wasn't a soldier and her lack of experience had doomed both her and the woman. Once those evil men realized the lady scientist was still alive, they'd also quickly do her in as well.

Well, you tried, Annie, the teen thought she could hear Mister Ellis say. His voice was bright and filled with pride for her. *I'd be proud to have you kicking down doors with me anytime,* he continued. *You're a real hero in my eyes!*

She saw her friend snap off a crisp salute and stand motionlessly, waiting for the final act to play itself out. Despite the chaos erupting all around her, Annie felt a sense of peace and calm settle over her as

Mister Ellis hovered there, willing her to remain stoic in the face of what was to come.

Keep firing while you're waiting, Annie, he gently reminded her. *No sense going down with rounds still in your magazine, right? Besides, you never know what could happen!*

The big, always friendly, man – her friend even unto death – winked at her and smiled, as if he were waiting for something big to happen.

Now I'm just imagining things!

She fired her rifle again and again.

"BLAM! BLAM!"

If Mister Ellis was still alive, he wasn't near her, that was for sure. Shocked, she realized that she now had few regrets about what she was doing. In fact, she only regretted her failure to execute it well enough to matter.

Well, that's worth something, isn't it?

From somewhere, Annie thought she could hear a man's voice – deep and resonant and filled with good cheer, crazily enough -- respond.

It sure is!

Not possible! The only men out there in the dark right now were the ones trying to kill her.

Suddenly, it was quiet in front of her.

The teen ceased firing in response, afraid to move for fear of giving her new position away, the one she'd rolled into. The man shooting at her had stopped, too, though she couldn't figure out why. She could also hear the other man – the one she hadn't been able to shoot – moving around in the brush off to her left. For some reason, he'd dropped his rifle and hadn't waited around to retrieve it as Annie kept shooting at him.

Score one for the girl from Lucketts!

The gods of fortune looked down on her just then and decided to intervene. Her kind of bravery was exceedingly rare and it deserved a reward. To be sure, she would eventually enter Valhalla, home to warriors, but at a time far, far in her future.

As one, they exerted their will.

"Now," the night whispered.

"POP! POP! POP! POP!"

The sound of Luke's suppressed AR-15 echoed in the air.

"YES!" Annie shouted and smiled from ear to ear. She'd always known the man who'd become her best friend, as well as guardian angel, was simply incapable of dying!

Luke exploded out of the night, firing his weapon and moving quickly toward the semiconscious woman – who by now had flopped over on her back and was weakly kicking her legs. In her pain and confusion, she was trying to sit up.

"Lay down, ma'am!" His shout echoed through the night. He hated making any noise, but there was nothing he could do about that right now. The woman had to lay flat and stay out of the way.

The gods dispensed one more gift. The mystery woman fell backwards and stopped thrashing around. Maybe she'd passed out. Luke didn't know and didn't care. She was still again and that was what counted.

On to other more serious problems, all of which he had to solve in the next second.

There were at least two men moving around in the dark and they wanted to kill Annie as well as the lady scientist. He wasn't about to allow them to, though, and instantly sized up the new tactical situation.

Sweeping his rifle around, he peered intently through his night vision scope and rapidly plotted out the scene. Satisfied, he quickly and silently moved to a new position before the man with the M4 could put a hole in him.

Well, I'm trying to put one in him, too, Luke thought to himself as he focused on what he'd do. "Two to the chest, face gets the rest" was one of his more frequent mantras.

His mind was moving at lightspeed and he quickly replayed the moment he'd finally closed the distance between himself and the men who'd shot the woman in the back. Fortunately, the round had struck squarely in the center of his rig's rear Level IV plate and trauma pad. He also took great pleasure in seeing just how magnificently little Annie had performed.

She's a cool customer!

He'd arrived on scene, moving as swiftly and silently as a jungle cat about to fall on its prey, there to see the teenager desperately fighting off a pair of terrorist killers.

The professional side of him noted approvingly that she was cycling her weapon at a constant rate, firing only a single shot at a time which – given her total lack of experience – was good for her. It would stretch out the single magazine he knew she had in her weapon and also give him time to close with their enemy. He could see that one of the men – probably the one whose rifle was still lying in the grass and dirt near the woman, who by now was in a semiconscious state -- was trying to sneak up on her from her left flank.

The other terrorist, after being peppered by panic fire from the girl, had scrambled into a low depression in the ground, behind which he was firing an occasional round to take her attention off his partner. Luke didn't know if that man had a pistol or a knife or even both. He only knew they meant to close in and then surprise the girl, killing first her and then the woman she was guarding.

Enough is enough!

The thought of the men killing the two females he'd been protecting threatened to drop a red curtain of rage over his eyes. Shaking his head, he breathed in deeply and forced himself to concentrate on his immediate task. He'd already flipped his NODs up and out of the way. The wet work he was about to do needed his night vision optic and his rifle more than anything else.

Annie stopped firing, perhaps in an effort to make sense of the movement in the night she suspected was occurring around her.

Time!

Luke moved rapidly to close the distance between himself and Annie and the woman that absolutely had to survive this firefight. Bursting from the dark, he fired his carbine at the spot where he knew the armed terrorist had sought cover as well as in the general direction of his partner, the one moving to outflank the girl on her left side.

So far so good.

He kept shooting and moving, working to suppress return fire and pinpoint where the two killers had gone to ground.

Up ahead in the dark, he heard a loud "YES!" escape from Annie.

Wonder of wonders!

After seeing him move in, the girl snuggled her rifle up to her shoulder again, making it clear from her position that she was looking for targets of opportunity to help him in his work. He shook his head briefly in admiration.

She's a player, bro!

Neither Annie nor Luke knew it, but she was down to a single round. With her adrenaline flowing and still being inexperienced, she wasn't able to tell from the weight of her carbine that she was so low on ammunition.

The gods knew it wouldn't matter in the end.

The girl had ably played her part in the great game. Now it was time for others to play theirs.

There!

Luke dropped to one knee. He'd managed to put himself between the females and the two killers moving around in the dark and so he took care to stay in the shadows. He didn't know if they had night vision, or at least a night vision scope on the M4 one of them still carried, but he didn't intend to give them an easy target even if they did.

Slowly lowering himself to the ground, he took extreme care to avoid sudden movements while he peered carefully through his weapon's optic. He was seeking his prey.

Movement! Direct front!

It was the terrorist with the rifle.

He had Annie in his sights!

He was snapped in and in the zone and his AR-15 was already snuggled up to his shoulder before he fired it. An intense scream followed, rewarding his quick action with a thud that sounded just like a sack of potatoes falling off the back of a produce truck. Sensing he once again had the initiative, he leaped to his feet and fired several more rounds off and to his left to keep the other terrorist from getting any closer to the girl and then he charged forward, firing into the ground ahead of him.

Very fleet of foot, Luke managed to close the distance between himself and his fallen foe in an instant.

The man was lying on his back, lifeless eyes clouded over and unable to reflect back what little moonlight there was. A bank of clouds – long and languorous in the night sky – had greatly dulled the moon's glow. He didn't have time to consider where it had suddenly come from, only that he intended to keep using it to his advantage.

Still moving rapidly, he brought his carbine up once more and looked through its scope in an attempt to find the other man.

He was chilled by what he saw.

The terrorist was now no more than five feet from Annie and advancing quickly toward her, knife in hand. His shout echoed like thunder.

"ANNIE! ON YOUR LEFT!"

She reacted almost instantly and tried to swing her rifle around and up in an effort to shoot the man who was trying to kill her.

Luke saw her tactic wasn't going to work and despaired briefly.

The man kicked her rifle away and tried to fall in on her. She quickly rolled to her right over and over again. Both of them were on the ground, the man scuttling after her, knife high in hand as he stabbed at the spot where she'd been just an instant before.

Luke tried to sight in on the killer who was intent on ending the teenager's life.

I'll hit her, too, if I fire at him!

Launching himself, he ran forward in hopes of reaching the terrorist before he could complete his evil deed.

He knew he was going to be too late.

Suddenly, Annie screamed.

"GET OFF ME!"

The man had her arms pinned to the ground with his knees and was raising his knife to shoulder height before he stabbed her to death.

Ellis knew that even if he could close in and shoot the man dead, the girl also wouldn't survive the attack.

He had to try, though, and ran flat-out toward the battling duo, throwing himself into the air in a last desperate attempt to reach the killer in time.

I just can't get to her!

Luke's heart filled with sorrow at what was about to happen.

A shot rang out. The man violently fell backwards, lifeless on the cold, hard ground.

He'd been shot right between the eyes.

Darren had finally managed to get close to his sister though he knew he wouldn't arrive at her side in time to help fight off the man moving in on her from the left. Frantically calculating angles, the boy was sick with dread.

I'm not going to make it!

Looking down at the big pistol he carried in both hands, he knew what he'd have to do.

The boy steeled himself to fire, not sure if he'd be able to or not. He thought of losing his sister to the bad man stalking her, though, and was filled with a strength and purpose he never knew he possessed. Running now, he raced to get close enough to the man to make sure he would hit him.

Before the moonlight had become so dull, he'd also seen Annie momentarily fend off the two bad men with her own rifle. It was an act of bravery that made his eyes practically drop out of his head. For sure, Mister Ellis had given her a few tips about how to use that rifle before he left to find the men waiting to attack them, but Darren had never in a million years figured his sister had it in her.

He admitted he didn't think he had it in him, either, yet here he was.

Almost there!

Mister Ellis, who'd moved in behind him, was shouting a warning to his sister.

"ANNIE! ON YOUR LEFT!"

At the same moment, the man leaped at her. She managed to roll away from him in barely enough time to avoid being gutted by his blade. And then she kept rolling as the man stabbed at her again and again. Each time, she barely avoided the downward slash of his wicked-looking knife.

"It's not enough!" Darren shouted to the night as he raced to get to Annie. She was fighting for her life, but with each roll she executed the man was closing the distance.

Now, he was on top of her!

They're just too close to each other for Mister Ellis to shoot him!

In the corner of his eye, he saw the ex-Army man desperately racing to get to his sister.

"Not enough time!" the boy shouted, this time to the ex-soldier. He could see in the man's eyes that he already knew it.

This is it! Annie's about to die!

He pulled up short, about 10 feet away from his sister and the man trying to stab her to death.

Sucking in a breath, he raised the pistol up to shoulder height and quickly sighted down the handgun's slide, putting the little dot at the front of it squarely on the killer's forehead. Saying a silent prayer and desperate to save his sister – the one who'd been so much a part of his young life -- he pressed the trigger.

"BLAM!"

Alec Holman's Glock was smooth, really smooth. He'd had the department armorer and gunsmith work it over, in fact, until both its action and trigger pull were like hot butter poured over popcorn. In the deputy sheriff's hands, it was like a magic weapon, even.

In a scared little boy's hands – one who was desperate to save his sister's life -- the outstanding quality of the pistol, with never a hitch or catch when it fired, was just enough to matter, and it helped save the life of a 17-year-old girl of uncommon valor and bravery.

Silence mingled in the night air alongside the smell of bullet propellant. Darren opened his eyes, afraid he'd see his sister dead, killed by the man who'd been trying to stab her.

Doubt filled his mind just then.

Maybe I was just too late.

He couldn't believe it.

Annie's alive!

There she was, lying on the ground in front of him and breathing heavily. Perhaps she couldn't believe the miracle of her survival after her crazed attacker's knife assault.

Relief flooded into him, followed by realization of what he'd just done. He'd just taken the life of another human being, evil though the man was.

Does that make me just as bad?

Fighting and shooting and killing in real life wasn't anything like he'd seen in all the war and action movies he'd watched.

Annie's fine now, and that's all that matters, right?

Darren thought he could hear a deeply resonant voice somewhere off in the distance reply to his question.

It sure is, son. It sure is.

Annie forced herself to calm down and take deep breaths. She really couldn't believe she'd somehow managed to avoid being stabbed to death, but they still had to prevent the end of everything and they didn't have much time left in which to do it.

Sitting up, she looked around momentarily. Off to her side, the woman she'd helped defend was trying to stagger to her feet and not doing a very good job of it. She was also trying to reach around to her back with her left arm, perhaps in search of a bullet wound.

That hit to her body armor must have really hurt, Annie surmised before quickly resuming her personal review of what had just happened. She looked around for a second and her eyes landed on the man now lying dead at her feet.

She couldn't help but gasp at what she saw.

Limp as a ragdoll, the terrorist was sprawled awkwardly on his back with one leg bent in an unnatural position behind him, as if all the life within had suddenly escaped, taking with it every part of his humanity. She also saw the bullet wound in his forehead, its edges glistening wetly in the ever-brightening light cast by the moon now that the clouds overhead were nearly gone.

Mister Ellis must have managed to shoot him.

She couldn't see how, though.

The terrorist had been right on top of her practically the entire time and there couldn't have been enough room between them for Mister Ellis to safely get a shot off without hitting her, too.

"No way," she said out loud, still confused.

Maybe he'd gotten an extremely lucky shot off?

Uh-uh. The angles just weren't right.

Well, then, who saved my life?

CHAPTER 19
ENDGAME II

Pondering on events, Annie looked around, still shaking from the thought of having come so close to death so many times over the last few hours. Just then, she spotted a slight movement nearby and her eyes locked in on it, partly fearful that yet another terrorist was going to attack.

She just as quickly relaxed and heaved a sigh of relief.

Her little brother stood silently about 10 feet away, eyes as dark and haunted as the night surrounding them.

"Darren!" She was thrilled to see that her little brother was safe and sound. "Come here!"

She opened her arms wide, beckoning to him. The boy remained firmly planted to the ground as if he'd been superglued there, not moving and not saying a word.

He just stared.

The look on her little brother's face was slightly unnerving, to be honest.

What's wrong with Darren? Something's eating at him.

Mister Ellis moved up behind him. He also had a solemn look on his face, and she saw him reach down slightly and then gently take something from her brother's right hand.

That's Deputy Holman's pistol.

She sucked in her breath just then, swamped by the realization of what had to have happened.

"Oh, Darren!"

She was, of course, unbelievably relieved that he'd saved her yet also deeply saddened by the price he'd had to pay to do it. Mister Ellis just nodded his head and moved off to take care of the lady scientist. They had a bare few minutes left, and he had to get her into his home right away.

Annie knew the world would have to wait for just a moment, though. Her little brother needed her. The 10 feet separating them disappeared in an instant and before she knew it she had him in a fierce hug.

"Thank you for saving me," she whispered, hugging him even tighter. Annie rested her chin on the top of his head, rocking him gently from side to side.

Darren gave no reply or acknowledgment.

She was afraid that he might have suffered much more mental trauma than she could ever wash away with sisterly love and endless hugs and gratitude, but she knew she had to try for her brother's sake. At the moment, there was no other world than the one existing between the two of them, big sister and little brother. They were both fighters and now they needed each other, as was right between all siblings confronting great stresses together.

"Come back, Darren," Annie whispered into his ear. "I need you." She exerted all her inner strength, willing his return to the here and now.

After a minute, her efforts paid off.

"I'm here, Annie," she heard her little brother say. His voice was muffled by her bear hug. "OOF! You're smothering me!"

Relief washed over her and she quickly released her grip on him.

"Darren!' she exclaimed in a voice filled with pleasure. "You saved my life!" Annie made as if to snatch her little brother up in yet another bear hug.

The boy deftly leaped backward.

"Okay, okay, don't get all weepy about it!"

They both laughed softly. Then they remembered just why they were here in Mister Ellis' yard. Their exclamation was simultaneous.

"We're running out of time!"

Annie quickly looked around while her brother picked up his satchel once again. They raced over to the big ex-soldier who, after all they'd been through, was now their best friend.

"I'm fine, Mister Ellis!" the woman gasped. "Put me down. I can make it now. We don't have much time!"

Luke set the lady scientist down on her feet. He'd picked her up from the ground as if she were a feather, and now he was trying to rush her into his home. Sizing her up momentarily, he could also see that she'd already regained much of her equilibrium or was at least pretending that was the case. Ellis was sure, though, that the bruising over her spine, beneath the body armor he'd given her, was seriously painful.

You don't take a hit like that and not feel like death warmed over!

"Are you sure, ma'am?" Only 50 yards separated the two of them from his home.

"I'm fine, I'm fine."

The mystery woman waved her hand away as she started walking, her mind focused on recalling the phrase sequence and number string she'd have to recite into a radio or phone – whichever one was more readily at hand – so that she could deactivate her failsafe.

"Okay, then," Ellis said to her, though he didn't sound all that confident.

She spared a second to look behind her. The man, the boy and the teenage girl were trailing about five feet behind. She was surprised at the tone of her voice as she spoke.

"Well, come on!" she told them all. "We don't have much time!"

At that, she turned back around and began a quick march toward the house once more.

The first hint of an idea also began to form in her mind.

It was a way to ensure nothing could be done with her creation, or the one her beloved Jay had made, and also a means of escaping the prison she'd erected for herself over the years.

It just might work, too.

She was sure now of what she'd do once she'd made things right. The urgent need to get to the man Ellis' communications equipment propelled her forward, giving her strength she didn't know she had. The pain in her back where she'd been shot by one of the now-dead terrorists – apparently, the last of the men who'd been after her all day (and she wondered why they were now just trying to kill rather than capture her) – hardly seemed to be a big deal, even. The body armor the man Ellis put on her had indeed done its job, and the fact she was still alive exhilarated her.

For a fact, she felt as light as air.

"We're nearly there, people." The woman didn't bother turning around to address them this time.

"KERRRR-WHAMMMMM!"

Luke Ellis' home exploded in a huge fireball.

CHAPTER 20
BARADAR

"HAH!"

Hasan Baradar exulted as he let his now-expended $AT4$ antitank weapon fall to the ground.

Still cackling with glee, he bent down and picked up his M4 and took off at a run to close the distance between himself and the people he'd just killed. He desperately needed to see their bodies.

The terror leader knew he hadn't directly hit that infernal woman and the man guarding her, but it didn't matter. The right kind of $AT4$ could, of course, function as an antipersonnel weapon but the ordnance in his wasn't that kind. Still, he was sure the disposable weapon's explosive projectile had blown up the house the four people were trying to use as cover. The shrapnel created by the blast was more than enough to flatten them all.

Probably, a propane tank or natural gas lines near the house ignited and then exploded, too, the terror leader thought to himself in Pashto as he ran toward the devastation he'd caused. Then he shouted at the night.

"I might have missed them directly, but they still died!"

Baradar capered a bit at that last exclamation.

The blunt-force nature of the AT4 was precisely why he liked it so much. You didn't have to have great aim when it came to buildings and people. As in horseshoes – a game he normally had no use for -- and hand grenades, you only had to be close.

Running toward the destroyed house, he planned to put a bullet in the head of each one of the four people he'd just killed. He also freely admitted to himself that the passions of the moment had clearly affected his aim, but so what? The God-cursed woman and the man trying to protect her had to have died in the fireball. That the boy and the teenage girl had also perished was icing on the cake, so to speak. They were Americans, after all, and their fates were already written in the Book: They were to die at his hands.

Baradar had never known such satisfaction. He now approached the scene of the havoc he'd wreaked.

Where is the woman?

She wasn't in front of him and he didn't see her lying on the ground. He didn't see anyone lying on the ground, in fact.

He quickly brought his M4 up and peered intently through its optic, seeking them out.

The woman must have crawled into the dark underbrush.

He was certain on that point. He began to look for a blood trail. He was sure she was dying of her mortal wounds. He dearly wanted to help her along, too.

Hasan Baradar needed certainty, though. Then he could leave America – which was unworthy of any mercy -- and return to his own country. His Taliban superiors would welcome him like a conquering hero.

The heat from the flames he'd brought to life washed over him in waves, giving him added satisfaction as he continued searching.

"Where are you?" he exclaimed loudly. "Show yourself, woman!"

"She's not here," Luke Ellis whispered into his ear. His voice was absolutely merciless and as cold as the grave.

Baradar tried to swing around so that he could shoot the man with his M4.

He didn't succeed.

A muscular forearm suddenly wrapped itself around his throat and jerked him backwards, lifting him up off his feet. His legs flailed uselessly as he tried to gain some sort of purchase so that he could fight back. The terror leader was tall for an Afghan, sure enough, but the man holding him in a death grip and choking the life out of him was at least 4 inches taller as well as heavier by 60 pounds.

The advantages of height and weight were Baradar's doom.

"I have a gift for you," the man choking him said in more-than-adequate Pashto.

The terror leader was at a loss.

Where did he learn to speak my language? He was fighting against oxygen deprivation and increasingly cloudy vision.

Then it became clear.

Of course. In Afghanistan.

A black curtain descended over his eyes and his last weak and pitiful attempt to free himself was just that: Weak and pitiful.

Regret that he hadn't killed more Americans flooded into him, though it barely had time to take form.

Suddenly, he felt a white-hot lance of pain at the back of his neck. The last still-conscious part of his brain told him what was going to happen next. A thunderbolt of light and heat and pure agony shot through his neck and up into his skull. It had been created by an exquisitely made and deadly serious knife.

He wanted to scream, but the demonically strong man holding him up in the air had slammed his hand firmly over his nose and mouth, and so he couldn't make any sound at all.

His eyes rolled up into his head just then, and all thought ceased.

Hasan Baradar fell headlong into the Abyss.

CHAPTER 21
COUNTDOWN

Luke dropped the dead terrorist to the ground, letting him fall in a lifeless heap. He felt neither satisfaction at killing him nor anger at what the man had done and had once been. He needed to die and Ellis meant to be the cause of his death, simple as that.

Looking down, he could see that his Yarborough knife – given only to graduates of the Army's Special Forces 'Q' course and named after William P. Yarborough, "the Father of Modern Green Berets" – was still in his hand. He quickly wiped the terrorist's blood from it using his pant leg and then stowed it in the sheath attached to the belt on his waist.

Inhaling deeply, he looked to his right.

Annie and her brother Darren were tending to the woman. She was badly injured, with a right leg that looked as inky black as the night sky. The remnants of her pant leg were soaked in blood, and it was obvious a part of her femoral artery had been at least partially torn, because there was so much blood.

After his house had been destroyed, and prior to the terrorist's arrival, he'd done what he could for her, risking plucking out a nasty chunk of very sharp metal from her leg, near where the major artery lay, in hopes of preventing continued blood loss.

Her blood had rushed out in a big, scary glob after he'd done it, but there'd been no arterial spray, which he'd feared. He wasn't a Special Forces medic, but he'd had enough first aid and life support training from the medics that he figured it was her superficial femoral artery, and not the deep aspect of it, that had been hit. If it had indeed been the deeper part, she'd already be dead, he knew.

Satisfied so far, Luke rifled around in his daypack once more and then took out two packets of rapid clotting powder and poured them into her wound. After that, he wrapped it in clotting gauze before he applied a Special Operations Forces tourniquet to her upper thigh above the wounded area, to buy her some time.

"She might not bleed out quickly now," he told Darren and Annie after making sure the woman couldn't hear them, "but that blood is still leaking out of her artery even so and we've got to get her some medical help fast." He looked down at his big black watch, its illuminated digital face counting down to Doomsday, and tapped it to emphasize his point to the girl and her brother.

They looked at him in stricken silence.

It was almost time to dance with Mister Terrorist, who was out there in the dark and making his way toward them. Ellis looked at the two young people, who'd both showed incredible bravery and courage just a few minutes ago.

"Go on, now," he told them both before he looked at the teenage girl. "Make sure she's comfortable and give her a little water while she waits," he said in a near whisper. "I don't know how long she has."

"Yes, Mister Ellis." Annie tried hard to keep from crying. She didn't know it was often a common reaction among troops after prolonged combat and violence, which was something she'd now experienced for herself.

Luke saw it all, of course, and he wanted to comfort her, but he had one more thing to do before he could completely devote himself to the woman as well as to Annie and Darren.

He had to make sure they were safe, and that meant dealing with the bad guy who thought he now had the upper hand.

Yeah, well... we'll see about that.

Ellis melted into the dark night and then dealt with the terrorist. On reflection, he found that it had turned out to be easier than he'd expected. Some small part of him was actually disappointed at how it had gone down, in fact.

Still, there's no such thing as a fair fight, now is there?

The man – now lying dead at his feet – was a fool and had rushed in expecting to find all of them already dead.

The former Delta Force man had been happy to disabuse him of that notion.

Luke felt slightly deflated, though. What was the point?

The point is, you've got to keep going no matter what, he heard a voice in his head remonstrate, as if it were talking to a moron. It sounded a bit like one of his old Special Forces assistant detachment commanders. The man had been a crusty old warrant officer back when he'd known him and no one on his Operational Detachment Alpha – or ODA -- team or even over in Delta could ever say with any certainty just what his true age actually was. They'd all agreed, though: He knew what he was talking about. The man was "snapped in," in other words.

Luke looked at his watch again. Five minutes to go and then they were done. No mulligans, no do-overs, no consolation drawings for second place, no nothing. *END OF STORY.*

That's what the woman had said and had even briefly shown him about the super virus she'd made -- to the limited extent she'd been able to, of course. But just from what he'd glimpsed and understood, he knew they were all done like dinner in a few minutes.

Luke breathed deeply and took stock of their situation.

"We have no radio or phone," he said aloud.

That was Point One.

"Even if we did, I'm not sure our lady scientist will last long enough to make it through her call, meaning we're all done for soon."

That was Point Two.

Ellis shook his head.

"Stop it!" His exclamation pierced the increasingly cool night air.

The teen girl and her brother exchanged looks at his remark and then sat silently, waiting. He was Mister Ellis and he was unbeatable, right?

Luke walked over to Annie, Darren and the woman. She was worse for the wear at this point. Kneeling down, he looked into her eyes.

She was lying on the ground and her head was in Annie's lap. Her brother Darren had taken possession of his ever-present daypack and placed it under her feet to elevate them and keep blood flowing to her heart and brain. The Delta Force veteran knew that if the woman's femoral artery had been completely severed, she'd have already bled out, so he did have some small hope for her still.

"How you feeling, ma'am?"

He gently placed two of his fingers against the carotid artery on her neck and counted the rise and fall of her chest as she breathed. Her pulse was weak and thready and it sped up as her heart fought to pump a decreasing amount of oxygenated blood to her vital organs, most especially her brain.

Ellis knew she'd likely go into shock and then lose consciousness in a bit if nothing else changed. The thought deeply saddened him. He'd come to like this mystery woman. She obviously wasn't an evil person or even just a plain old bad one.

No, she was just someone who'd made a galactically bad mistake in the past and was now trying to fix it.

He smiled at her, hoping to lift her spirits. It was the least he could do.

"I'm fine, Mister Ellis," the woman replied, her voice just as wan and diminished as her appearance. She knew what lay in store for her now.

"I tried to make it right, didn't I?"

"You sure did, ma'am. I can't fault you for the effort, now can I?" Luke's voice was a bit brighter than the occasion called for, but so what?

Annie and Darren nodded at the big ex-Army man's remark to the woman they were trying to comfort. The girl took a bottle of water, poured some of the liquid over a bandana Luke had given her and then cleaned the dirt off her forehead and cheeks. Her skin felt cold and clammy.

Both young people remained silent. What more could they say?

Inside, Ellis raged at the unfairness he saw all around him.

He only had a small IFAK or "Individual First Aid Kit" in addition to his tourniquets. It wasn't enough, though, because the woman needed an intravenous to replace the blood volume she was losing. He didn't know her blood type or the kids' and he didn't have time for that stuff anyway, even if he had IV solutions or a way to safely give her whole blood or plasma. She needed immediate top-level medical intervention from a Special Forces-trained medic, at minimum.

Luke wasn't sure he'd ever been in a tougher situation, though he'd seen more than his fair share of life-or-death events during his Army career. After all, a human extinction level event was likely to occur if this woman couldn't contact her failsafe in the next few minutes and try as he might, he couldn't recall ever having to deal with that particular mission set before.

Back to reality, Luke.

The clock was ticking. That was now Point Three.

Ellis thought back to just a couple of hours ago. It was after he'd convinced her to be honest with him. He chuckled briefly. In her own weird way, the woman had actually been trying to reassure him.

"Even if we fail, it might not all fall apart for a couple of weeks or even a couple of months, so we've got that going for us," she'd told him matter-of-factly.

"Why so, ma'am?"

Luke had been listening to her speak as they maneuvered through the woods. He was looking for any angle he could turn to their advantage as they struggled to survive.

"It all depends on the system my best friend – who was also one of the world's most brilliant computer scientists -- created to keep me from being murdered by my own government, and whether it still has access to a stock of the virus I created or if it just has my data."

"You don't know if any of your super bug survived, then?" Ellis was no scientist.

"It's not a bug. It's nothing that's ever existed in nature anywhere, and after all these years I just don't know what my system still has." Her voice was firm on that point. "Anyway, my friend Jay designed it to compartmentalize and keep from me certain information. That was for my own protection," she quickly added.

"Give me a worst-case scenario, then." Luke needed to know. The curiosity was too much.

"If it does have access to my virus, then we're all dead in a couple weeks. If it no longer has any stock stashed away somewhere, then it depends on how quickly someone can take all my data, once my program releases it, and then recreate it. That would probably take a couple of months, at which point some lunatic nation will, of course, fail to contain it – or even deliberately release it -- at which point it's in the wild, at which point we can all start dying."

Satisfied with her summation, the mystery woman shut up once again. Looking back, Luke recalled being momentarily struck dumb, and for a good reason.

Time check.

Luke looked at his watch again.

Three minutes to go.

He walked over to the woman and sat down beside her.

"Ma'am, there's got to be something we can do." Luke kept all fear out of his voice and even reached down and took the woman's right hand in his. Her skin was cold.

Annie and Darren leaned in slightly to listen to the two adults.

The lady scientist opened her eyes and looked to her right at the big man who'd done everything he could to get her to a radio or a phone.

"I don't know, Mister Ellis," she said to him. She was tired and felt like she wanted to go to sleep for a long, long time, if not forever. "Do you know where any other radios are at?" She didn't really expect the man to answer in the affirmative and she was too weak to look at her own watch.

"How long now?"

"About two minutes, ma'am. What else can we do to stop this?" Luke wasn't pleading or begging, just asking her to think of something. What else he expected her to do at this point, though, he couldn't say.

"For want of a radio, the world was lost, wasn't it, Mister Ellis?" The woman wasn't delirious. Just resigned.

"Well, ma'am, if it's a working radio you need, I'm kind of out of stock on that item and my supply sergeant isn't around. The one I took from the bad guys is encrypted and it self-destructed somehow."

The ex-soldier's voice held just a hint of unexpected laughter in it as he and the girl and the boy and the woman sat there, counting down to the end.

Darren's eyes suddenly widened and became as big as saucers. Filled with excitement and relief, he jumped to his feet, startling his sister and Mister Ellis. The retired soldier had never seen this side of the boy he'd known for the past year.

The 12-year-old finally remembered just why he'd been toting his satchel the entire day rather than just ditching it to lighten his load.

———

"Radio? Radio? RADIO???"

The boy practically screamed the third recitation of that word as he excitedly jumped up and down. Annie, ever the big sister, tried to calm her little brother down. She squeezed the hand of the poor woman lying next to her before speaking.

"Darren, take it easy! What's gotten into you? You're acting crazy!"

"I'm not crazy, Annie!" The 12-year-old grabbed at his satchel and fell to his knees. He furiously began digging around in it.

"Tell me what you're doing, son," Luke commanded. The boy ignored him as he dug deeper into the sack he'd been carrying during their flight through the woods.

"NO TIME! Mister Ellis!"

Well, at least he's supplying some entertainment, the ex-soldier thought to himself, and so he sat and took in the show, glancing once more at his watch.

Only about 90 seconds now.

Annie's eyes widened as she watched her brother do his best to imitate a badger burrowing into the ground. Various junk electronic parts began flying out of his bag, there to land on an ever-growing heap behind him. She thought she even saw a few big, ugly beetles and at least one garter snake, hissing as it too tumbled through the air.

"AH HAH! THERE YOU ARE!"

Darren's voice – uneven and scratchy in the way of boys about to move into their teen years – rang like a clarion call. He jumped to his feet once again and held his treasure aloft.

Even the lady scientist -- fatigued as she was – gasped in shock and surprise.

"It can't be!" Though raspy and sere, her voice suddenly seemed a bit stronger. Then she turned her head to the girl who'd been at her side the last hour. "Help me sit up!"

The girl quickly obeyed, reaching for the woman's back.

She was heavy. Maybe too heavy, as exhausted as Annie now felt.

"Mister Ellis, help me!" she beseeched her friend, but the man wasn't listening for the moment. He was already on his feet and staring at her little brother, amazed.

"Son of a...!" Luke exclaimed, suddenly fully focused on what it was Darren was holding over his head. The boy held it aloft like an MMA fighter triumphantly displaying the championship belt he'd just won.

It was a radio, and it was working even as the boy capered about like a madman.

"IT WORKS! IT WORKS! IT WORKS!" Darren exulted loudly. "WHOO-HOO!"

The sweet sound of white noise interspersed with a Tower of Babylon-like mish-mash of clearly human voices spilled out into the night.

"DARREN! ON ME!" Luke commanded. He had once again deployed his Command Voice. Not surprisingly, it worked yet again.

"YESSIR!" the 12-year-old boy yelled. He ran over to the big man, who scooped him up like he weighed nothing and then raced back over to the woman and Annie, who by now had managed to prop her charge up.

"Explain how your radio works, Darren!" The retired Delta Force operator was in the zone now, one part of his mind counting down their remaining time, the other part racing ahead to what he could do to help their lady scientist cancel Doomsday.

"I've got it on now, Mister Ellis!" the boy exclaimed. "All we need is the right frequency!"

Ellis looked at the woman they'd all gathered around, crowding in and willing her to succeed. She quickly supplied the answer.

"Any frequency from 27.015 to 27.055 megahertz, Mister Ellis!"

"Those are CB radio frequencies." Alone among the four of them, the ex-soldier's voice was now calm and even-toned. Luke looked at the boy once more.

"Your radio picks up CB frequencies, right, Darren?"

A smug look stole over the 12-year-old's face.

"Duh! It sure can! Here, I'll dial it in!" Moving in a blur, the boy's hands danced over the radio's short, stubby knobs.

He landed on 27.035.

Everyone instantly fell silent, though Darren couldn't prevent his feet from dancing around in delight just a little bit.

"Give the radio to our lady friend, Darren," Ellis ordered.

The boy quickly slapped it into the woman's open right hand, which was lying on her lap.

"Mister Ellis, help me raise the radio high enough so that I can speak into it." The woman was weakening quickly now. She gritted her teeth and forced herself to live just a little bit longer.

"You got it, ma'am!"

Luke's big hand took the mystery woman's small, almost-birdlike hand in his own and brought the radio to her lips.

Less than 50 seconds to go.

The girl, her brother and the big former Special Forces soldier all looked at the woman, waiting for her to speak into the radio's built-in microphone.

She licked her lips, suddenly enormously thirsty. Pressing the send button, she started speaking, though her voice was weak and reedy. It didn't matter, though. Her failsafe would instantly be able to verify it was her. Its processes moved at the speed of light, after all.

"Ozymandias, Ozymandias... do you copy? Over."

The woman stopped speaking and waited. Her three companions were stock still and stone silent.

40 seconds to go.

"Affirmative, Athena. Begin your transmission. Over."

Annie couldn't believe it. The radio voice – the woman had called it "Ozymandias" – was crystal clear in the night air. Crisp and clipped, it was almost inhuman in timbre. She didn't understand why it spoke like that, though. All the other voices she'd just heard coming from her brother's radio had sounded completely nonsensical, as if the vast radio communications networks covering the United States, or maybe even the world, were all suffering a major epileptic seizure.

Not Ozymandias, though.

The woman spoke once more.

"Copy, Ozymandias. Transmission begins. Vishnu, Vishnu. Now I am become Death, the destroyer of worlds. Over." She released the radio's push-to-talk button, waiting on Ozymandias to reply. Her breathing was ragged now and she struggled to remain upright.

Luke reached around and placed his free hand on her back, steadying her.

30 seconds.

The radio blasted out the inhuman voice once again. Ozymandias spoke.

"Look on my Works, ye Mighty, and despair. Over."

The voice coming through the radio sounded even more inhuman than before, as if it were on the verge of making a momentous decision and it wanted to ensure it didn't allow any emotion to affect what it would do.

The woman nearly toppled over before she could send her reply. Luke's arm moved quickly, catching her and preventing her fall.

"You can do this, ma'am!" Ellis' voice was low and urgent. He looked only at her and spoke only to her. No one else in the world but him and the woman – and this Ozymandias – existed. He despaired for just a second, though, before he caught himself. He could tell the lady scientist clearly had little time left.

Luke leaned toward the woman once more and willed his great physical strength into her, hoping to support her however he could. He knew the universe didn't work that way, of course, but it's what he'd always done whenever he'd had to comfort one of his mortally wounded soldiers.

25 seconds.

The woman looked like she was about to faint. Annie and Darren began to weep a little, both in sympathy for this lady they barely knew but also in fear that they were simply too late.

"C'mon, ma'am." Ellis stared intently at her. "Wake up! You have to make this right!"

"Make this right." The woman's voice was barely audible for a second. She exhaled in a sigh but then stopped.

Luke, Annie and Darren waited, motionless and intent.

Suddenly, her eyes – hazel in color and now clear and bright and sharp – flew open and she sucked in air in a great "WHOOSH!"

20 seconds.

The woman sat up straighter, this time needing no help from Ellis. She hit the radio's push-to-talk and spoke in a firm voice.

"Object3Wee8Utter6Break1Duece7Welt Zero. Control, control, control, 3-Point-One-Four-One-Six-Seven. Over" She released the send button and waited along with her three friends for the AI program to acknowledge her deactivation command.

Silence.

15 seconds

Luke wanted to grab the radio and scream into it.

12 seconds.

Still no reply. All four of the people there in the dark night, on the ground behind the blasted ruins of what had once been Luke Ellis' home, prayed for a miracle.

10 seconds.

It was as if the voice of Ozymandias – an immensely powerful AI program and one that could seemingly be everywhere all at once, with no amount of security able to stop it nor any other program able to defeat it—was deciding whether to obey its mistress one last time.

5 seconds.

The man, the woman, the teenage girl and her little brother all sighed as one.

3 seconds.

The trio leaned in to embrace the woman they'd nearly died for to get her to this point. She hugged them in return, crying softly.

Now came a miracle.

The inhuman voice boomed once more from the 12-year-old boy's homebuilt radio.

"Deactivation command acknowledged and accepted, Athena. Over."

Three of four people – Luke Ellis, Annie, her little brother Darren -- shouted at the starry sky.

"YES! YES! YES!"

The trio's collective voice rose to the heavens, there to please the gods looking down on them from very high above. Even the woman –

now on her very last leg and finally ready to surrender to sweet oblivion – smiled broadly. Her spirit was still strong, though her flesh was very weak and nearly spent.

She had one more thing to do before she left.

Pushing the radio's send button yet again, she broadcast a command to Ozymandias she never thought she'd utter. Before she'd met the man Ellis, she'd always believed her AI's life would end just before hers did.

It's different now.

She watched the man first sweep the teen girl into his muscular arms and then the boy as well. He hugged them both, a broad smile playing across his face. They hugged him back, fierce in their determination to never let the moment go.

She now saw everything. Only Jay had been this man's equal when it came to goodness, though she knew Mister Ellis' version of "good" was far different than that of her dearest departed friend's.

She didn't know why that was, though, and didn't have the time to think on it, either.

Good is good, right?

She looked up into the sky as if she expected a reply from the vast, unknowable universe.

No answer.

She sighed once again, this time in contentment.

"I suppose I'll have to discuss that with Jay when I see him," she said aloud, though none of the three people there with her noticed. She no longer feared death even as it began to creep in ever so softly. Her legs grew cold and an icy feeling began moving up her body.

"Not just yet," she remarked, surprised a bit at the strength in her voice.

Time to speak. She licked her lips.

"Ozymandias, Ozymandias. Do you copy? Over."

"Go ahead, Athena. Over."

The man and the boy and the girl stopped their celebration and looked at her, quizzical expressions playing out on all three of their faces. Hadn't she shut her program down?

None of them knew it, but her deactivation command had been followed by a special remark meant to transfer control of her AI program to a person of her choosing. She just wasn't sure it would work, and that was probably what had caused Ozymandias' delay in accepting it. It was unbelievably attuned to the stresses in her voice.

She looked once more at the big man who'd saved her in all the ways that counted, and then spoke.

"Luke Ellis. Over."

"Acknowledged. Over."

Had the AI's voice warmed up just slightly in excitement at its new mission and new master? She couldn't tell. The woman looked at her three saviors, but especially at the man Ellis. She beckoned to him once again.

"Mister Ellis? There's something you need to do for me. Would you, please?"

Her voice was sure and vibrant and strong for the last time, though hints of what was about to happen to her were also contained within it.

"Uh, sure, ma'am. What do you need me to do?"

Luke wasn't sure just why the woman had summoned her AI program yet again. After all, he thought she'd permanently deactivated it.

"Just speak your name into the radio. Ozymandias needs to hear it for just a second."

"Ummmm... why?"

"I want to make sure it can never again inflict my creation on the world, is all. To do that, I need it to hear someone else's voice." The woman hoped her own voice wouldn't reveal her very, very trivial lie.

Luke thought about her request for a second. Then he decided.

"Okay, ma'am." The ex-soldier could tell there was nothing malign within the woman he'd risked his life to protect.

She in turn looked directly at Ellis. There was no dishonesty in his eyes, either.

Luke sat beside her for the last time. Her strength was waning fast now that she'd completed the most important part of her task. This little thing she was going to do was an unalloyed good, at least in her opinion.

She lifted up the radio again. This time it felt like it weighed a thousand pounds.

"Please take the radio, Mister Ellis, and speak only your name into it." Black spots began to appear at the edges of her vision.

Soon, soon... she heard a voice in her mind remark. She thought she could also see her parents off in the distance. They wanted her to come to them. And was that Jay waving at her? She thought so.

The ex-soldier – who'd once been a top-flight Delta Force operator -- lifted the radio to his lips and repeated his name.

"Luke Ellis."

He released the push-to-talk on the radio and waited.

Almost at once, the AI program replied.

"Acknowledged, Luke Ellis. Will send contact and control instructions shortly. Over and out."

What?

What did the program mean by "contact and control instructions?"

Now Luke felt his smartphone vibrate strongly. Reaching into his cargo pant pocket, he pulled it out. The screen glowed brightly and displayed little file folders moving into his device's storage cache even though there was obviously still no cellular service available, if the lack of reception bars on his touchscreen was any sign, that is.

Luke looked at the woman, utterly confused now. "Ma'am, what's going on here?"

She answered him by falling over onto her side, a long, low exhalation the only sound she made.

Annie yelped in surprise and Darren froze. He was afraid for the woman and sure now of what was happening to her.

She was leaving them.

CHAPTER 22
DEPARTURE

LUKE WASN'T SURPRISED AT THE WOMAN'S IMMINENT departure but he was still saddened. He leaned in close to her and could tell she wanted to say something to him, though when she did finally manage to it was in a barely audible voice.

"Mister Ellis?" Her voice was as dry and desiccated as sand.

"It's just Luke, ma'am. Call me Luke."

"Okay, Luke." Her breath wheezed and rattled. She coughed weakly and paused for a moment to gather her rapidly diminishing strength.

Ellis had known Death his entire adult life and he knew that it had arrived to claim this woman. He squeezed her hand in reassurance and fell into respectful silence. He would stay by her side until she left.

The woman also knew she had just a minute to live. She made one final heroic effort and pushed back the black spots that had by now almost completely stolen her vision.

Time for a revelation.

She calmly focused her hazel eyes on Luke's piercing blue ones.

"My real name is Elizabeth Elliott. My parents were Howard and Janet Elliott and they called me Lizzie."

Luke knew what to say, though he struggled for a moment to keep his voice steady.

"I'm very pleased to know you, Lizzie, and I'm sure your parents are very proud of you. I know I am." Luke was surprised at the depth of feeling that had stolen over him.

I barely know this woman.

Maybe he was going soft in his old age? Ellis knew that wasn't true, either. Rather, he'd just gone through the crucible with her. Doing so created a bond few people ever experienced. Behind him, he could hear Annie weeping softly while her brother Darren fought unsuccessfully to suppress his own small sobs. The moment threatened to overwhelm them all.

"I don't have much time, Luke, and I need to tell you something else. Please come closer." The voice of the woman -- whose real name was Elizabeth Elliot but whose parents called her Lizzie -- was now barely more than the merest whisper.

Ellis leaned in as close as he could. If there had been even the slightest breeze, he didn't think he'd have been able to hear her regardless. Fortunately, the night was still and it waited and watched.

Elizabeth Elliot told him what she'd given him.

"Ozymandias has destroyed every bit of my creation, Luke, and it will make sure it stays destroyed. I hope you know that."

"That's great, Lizzie." Luke was clearly relieved at the destruction of her super virus. Saying nothing more, he opted instead to just continue holding her hand. Something told him the woman wasn't finished just yet.

"Ozymandias belongs to you now, Luke."

Luke was stunned.

"I... I don't understand." The woman was now just seconds from death and he could see she was fading fast.

"You control Ozymandias now, Luke," she gasped. "You can't pass it along to anyone else, but you can order it to self-destruct if you want. When you told it your name it analyzed your voice and then linked with you. Soon, it will tell you everything you need to know about it."

Ellis felt like he was in a confessional.

"Elizabeth, uh... Lizzie. I don't know what to say."

For the first time in his life, or at least since he'd been a young boy, Luke was at a real loss and stunned at what the woman had done. He was also afraid of what might happen if anyone ever managed to wrest control of Ozymandias from him. During their flight through the nearby forest, she'd told him about the AI program's unbelievable reach and presence. It was literally everywhere, all the time, and it never slept. Its capacity for good was tremendous, but so was its ability to do great evil if it ever fell into the wrong hands.

Though he didn't know it yet, Elizabeth had guaranteed it wouldn't. Now it was time to reveal her last secret about the program poor Jay had built for her.

"Luke?"

Elizabeth's heart was racing and she took in air in shallow gulps, like a goldfish pulled from its little water bowl and thrown onto the carpet by a careless child. The black spots obscuring her vision had also become deeper and darker. She was afraid she'd die before she could reassure the poor man who'd done so much to help her.

No, you can't die just yet, a stern voice in her head declared. She thought that maybe it sounded like her father.

"Yes, Lizzie?"

The rough and ready former Delta Force operator's voice was husky. He held the increasingly cold and clammy hand of the woman whose name he'd finally just learned and prayed she'd live just a little longer as he tried to comfort her. Taking a moment to reflect, he noticed Annie and Darren, both barely visible from the corner of his eye. They were afraid to approach, though they clearly wanted to.

"In a minute," he whispered to them, nodding solemnly. The boy and the girl silently looked at him. They knew what was occurring and stood at a respectful distance.

He leaned in once more. The woman needed to tell him something important.

Elizabeth coughed softly, too weary to keep taking in air and then forcing it out. The reassuring symphony echoed in her ear one last time.

Soon, soon... she heard angelic voices singing to her.

"Luke," she gasped. "I made sure Ozymandias was limited only to two controllers. First, there was just me, and now there's just you. Once you're gone, it will remove itself from existence." The relief in her voice was clear.

"I'm glad to hear that, Lizzie."

The big ex-soldier was relieved at her revelation. He held her tiny hand in the warm furnace of his own. He wasn't at all sure he even wanted the responsibility to begin with – and he knew he had a decision to make about that – but he also was mighty glad to learn the AI program wasn't going to live forever.

Elizabeth's struggle wracked her body. Luke placed his index and forefinger on her carotid artery one more time. Her pulse was like the fluttering of a hummingbird's wings: All speed with hardly any substance.

"It's okay." The retired soldier now knew what to do, what to say. "It's okay to go, Lizzie."

He received a short, painful gasp of a chuckle from her in return. He couldn't help but smile for a second and laugh with her.

"What's so funny, Lizzie?"

She answered him.

"Well, Luke, you'll be glad to know that Ozymandias is sending you some files that are very special and that are going to help you immensely. They'll help you fix what I broke as well as allow you and your friends to bring about a little justice. They're my gift to you. Please do right by them."

Ellis knew enough not to ask about the files' contents, preferring instead to comfort his new friend just a bit longer as she crossed over. He nodded at her instead, tears welling up in his eyes just a tiny bit.

Truth be told, it was a rare Green Beret or Delta Force operator who hadn't shed a tear on occasion at the loss of a battle buddy or a good friend or family member.

"Time enough for all that file stuff later, Lizzie. You just relax now. Everything's going to be alright."

"I know, Luke. I know."

Ellis had to strain to hear even her labored breathing now, so shallow had it become. He sniffled once and then looked at Annie and Darren.

"Would you both like to say goodbye to Elizabeth?" he asked the pair. "That's her name, by the way. Elizabeth Elliott. Her parents loved her and called her Lizzie."

The teen girl and her brother rushed to join him and the woman they now felt an incredible kinship with. They all put their arms around her and hugged.

As always, Annie spoke first, though this time between tears.

"Goodbye, Miss Elliott, and thank you for saving all of us."

"We should always do what's right, young lady," Elizabeth whispered in her ear.

"I'm Annie, Miss Elliott. Just call me Annie."

"Annie," she whispered. "Such a beautiful name..." Elizabeth's voice trailed off as she looked the girl's brother over, though she could barely see him now through the black haze. The boy was looking carefully at her.

"You can call me Darren, Miss Elliott."

The boy moved his hand to her shoulder and saw that her eyes were now closed. He didn't think she'd speak again, but she surprised him.

"Darren. I'm very pleased to meet you, Darren."

At first, the boy wasn't even sure she'd spoken, so low had her reply been, but the lady scientist opened her eyes and looked at him for a second before slowly closing them again.

Luke squeezed the woman's hand one last time and received an almost imperceptible squeeze in return.

And then she became still.

Elizabeth felt a great weight lift from her shoulders. She felt as light as air, in fact. She wasn't struggling to breathe, either. Plus, her vision was clear once again.

"Isn't that just amazing?" she asked Luke and Annie and Darren.

They didn't respond, as if they couldn't hear her any longer.

Oh.

Oh?

Oh, yes.

She was almost irrationally satisfied at the way things had turned out.

Well, I guess it's time to leave, then.

And so, she did.

Epilogue: Crispy

"We're letting Luke and those kids go, right Crispy?" Killdozer asked his boss on this operation. He also knew the other two men in their snatch-and-grab team – Bruiser and Hardcase -- wanted assurance on that point as well.

They were all looking closely at Crispy and not saying a word. Composed of former Army Special Forces, Delta Force, and Navy SEAL Team Six operators, the small team was employed by a very special private military contractor security company, one that worked almost exclusively in a black ops capacity for an extremely limited clientele. Oftentimes, the clientele included certain US government agencies as well as people formerly with the government, but who now worked in a more independent manner. The four of them figured the latter circumstance was the case in this instance.

"You better believe it," Crispy reassured his three team members.

Killdozer and the other two men heaved a sigh of relief, glad they wouldn't be forced to do something none of them were prepared to do at any rate. They'd all been utterly stunned when they saw Luke Ellis appear from the dark after the woman had gotten shot in the back by those two Afghans as she and the kids approached that house. Too far away once they'd infiltrated the area, they'd been working for hours to close the gap and snatch her from the hands of the terrorists rampaging in and around Lucketts, which was where their intelligence briefing had informed them she'd be. Their mission was to take her from the Afghans, get rid of those men, and then spirit the woman away from danger. After that, she'd be out of their hands.

"Ellis saved my behind over in the Sandbox twice," Crispy spoke again. "Besides, the woman's dead and I'm not waxing any kids and I'm especially not taking out Luke." The burly former special operator's voice made it clear he wasn't willing to entertain any dispute or argument on that point. He was a gunslinger and he'd do what he had to if anyone on his team cared to disagree with his directive, because Luke Ellis had been that important to him in the past.

Killdozer was relieved. "No complaints from me, stud," he said.

Ellis had been one of his mentors back in the day and had also kept at least two of the three other men on his current team from getting killed at one time or another. In Killdozer's case, he'd almost gotten himself blown up by a jihadi who was preparing to use his cell-phone to remotely detonate an enhanced improvised explosive device he'd concealed near his team's GMV 1.1 – or "General Mobility Vehicle 1.1." They'd all been congregating around it, except for Ellis – callsign Blade -- whose sixth sense about such things had saved them all. He'd spotted the jihadi just in the nick of time, putting him down with a clean shot from his assault rifle as he was attempting to punch in the right number on his cellphone.

"I'm cool, too, Crispy." This came from Bruiser. Like the others, he'd also served in the past with Luke Ellis.

Hardcase chimed in last. "No way, we're taking out Luke Ellis, Crisp." He'd served with the Navy's "Development Group," or SEAL Team Six, and had shared trigger time with the Army Delta Force professional, as well, and liked him immensely.

Looking at the trio, Crispy knew he had to give them the latest piece of intel.

"The boss is torqued big time at how he got played on this one. We're not a "kill Americans assassination squad," and snatching the woman was supposed to help protect US national security, or so we were led to believe. Taking her from those Afghan jerkweeds was supposed to be the mission set, not all this," he said, waving his hand to indicate he was talking about the entire day.

The team leader continued with his update.

"The boss was fine with whatever we had to do to those guys, believe me, but he told me personally that Ellis is off limits." Their boss, who owned the company, had also been saved by the ex-soldier once on a really nasty op up in a region on the Afghanistan-Pakistan border where they weren't even supposed to be.

"If it wasn't for Luke, I wouldn't be standing here, writing out big, fat paychecks to you guys," he'd told Crispy on his secure, encrypted satellite phone after learning the former Delta Force operator was also running around in the woods and trying to protect the woman. The man continued speaking once again.

"Get out of there, ASAP, and go to ground. I'm shutting everything down and doing the same thing myself. We'll hook up and bring you four in from the cold in six weeks. Take the time to clear your six and then get hidden, because the blowback on this one's going to be huge." With that, the man clicked off.

The team leader looked around once more. Fortunately, all three of his guys were completely in agreement with him on the matter of Ellis' continued survival. They'd all been part of the Brotherhood, after all, and they'd all bled together as well. He also knew that if the four of them stuck together, they had a really good chance of riding out the inevitable storm that would ensue from their decision not to eliminate anyone who knew about the woman they were supposed to grab.

We ain't killing Luke and we certainly ain't killing those kids.

Crispy was mightily impressed at how that girl and the boy with her had managed themselves during the little firefight they had with the two Afghan terrorists. He thought that kind of courage merited special consideration and so did his boss, especially after discovering how badly he'd been set up.

"Some people are gonna pay for that," the man had told him in an angry voice.

Looking closely through his night vision binoculars once more, Crispy saw Ellis and the kids start moving away. "Heading toward that blown-up house, no doubt," he said aloud to no one in particular. There was really no need for extreme quiet any longer. They were now just there as observers from a distance.

He saw movement from the edge of the field surrounding the wrecked and ruined building and moved his binos over to focus on it.

A man appeared, limping badly and leaning heavily on his M4. It was the cop -- the one who'd crazily charged all those Afghans TWICE, his boss told him after seeing the drone footage and first suspecting that it might be Luke Ellis up ahead with the woman. Each time, the badge had managed to kill more bad guys than he really had a right to. Crispy didn't know if the man had any prior military training, but there was no doubt about his courage. The former Special Forces assistant detachment commander shook his head admiringly at the cop's sheer bravado and crazy brave attitude.

"The guy's nuts," he whispered. Looking at the cop once more, he saw the man yelling and waving at Luke Ellis, trying to catch his attention. After a moment, he finally succeeded.

Crispy saw Ellis and the two kids turn around and catch sight of the wounded man. They all broke into a trot toward him, finally meeting up in the middle of the field. He had to admit it: The group hug among the four was impressive.

"Guess they're all part of the Brotherhood now," he said, satisfied at the thought.

Turning around, he looked at his team. "Let's bail, guys. We're going to disappear for a while until the boss sorts all this out."

With that, the four men melted away into the night, with Luke and his little band of now-warriors never even knowing they were ever in the vicinity.

EPILOGUE
FEBRUARY, SIX MONTHS LATER

Annie and Darren

ANNIE, DARREN AND THEIR FATHER MARK AND MOTHER Janelle sat around their dining room table stunned. Two men had just left, both delivering no small amount of amazing news to them all.

"I can't believe it!" Annie, now 18 years old, squealed happily.

The first man who'd visited their home had just informed her that all four years of her education at the University of Virginia, come late August when it finally reopened, were now fully paid for. That fact amazed her, as the school had had to rescind all scholarships last year in the aftermath of the terror attacks which had caused hundreds of millions, if not billions, of dollars in damage to the campus.

The university had an endowment fund, of course, but not nearly enough of one to cover everything, plus the school's many alumni were currently in the same boat as everyone else and the state was dealing with its own financial problems at the moment and also couldn't help. Neither could the federal government, the university had learned. Ergo, no scholarships for quite some time to come and right now her parents just couldn't afford to pay for it all, which was something she was fine with. She could wait.

But now?

Now I don't have to!

To top it all off, the man – who'd flashed an impressive set of credentials at her parents and who said his name was Mister Brown -- had handed her his very, very impressive smartphone. "There's someone who needs to speak with you," he told her.

She took the phone and put it to her ear. "Hello?"

"Hello, Ms. Dedham," the woman on the other end said to her. "This is Doctor Naomi Shapiro, and I'm Dean of the Harvard Medical School."

Annie didn't know what to say. She'd hoped to go to medical school and become a physician someday, but that was far off in the future, she knew. She had to say something right now to the woman on the phone, though.

"Ummm... hello, Doctor Shapiro. It's nice to talk with you, though I don't know what this is about." Annie was genuinely at a loss as to why such an important person would call her all of a sudden.

The dean told her.

"Well, Annie, the President of the United States – who is apparently a friend and admirer of yours – asked that I call to inform you of your acceptance to our medical school once you graduate from the University of Virginia. We're going to hold a seat open, and at absolutely no cost to you or your parents, of course."

"You're kidding, Doctor Shapiro."

The 18-year-old had trouble keeping the excitement out of her voice as well as the tears from her eyes. Her parents had heard the woman on the other end identify herself and then give their daughter the news. They'd hugged each other fiercely.

Her brother Darren just stood there, mouth open and eyes wide in shock.

What a dork! she laughed inside, loving him more than ever.

"I never kid, Ms. Dedham. Harvard Medical School can certainly use a young woman like you."

Annie could barely recall the rest of her conversation with Dean Shapiro before the woman ended by telling her she'd be checking on her studies from time to time. After that, she'd clicked off. The 18-year-old was slightly dizzy from the shock of it all. Hands shaking, she gave the phone back to Mister Brown, the government man who'd come to their home.

He took it, then entered a number and waited until it answered.

"Send him in," was all he said before retreating to the rear of the dining room to watch the goings-on.

There was another knock on the door.

"I'll get it!" Darren informed his sister and parents, racing off to see who was visiting next.

They could make out the sound of the boy opening the door, and then muffled conversation between Darren and whoever was out there.

"HAHAHAHAHAHAHAHAHA! THAT'S AWESOME!" they heard him shout. His feet pounded on the hardwood floors as he crashed back into the dining room, a tall, serious-looking man -- olive-skinned and in serious shape -- trailing behind him.

"MOM! DAD! ANNIE! This is Mister Lopez!" The boy's voice raced at breakneck speed. "He says he knows Mister Ellis and that he's here to teach me about all kinds of cool radio and other communications! And you won't believe the equipment and computers his assistants are bringing in for me. I've never seen such expensive stuff in my life! And there are other people Mister Lopez says will be waiting to help teach me anything else I want to learn! Plus, he says we'll never have to worry about any school or college tuition for me ever again!" Darren hopped excitedly from one foot to the other.

"Mister Lopez," now retired but formerly of the US Army's Operational Detachment Delta – better known as Delta Force – just nodded solemnly, though with a twinkle in his eyes. While setting this up, Luke Ellis had told him all about the boy's role in helping save the world through his homebuilt radio handset as well as what he'd done to save his sister.

"That boy has Special Forces written all over him," Luke said. "Let's see if we can help him figure that out."

And so here he was, tasked by both his friend Luke as well as by a grateful President of the United States to do everything he could to reward the young man for what he'd done on a late August day just six months ago...

"Oh my God!" Mark and Janelle Dedham exclaimed in unison.

First their daughter and now their son?

Something had to have gone on last August – during that horrible day – that neither of their kids had revealed to them. They'd certainly huddled and discussed things in many a whispered conversation since then, that was for sure, but not a peep out of them about what they'd seen or done. Apparently, it was enough to attract the notice of the President, though, a fact that left them dumbfounded, as did the letter he'd personally addressed to them on White House stationery, complete with the Seal of the President of the United States.

They read it yet again, not believing what their eyes were telling them.

Dear Mr. and Mrs. Dedham, it began.

Please accept the sincere thanks of the people and government of the United States of America for all that your daughter and son did to help our nation last August. Words cannot begin to express my personal gratitude as well. I hope to speak with all four of you in person soon here at the White House in my personal residence as well as in the Oval Office. We all have an amazing story to share with each other.

The letter became even better after that.

In the meantime, Mister Brown – the man presenting this letter to you – will be working to ensure your new market is rebuilt and up and running as soon as possible. I've given him one month to make sure it's finished, and he's able to draw on all the resources of my government and the private sector to make it happen. To that end, I and a friend of your daughter Annie and son Darren have arranged the deposit into your bank account of all the funds necessary to construct a new facility sufficiently fitting for a family of your impressive accomplishment, courtesy of the United States Treasury. The Treasury will also be paying off your home's mortgage later this week. Please feel free to let Mister Brown know just what sorts of improvements you'd like to make to your home and he will also make sure those are taken care of posthaste.

Again, thank you on behalf of a grateful nation.
Sincerely,
Thomas C. Masterson, President

Mark and Janelle looked at their kids once again, still disbelieving everything that was happening right now.

"Annie! Darren! Just what went on that day with Mister Ellis? You have to tell us!" The man and woman looked at their 18-year-old daughter, expecting an answer.

Overcome with joy, all she could do was laugh very, very hard.

I knew it, I knew it! Mister Ellis has been watching us all, biding his time and waiting!

Always modest, the 18-year-old was just grateful to be alive after everything they'd all gone through, and that was due to her brother and to the big ex-Army man who'd melted away once he'd gotten her and her brother and Deputy Holman to safety after their long night's march through the Loudoun County woods surrounding Lucketts, their town. Mister Ellis had even carried the deputy in his arms and on his back many times during the night until they were well away from danger.

In the morning, he'd left them at the big community park, where an emergency shelter and medical services had finally been set up. The entire area was protected by National Guard units that had rolled into town a few hours before. Hundreds of people were sitting on the grass, drinking water from plastic cups and trying to stay warm under thin, silver thermal blankets. Medical tents were overflowing, sadly. Too many people had lost their lives over the last 24 hours.

"I have to go now," Luke said to them. The first rays of another late-August morning were firming up.

The four of them looked at each other for a moment.

"We look terrible!" Annie exclaimed, drawing laughter from Luke, Darren, and Alec Holman, the wounded lawman. Then they all fell silent once more.

As if he could read minds, Ellis just nodded at her and then shook Alec Holman's hand and received one in return. The two men didn't need to say anything to each other. They now shared an unbreakable bond developed only by men who'd fought in combat together.

Looking at Darren, Luke put a hand on his shoulder. "You keep this up, and I'll have to get them to make a movie about you, son."

The boy didn't say anything. He knew the man who'd done so much for them all had to leave, but that didn't mean he had to like it. Instead, he grabbed him around the waist and hugged for all he was worth. After a minute, he released him and then stepped back, tears in his eyes.

"When will we see you again?" To Annie, her brother's voice sounded mournful.

"Soon, Darren. There are some things I need to do first, though. I'm pretty sure the Army is going to need my help for a while, and we all know the government will, too. But once that's taken care of, I'll be back. You can count on it."

In response, the boy slowly raised his hand and gave Luke a thumbs up and then stepped back, thinking whatever thoughts it is that 12-year-old-boys of outstanding courage think.

The former Delta Force operator finally looked for a moment at the most courageous teenager he'd ever met.

Annie walked up to him. Luke gave her a long hug and then stepped back and gave her a crisp salute.

"I'll be back, Annie. I can't tell you how brave you were last night.

Just know that I'm so proud of you, and I know your parents will be, too." Ellis' voice threatened to break for just a second.

Annie could only sniffle a bit in return and look at him miserably.

I don't want Mister Ellis to go, but I know he has to. This isn't over, is it?

He had a secret that Miss Elliot – Lizzie – had entrusted to him. He also had to seek justice against the people who'd done all this to everyone.

Luke looked at her and nodded his head once again. He knew the girl would understand more than the others. Stepping back, he spoke to them all one last time.

"Until I do return, I'm trusting all three of you to say as little as possible about what we went through together. I have to take care of some business and make sure that the right people know what went on and what we and Lizzie Elliot experienced, as well as what she did to save us all. I promise you, the truth about everything will soon come out. Just sit tight for a little while."

With that, the big ex-soldier turned around and walked down the shoulder of the road on which they were standing. The three of them – lawman, boy, and 17-year-old girl watched him melt away into the early morning mist and fog.

Alec

"C'mon Deputy Holman, just one more leg extension! You can do it!"

The physical therapist – a woman almost devilishly obsessed with breaking the young lawman's spirit so that she could build it back up again -- added to the weight against his lower leg by pressing her hand down on the padded bar lying heavily against his shin. It instantly added another twenty pounds.

"C'MON!" she exhorted. "WORK!"

Alec Holman's cheeks were red and they puffed out as he

exhaled loudly, hoping the vein popping out on his forehead wasn't a precursor sign of a stroke or something.

Wouldn't that be a bite, he thought, *to survive all that I survived in August only to vapor lock here on this machine?*

He couldn't help but grunt loudly and laugh as he slowly raised the weight stack inch by inch.

"Just a little bit higher, Deputy! You've got this! DO IT!"

Alec wanted to curse the physical therapist. She refused to let him give up!

Summoning his final reserves of strength, he raised the weight stack to the maximum up position.

"AAAAAAAAGGGGH!" The lactic acid in his nearly healed left thigh burned like a blowtorch.

"Hold it, Deputy! HOLD IT!"

The woman was the Devil, pure and simple.

Alec felt pain wash over him like an unending series of tidal waves, but he didn't let the weight stack fall. Time had no meaning now as his leg writhed and spasmed in agony.

"AWESOME, DEPUTY! Lower the weight now!"

"AAAAAAAGGGH!" the lawmen shouted yet again as he slowly lowered the weight back to the fully down position, the lactic acid in his leg finally easing off.

Alec could see the physical therapist's ecstatic look. She'd told him before that no patient of hers had tried so hard to heal himself so quickly as he had.

She also knew why that was.

"I'm trying to get accepted to the FBI Academy," he'd confessed during one of their extended torture sessions. "They won't consider me until I'm fully healed and certified as one-hundred percent capable."

Holman thought on that one for a moment.

The therapist knew he'd been seriously wounded in last August's terror attack along with many other law enforcement people, but he refused to talk about the details.

"I was just in the wrong place at the wrong time," was all he'd reply whenever he was asked about what had happened. "Other people paid a far higher price than I ever did or ever will," he would always say before making it clear no added discussion would be tolerated.

To keep his mind off the dull ache in his thigh, he watched his therapist walk over to the desk area. She'd been called there by the people staffing it. They were now engaged in animated conversation. Occasionally, one of them would look over at him. She took the phone another one of them handed to her and listened. Nodding her head, she said something into it and then handed it back to the desk staff before marching off to the front of the medical building the physical therapy department occupied.

He idly wondered what that was all about.

The lawman had seen the attack and the damage done to all of them that fateful day last August, every man, woman and child. He knew what they'd all narrowly avoided and he also knew the best chance he had at making sure nothing like it ever happened again was with the FBI.

The trouble was, the Bureau was still trying to recover from its own grievous wounds. It had finally gotten a new permanent Director just a couple weeks ago, and Congress and the President were working hard to help, but it was going to be some time until any new agent applications would be considered. From what he'd heard, background investigations were also months and maybe even years behind schedule now.

Alec sighed a bit at that.

Nothing I can do, though, except keep working hard, he thought to himself. *It'll come someday.*

The lawman wasn't sure when that would be, though, so he did what he could to heal himself while his department waited for him to return to duty. His limp was gone now, he felt strong, and he was finally ready to schedule both his duty physical and the fitness test that would follow it.

"Loudoun County, get ready for the return of Robo Deputy!" he'd joked on more than one occasion. There was absolutely nothing wrong with being a deputy, he knew, and he liked what he did, which was more than he could say for many men and women in law enforcement these days.

Leaving aside the matter of just how many men and women manning the thin, blue line had lost their lives back in August, there was also the issue of the wholesale resignations departments across the country had experienced after the attacks. It had been open season on many of them even before that day due to budget cutbacks and other municipal initiatives, and more than a few of his comrades had decided that more welcoming climes and less hazardous careers were now in order.

Not me, though. No brain, no pain!

Looking around, he saw his physical therapist return with a tall, well-dressed man in tow. She had a smile on her face.

"No way," Alec said in a low whisper. "No. Freaking. Way."

The man was the new Director of the Federal Bureau of Investigation, and he also had a smile on his face.

Therapist and FBI Director both came to a halt in front of him. The woman couldn't stop grinning. She had a cute smile, he had to admit, surprised that the stern young woman who tormented him daily could actually be pleasant when she wanted to. He returned his attention to the man and waited.

"Hello, Deputy Holman, I'm Jason Kelleher and I'm very pleased to meet you. May I shake your hand? No need to stand, though. Just stay off that leg."

Kelleher knew all about this man Holman, having discussed him with the President of the United States just yesterday, in fact.

"We need a man like him, Jason," President Masterson told him. "Especially as you try to rebuild the Bureau."

"Of course, Mister President," he replied, not sure just what Masterson wanted him to do. He had an entire personnel directorate – one that was slowly rebuilding after several of them had been killed by the terrorists, while others had resigned or retired -- to oversee matters like that.

And then the President filled him in on everything that one Deputy Sheriff Alec Holman of the Loudoun County Sheriff's Department had done last August.

Everything.

And now here he stood, as eager as his old friend, the President of the United States, to bring this young man into the fold, so to speak.

Amazing, simply amazing, was all he could keep thinking, trying to imagine what this deputy sheriff had done last August.

Yes, indeed. The Bureau certainly could use a man like Alec Holman.

Luke

Luke Ellis stood within the shadows of the dark February night, admiring the broad, expensively appointed and enclosed patio. He was waiting for the younger man and the older woman to step out onto it from the warm sanctuary of the mansion she owned.

Though the estate was normally heavily guarded by all manner of electronic surveillance and anti-intrusion devices – including sonic and infrared as well as more traditional motion detection -- that made it nearly impossible to penetrate without being discovered, Ellis had managed to do so with ease. No alarms went off and all computer screens showed every security system working as normal, though. For some reason, all those devices had suddenly gone down while closed circuit monitors inside projected the same old scenes they always did, as if nothing was out of the ordinary, which was really the farthest thing from the truth.

Luke knew how the phenomenon worked and just what had pulled it off, though no one else did. The men in the woman's human security detail – courtesy of her employer, naturally – were now comfortably stashed away in the property's carriage house, hogtied and unconscious. They wouldn't wake for several hours and then they'd have a splitting headache. Ozymandias had verified they didn't know anything about what the woman had been up to and so their lives had been spared.

Two Augusts ago, the woman had been serving with a deliberately obscure intelligence agency as head of its Afghanistan desk, though she was now in the private sector and very well-compensated for her work. Luke had her salary history, including payments into her false front and hidden bank accounts. He even had the ones in certain other countries where the banking laws were very, very loosely interpreted and where client data was guarded more closely than the most top-secret of top-secret intelligence held by the United States. He also had records of the payments made to her and the younger man by several very rich men who'd been funding international terrorism for the last 20 years now.

Luke had learned just why, but addressing that issue was definitely for another day.

Back to the duo if front of him.

The younger man had worked for the woman before she'd left their intelligence agency shortly after the Afghanistan withdrawal debacle less than two years before. He was supposed to have died in the terror attack after a massive bomb blast vaporized the building he was thought to be at, along with everyone else in and around it. Certainly, no part of his body had ever been found, but that's how powerful the bomb had been. Or at least the authorities had assumed as much once they'd been able to examine the ruins of the building, such as they were.

Luke thought that was funny.

Like Jesus, here he is. Raised from the dead.

No, in the young man's case it was something much simpler than the Resurrection. Just the week before, he'd finally resurfaced and contacted his partner in crime using very, very good tradecraft. It didn't matter, though. Ellis had known about him and where he was hiding ever since Ozymandias had sent him the man's file.

In keeping with the plan, the pair had concocted after stumbling onto Lizzie Elliot's existence and just why she was so important – courtesy of an inadvertent file breach due to a single careless slip-up on the part of one of the very few people who knew about her-- she'd finally brought him in from the cold.

And now here Luke was, waiting for the final act in this particular play to begin. No doubt, the two of them would have drinks in hand as they stepped out onto the patio to celebrate their great good fortune. Both were now fabulously wealthy, for one, courtesy of those very rich men, and the younger man also had a new identity, complete with extensive plastic surgery and a passport from a Caribbean nation famous for its no-questions-asked attitude.

It had taken Ozymandias about 30 seconds to find the man out.

Luke found that funny as well, and even smiled at the thought before he became serious once again.

Work now, laugh later. Time to focus, Luke.

Ellis heard the sounds of conversation approaching the patio entrance. The man and the woman were coming. He melted farther back into the shadows and waited.

The woman was the first to appear. The man had held the double doors open for her before following her out onto the patio.

She spoke idly, chatting with her former subordinate as they drank a very fine, very expensive brandy from the snifters in their hands.

"When will you be leav---" She froze, eyes wide, seeing Luke Ellis appear from the shadows, gun in hand.

Before she could give warning, the younger man stepped out onto the patio and looked at her.

"What's wrong, Sandy? You look like you've seen a ghost. Hey, I'm the only one who's a ghost," he said, chuckling at the inside joke.

Then he looked around and his knees trembled.

The woman was pointing to a man with a gun.

How did he get in? He heard a voice in his head ask. Sandy's estate was guarded more closely than CIA headquarters, which was just down the road, in fact.

Andy fell silent, too scared to talk. He was no field guy and had never come anywhere close to actual danger in his entire life, though that was no longer the case.

Gun never wavering, Luke moved closer to the pair.

"Sit down, both of you." He pointed to the chairs around the dining table that took up only a small part of the massive patio.

"Who are you?" Sandy asked. His face looked familiar, she thought, as if she'd once seen him in photos or drone footage shot during a raid on a terrorist stronghold in Helmand Province some years ago...

"I'm no one," Luke answered. "Who you two are, though, and what you helped our enemies do, is far more important."

"I don't know what you mean," she shot back. "You've invaded my home and police are on the way. Get out before I have you arrested or something even worse happens to you!"

She pressed a small stud on the side of her watch. It was designed to set off every alarm on the estate. She knew how to deal with the lower classes like this man. No doubt her security deal was racing toward her even now. It was important to hold the intruder's attention and play for time so that they could grab him and then deal with him properly.

Petrified with fear, Andy sat still and remained silent, hoping not to draw the man's attention. He didn't think Sandy realized the implications of what this stranger had just said. He knew who they were, and he obviously knew what they'd done.

"No one's coming to help you, ma'am," the man assured her. "It's just us three now."

Sandy paused to listen. No sirens, no pounding feet, no nothing. Dead, flat silence all around them. How had this shabby man managed to penetrate every single one of her security layers?

Time to bargain, then.

"What do you want? Money? I've got plenty of that, plus a couple

FIRST STRIKE: LOUDOUN COUNTY

of really nice, really new cars. I don't have any drugs but take everything else." She held her wrist up. "This watch is worth $50,000," she said.

Sandy was worried now. The man, whoever he was, hadn't reacted in the least to her offer of money, watch and super-expensive cars.

Andy tried to sink even lower into his chair. The man saw him move slightly, looked at him and then dismissed him like he was some sort of uninteresting insect or a dead tree leaf or something.

He noticed that his gun never moved off of either of them, though.

"What do I want, ma'am?" Luke asked. She nodded her head in return, waiting for him to tell her. The man with her had the good sense to just stay silent and not move, Ellis noted.

"Yes. What do you want?" she demanded.

"Why, I only want one thing. It's what Elizabeth Elliot asked me to obtain on her behalf, just before she died. Do you know what that is, ma'am?"

The duo's eyes grew wide.

Elizabeth Elliot!

The man knew Liz Elliot, the woman realized. Not just knew *of* her. No, he really knew her. He said he'd been with her when she died, in fact.

Dread realization stole over Sandy. Andy had long ago reached that point.

The man was the same one who'd held the Afghans off that August day and night and then somehow managed to convince the snatch-and-grab team to disappear as well.

It was Luke Ellis in the flesh, standing right here with them both.

Andy began to blubber slightly. Sandy looked at him and felt disgusted. She wouldn't give Ellis the pleasure. A plan quickly formed in her mind. She was surprised at how firm she managed to keep her voice.

"Look, I don't know what you think you know, but I can make

you rich beyond imagination."

Luke wasn't swayed.

"Let's go," he ordered the pair, motioning toward the patio exit with his pistol.

Andy found he couldn't stand up. He didn't want to die tonight, out on Sandy's lawn, executed by this man like some animal. And so he blubbered even more, tears running down his cheeks while a dark stain slowly grew on the front of his pants.

Ellis felt embarrassed for him, but that was about it.

So be it.

He looked at the woman.

"You feel the same way, ma'am?" His voice was like the grave.

Sandy was braver.

"I'm not going anywhere with you," she declared and crossed her arms. "If you're going to shoot us, shoot us here, right now." She gambled that the man was bluffing and that they both were of more value alive than dead. Both knew secrets about the entire operation that only a very few other people knew.

The former Delta Force operator had known it would come down to this. He rolled his eyes and sighed theatrically.

"You're right, Sandy. I'm not going to shoot you two."

Sandy exulted inside.

Hah! I knew it!

She had more than a few bargaining chips, something she knew Ellis was aware of.

Beneath her, Andy almost sobbed with relief. They'd both live another day. After that, they had information to trade, and more than enough of it to buy them their freedom and still ensure they'd be wealthy at the end of it all.

Sandy also smiled slightly in triumph. Eventually, she'd show Ellis who was boss. Or, more precisely, the people protecting her would show him. It would be a permanent surprise for the man, too, if she had her way.

He puzzled her, though, because he seemed unfazed by it all, as if he'd known everything would turn out like it just had. A strange look also stole over his face just then, like he was regretting what he was going to have to do.

That's understandable. I called his bluff. I knew he wouldn't shoot us down in cold blood. He's too honorable for that.

The thought of his weakness in this regard made her sneer at him inside.

Luke was indeed regretful, but not at the thought of having to shoot the traitors in front of him.

"No, Sandy. I'm not going to shoot either of you. You know it and I know it."

Ellis saw a victorious gleam steal into the woman's eyes.

I wonder how long that's going to last?

"I don't know about old Andy here," Luke continued, using his pistol to indicate the younger man, "but you're probably a good poker player, aren't you?"

"I've won a few hands," Sandy replied, waiting for the man to get to the point. In her opinion, verbal games like these were silly, but they were what men like this one played when they weren't allowed to play with guns, weren't they?

"Yeah, I just bet you have."

Time to wrap this up, the former Delta Force operator thought to himself.

Luke's shoulders slumped a little, as if he'd have to accept defeat at the hands of the woman dueling with him.

Then he smiled broadly.

Sandy frowned once more.

What is this foolish man playing at? I've beaten him! He knows we're too valuable to kill. All that's left is to haggle over my price!

What he did next stunned her.

"No, I don't play much poker, Sandy. The price just goes up and up and, before you know it, you're in way too deep and trying to figure out where all your money went."

Luke pointed at the other end of the patio, where a long bar stood in the deepest part of the shadows.

Sandy's eyes followed his arm, and then they widened once more. She heard Andy began to blubber yet again.

Crispy, Hardcase, Killdozer, and Bruiser appeared from the shadows.

"They're all yours, guys," Luke Ellis – callsign Blade -- told the quartet as he holstered his pistol and headed for the patio exit.

Crispy spoke.

"Thanks, Blade. See you when I see you, bud."

"Yeah, same here, Blade," the other three former special operators said to their old comrade.

Luke looked at his old fellow special operators. "Likewise, guys. Stay frosty, huh?"

"Always, Blade," all four replied in unison and then chuckled, also in unison.

That done, the quartet turned their attention to the man and the woman who'd played them and their boss.

Luke looked one last time at the woman. Amazingly, he even felt just a tiny bit sorry for what was going to happen to her and her partner.

She looked like she'd been forced to suck on an extra-large lemon. The man just looked pathetic.

Maybe I really am getting soft in my old age, Ellis thought to himself as he walked out the patio door, making sure to shut it firmly.

Crispy spoke to the woman first.

"Our boss sends his regards, Sandy, and so does the President of the United States." Killdozer and Hardcase each held a black hood while Crispy and Bruiser had flex cuffs.

The older woman's face went pale. This time, the young man did manage to faint.

Luke listened for a moment to the goings-on inside the patio and then shook his head and looked up into the cold night sky as he walked away into the night.

"I told you I wasn't going to shoot, you Sandy," was all he said.

Coming Mid-Summer 2022

Second Strike: Danger Close!

The United States is still struggling to throw off the massive terror attack it had experienced just six months before and Luke Ellis, retired US Army Delta Force operator, is facing his greatest challenge. His country's enemies, sensing the American eagle has been seriously wounded, prepare to attack across all domains. What Luke does and how he uses Ozymandias, the powerful all-seeing and all-knowing artificial intelligence program he alone controls – or does he? – will determine the fate of the nation.

ABOUT THE AUTHORS

A.W. Guerra is a retired U.S. military officer and an all-around jack-of-all-trades and enthusiastic and determined master of none. After his military career he spent more than a decade in airline operations management. Now a prolific freelance writer, he has previously published the solo fiction novel "Motown: The Vampire Must Die (Ninja, SEAL, Believers: Book I of the Brushfire Organization Series)." It is available exclusively on Amazon (Kindle and Paperback).

Kelly Hoggan is an aviation security consultant and founder and CEO of H4 Solutions. Before establishing H4 Solutions, Kelly served in numerous senior level positions at the Transportation Security Administration. He also spent 17-plus years working directly in the airline industry. Kelly is a terrible golfer with a 23 handicap. This is his first novel.

Made in the USA
Columbia, SC
20 May 2022

60701768R00161